THE CASE
OF THE
WAYWARD WIFE

"If Hollywood gives an Oscar for pornography, this portfolio wins it. Sixty-six highly artistic color poses of starlet Valerie Kiss . . . co-starring a young Apollo blissfully unaware of the hidden camera.

"Entertaining . . . except that Valerie Kiss is suddenly my client, and one person is already dead over this lurid little portfolio.

"A nice way to start a caper . . ."

Here is the famous Peter Chambers in a racy triple case: an irresistible client, an unmatchable finger-print, and an impossible killing.

The new

Peter Chambers

Mystery

Kisses of Death

by

HENRY KANE

WILDSIDE PRESS

ONE

I was seated in my briefs in the kitchen having breakfast. It was Saturday, June 17, nine-thirty of a hot day in spring. Friday night's newspaper was propped against the sugar bowl and I was sipping coffee and reading about murder, rape, divorce, delinquency, and political missile rattling, when the phone rang. I relinquished the literature, went to the living room, picked up the phone, said, "Hello?"

"Mr. Chambers?" It was a woman.

"Yes," I said.

"Peter Chambers?"

"Yes," I said.

"May I see you, Mr. Chambers? On business?"

"Yes, of course. When would you like?"

"Right away, if you please."

"Who is this?"

"Mrs. Kiss."

"I beg your pardon?"

"Mrs. Valerie Kiss."

"Do I know you, Mrs. Kiss?"

"No."

Kiss. It is a name. It is not somebody making a joke at nine-thirty in the morning during breakfast. Once before, several years ago, I had had a client by the name of Kiss— Justine Kiss. I had then checked the Kisses in the Manhattan telephone book. There had been eighteen Kisses listed. Kiss is a name.

"Are you a relative of Justine Kiss?" I said.

"No. Why?" She sounded annoyed.

"Just that Kiss is an unusual name. I thought perhaps Justine had recommended—"

"Mr. Felix Davenport recommended you to me."

Felix Davenport was an old friend, a well known actor on the Broadway stage, but for the past three years Felix had been living on the West Coast wasting his talent but

earning a huge income as the straight man to a comic in a
television series.

"Oh," I said, "you're from Hollywood?"

"I'm from New York."

"But Felix—"

"Look, please, Mr. Chambers, it's very important that I
see you as quickly as possible. May I come over?"

"Sure. Do you know the address?"

"Yes."

"How soon will you be here?"

"Fifteen minutes all right?"

"Fine," I said.

"Thank you," she said and hung up.

I was showered and shaved. I cleaned up the kitchen by
putting the dishes into the sink. That took two minutes. I
dressed quickly but carefully as is fitting when the client
is a lady and the lady is a stranger. That took ten minutes.
With three minutes to spare, I was about to light a cigarette,
when the bell rang. My lady was either prompt by habit or the
matter was as urgent as she had intimated.

The matter was as urgent as she had intimated.

TWO

SHE WAS tall and willowy with beautiful ankles. She was long
legged and tiny waisted and high hipped and provocatively
chested in an expensive green summer dress without sleeves.
She had a small nose and enormous eyes, the nose tilted and
the eyes brown. She had poise, she had posture, she had
presence, she had luminous auburn hair expensively coif-
fured. She carried a black patent-leather handbag and the
graceful ankles, nylon sheathed, rose up out of spike-heeled
black patent-leather pumps. Her skin was fair, white, smooth,
and carefully tended, and her hands were long-fingered and
delicate. She was distressed; naturally she was distressed
—she had insisted upon visiting a private detective early on
a Saturday morning—but she did not stress her distress; she
was contained, reasonably calm, somehow remote. She had
quality. It was written all over her. She had class, Class A.
She smiled and said, "Mr. Chambers?" and she extended her
hand and I took it and shook it. It was cool and dry with a

firm but not flirtatious clasp. She shook my hand and then let go. She said, "I know I am an intrusion so early on a Saturday morning but you must forgive me."

"That's the kind of business I'm in," I said.

"Thank you for being so sweet," she said. Her voice was deep, slow, trained, cultured, somehow familiar. All of her was somehow familiar but I could not place it.

She sat down in a soft-pillowed easy chair, sank in. She crossed her legs and the slender ankles plumped up to the kind of rounded calves that caused one to become rampantly curious about the thighs, so I looked away.

"Do I know you?" I said.

"Do you?" she said.

"I feel as though I do but I can't put my finger on it."

She looked upon her wrist watch which, like all the rest of her, was obviously expensive, and she said, "We have an appointment at eleven o'clock."

"We?" I asked.

"At 527 Madison Avenue. At eleven o'clock. It'll take us about ten minutes to get there from here, yes?"

"Yes."

"Before that, I have about ten minutes of explanatory matter for you. But before *that,* if you so desire, you may talk about whatever you want, ask any questions you wish."

"Do I know you?" I said again.

"My name is Valerie, Valerie Kiss, Mrs. Jonathan Kiss. Does any of that mean anything to you?"

"Not a thing. But I'd swear I—"

"My professional name was Valerie Dayton. Any bells?"

Bells, not gongs, little bells, began to tinkle. Valerie Dayton. Sure. Of course. Seven, eight years ago, it had been a stage name, a motion picture name, a television name. I had seen her in a couple of lead roles on Broadway, I had seen her in a couple of secondary roles in movies, and I had seen her in countless supporting roles in countless television epics: westerns, easterns, southerns, violence-shows, and emasculated social-significance dramas. "Sure," I said. "Valerie Dayton. Sure."

"I married," she said, "and I married well. Second marriage, as a matter of fact. First marriage still had to do with the career, but I got wise, it was not for me. I didn't have —" She shrugged and scraped out her cigarette. "—the guts, the drive, the perseverance. I had the talent and the training but I just couldn't take the grind. I got married and quit show business."

"When?"

"Three years ago. I married a rich-type fella, a banker-fella, and I retired, sour grapes sort of, from show biz."

"Which explains the recommendation from Felix Davenport."

"A long time ago Felix told me, 'If you're ever in real trouble, see Peter Chambers. He's in the phone book.' "

"Are you in trouble, Mrs. Kiss?"

"I believe so."

"You *believe* so?"

"I'm not sure."

"What kind of trouble do you believe you're in?"

"Blackmail trouble."

That's trouble, even if you only believe you're in that kind of trouble. I sighed and extinguished my cigarette. It was not going to be easy for the lady. Blackmail trouble requires confession and confession is difficult when you must look upon the eyes of your confessor and is doubly difficult when the eyes of the confessor are straining not to look upon the curves of your calves. I glanced at my watch. There was time. I stood up and said, "Would you like a cup of coffee, Mrs. Kiss?"

"Oh yes, very much, thank you."

"Be with you in a minute," I said and went to the kitchen.

THREE

THERE IS a conundrum for the gods always asked by every host—why is it that stale coffee is invariably praised by an unexpected guest? I heated up the old coffee, poured it into my best china, and brought it to the living room, a cup for her, a cup for me. I sipped once, enthusiastically if emetically, and put the cup away on the mantel. She sipped and continued to sip and drained the cup and said, when she handed it back to me, "Delicious, absolutely delicious. Perhaps some day in different circumstances I shall inquire into your secret of making coffee."

"Blackmail," I said.

"Pardon?" she said.

"Eleven o'clock at 527 Madison."

"Yes," she said and suddenly coffee was no longer of the essence. For a moment her lower teeth caressed her upper lip and then she stood up and amenities vanished and small talk was dead. She paced, clasping and unclasping her hands. "I'm not sure," she said. "Actually, I'm not sure."

"Mrs. Kiss," I said, "*are* you being blackmailed?"

"No."

"Then what—"

"I believe I'm about to be blackmailed."

"Oh."

"But even as to that, I'm not certain."

"Oh."

"But I don't believe there can be any other explanation."

"For what?"

She sat down again. "This morning, Mr. Chambers, at a quarter after nine, I received a phone call, a most peculiar phone call."

"At your apartment?"

"Yes."

"Where do you live?"

"Brentwood Apartments. Seventy-fifth and Central Park West. Twenty-fourth floor, penthouse apartment. The call was from a woman. She said she had some interesting pictures to show me. She asked me to be at her office, 527 Madison Avenue, at eleven o'clock. I asked her what sort of pictures. She said it was something she didn't care to talk about over the phone. I told her I'd be at her office at eleven."

"I see," I said. "Pictures. What sort of pictures, Mrs. Kiss?"

"I don't know."

"But you must have *some* idea."

"I have no idea."

"But you *are* assuming that this is some kind of blackmail deal. You've stated that you believe that you're about to be blackmailed. That's correct, isn't it?"

"Yes, that's why I'm here."

"Then you must have some idea about those pictures."

"None. No idea."

It didn't make sense. It never does when the client is lying. Clients have many reasons for withholding the truth. Embarrassment is the chief reason when the subject is blackmail. The very basis of blackmail is material which one wishes to keep undisclosed. Confession is never easy. I switched the tack. I said, "Did you discuss this with your husband?"

"My husband wasn't at home."

"At nine-fifteen on a Saturday morning?"

"He went out, at about nine o'clock, on some sort of business."

"I see. So you got this phone call. Then what did you do?"

"I looked you up in the phone book and I called you here."

"For what purpose?"

"I wanted somebody on my side. Somebody with experience. Somebody who could protect me."

Softly I said, "You felt . . . you needed protection?"

"Wouldn't you?"

"Not unless I was aware that pictures existed that might be incriminating."

The brown eyes were stubborn. "I am not aware of any such pictures."

"Now look, Mrs. Kiss." I sat down near her. "A private detective is in a profession which is something akin to a doctor, a lawyer, a psychiatrist, sometimes even a priest. There is a need, perforce, for intimate disclosures, confidential communications. That is, if you trust the person to whom you come—"

"Felix said you were the best. He mentioned you frequently, as the best, honest, honorable—"

I did not take a bow. I shrugged. "Then you're going to have to trust me, Mrs. Kiss. My purpose is not to pry. I have no personal interest. But if I'm to work with you on this, if you want—as you have put it—my protection, then you must acquaint me with the facts. I must have something concrete to know what in hell I'm working on. You can even tell me to mind my own damned business, you can even point-blank refuse to tell me, but wriggling around, being evasive, fabricating, lying—that's out. Please, do you understand me?"

"Yes," she said.

"All right, then, please, this question. Have you ever posed for photographs that you wish you had not posed for?"

"No. Never."

"How old are you?"

"Thirty-two."

She didn't look it but what woman does? Thirty-two is a happy age. A woman of thirty-two is wise, experienced, fulfilled, sophisticated, at the bloom of her beauty but with sufficient guile and knowledge to keep that beauty never looking more than twenty-five.

"How long have you been an actress?" I said.

"Off and on, since I was graduated from college, since I was twenty-two. Modeling and acting. At the beginning I did a good deal of modeling and a little acting. Later, it was a good deal of acting and a little modeling."

"Now going all the way back, right to the beginning, did you ever pose for the kind of pictures—"

"No."

"The kind of pictures that somebody could unearth and, now that you're married, use against you for the purpose of blackmail?"

"No! Absolutely no!"

I leaned back in my chair and surrendered to confoundment. What in hell was she trying to pull and why? Sure there would be a fee, probably a handsome fee, but I was beginning to feel that I was in the middle of something, that I was about to be used but not for the purpose expressed. I don't like to be used for purposes unexpressed no matter how handsome or ugly the fee. I lit a cigarette, dragged in smoke, and took one more shot out of her. I was determined. Fee or no fee, handsome or ugly, unless I received a satisfactory reply, I'd throw her the hell out.

I smiled and I said politely, "Mrs. Kiss, let's forget the past and keep it in the present. You say you've been married for three years?"

"Yes." And now the big brown eyes were alive and interested.

"In those three years, Mrs. Kiss, were you ever in circumstances wherein a picture or pictures could have been snapped—all unknowing to you—which might prove, er, embarrassing?"

The brown eyes had long lashes and now the long lashes fluttered and the brown eyes avoided my eyes. A faint glint of perspiration shone on her forehead but of course it was a hot morning. She clasped her hands in her lap, seemingly gently, but the blood was out of the fingertips.

I pushed it, without push. Quietly. "What say, Mrs. Kiss?"

"If you please . . . I . . . I'd prefer not to answer that."

Better. Much better. Now it was in the groove and I was in the act and I knew why I was being used and I was willing to accept a fee. It was the age-old deal: hanky panky. A married lady had indulged herself in hanky panky. Hanky panky requires a partner. The partner had arranged for pictures and now he was maneuvering to make the hanky panky pay off. Sure she needed protection. Smart gal. If he was selling and she was buying, it was smart to bring an expert to consummate the deal, to pull in all the loose ends, to make it *one* deal, finished and final. *Caveat emptor!* Let the buyer beware! Smart gal, and smart to prefer not to answer. Why bleat the whole deal to the private richard before you know how bad the evidence is? A couple of night club photos drinking at The Stork could be explained away, without pay, and without incrimination. Let us wait and see before we bleat. Hanky had called to make the panky pay off, *but a woman had called!*

"You said," I said, "it was a woman who called. Correct?"

"Yes. A private detective."

Private detective. Smart, all around. It wasn't a couple of drinking photos, hanky and panky slobbering drunk, grinning into a camera at The Stork. It was a real deal with all the trimmings.

"Who was the woman who called?"

"Marla Trent."

"Stinks," I said. "You're all wet on the blackmail."

"I . . . I don't understand."

"I know Marla Trent. You remember the recommendation Felix Davenport gave me? That recommendation goes double in spades for Marla Trent—from me. Marla Trent wouldn't mix in blackmail, not on your life, or her life, or mine."

"Please, Mr. Chambers, let's go and find out."

"You bet," I said. "I'm quite anxious now because I'm curious. Is there anything else you'd like to tell me?"

"There's nothing."

My client was still under wraps, hoping against hope, but the glint of sweat on her forehead had now accumulated to beads. She stood up, opened her bag, and patted powder on her face. It *was* a hot morning.

FOUR

MARLA TRENT was Marla Trent Enterprises, 527 Madison Avenue, New York City. Marla Trent was a lady eye, the very tip of the top of the heap—the famous Private Eyeful. Marla Trent had no need to put her breast a foot forward to win, hands down and buttocks up, the accolade of Most Beautiful Private Detective In The World. Marla Trent was rich and successful, as were her clients. Marla Trent would as lief traffic with blackmail as a leaf would lief traffic with a whirlwind. Marla Trent was acute, astute, a beaut, and, of all things, a Ph.D., and with her figure yet. Marla Trent, in the preen of her teens, had once been runner-up to Miss America in Atlantic City, runner-up only because the dazed judges had not yet been ready to accept Juno as representative of the All-American Girl: Marla Trent stood five-six in stockingless feet and juttingly measured a justly proud 38-23-38 which is about as much woman as any man can dream to handle.

I admit to having dreamed but there had never been the opportunity to transfer the dream to reality. Marla Trent had always been the friendly enemy, the competition. Macy does not attempt to seduce Gimbel; nor Tiffany, Cartier; nor Lockheed, Boeing; nor Squibb, Parke Davis; etcetera all the way down to private detectives. There is a seemliness and a regard where mutual respect exists: the competition does not attempt to buck or pluck (or whatever rhyming word) the competition. I had worked in intimate concert with Marla Trent on intermittent and casual occasion but we had never worked in intimate concert for any length of time, to my regret.

Now at eleven o'clock Valerie Kiss and I presented ourselves at the spacious offices of Marla Trent Enterprises and I nodded to the receptionist, Miss Rebecca Asquiff, hatchet-faced and gimlet-sharp.

"Mrs. Kiss for Miss Trent," I said.

"How do you do, Mr. Chambers," gritted Rebecca. Miss

13

Trent will be with you very shortly," she said. "Please sit down."

We sat together on a beautiful, custom-made, modern-type bench (modern-type means built for show but not for comfort) and as I wriggled to prevent the displacement of my coccyx, I said, "I'll talk to her alone first. Sort of pave the way."

"Whatever you say, Mr. Chambers."

A boy came out, tall and manly but more feminine than Rebecca Asquiff, and he smiled and said, "This way, Mrs. Kiss."

"I'm Peter Chambers," I said. "I'll see Miss Trent alone first."

"Well, she's waiting in the library."

That meant—why keep Mrs. Kiss sitting on a modern-type bench in the reception room when instead she could be comfortable in the library while you and Marla Trent talked in Miss Trent's office?

We were led to the library which was a vast, cool, dim, book-lined room with an enormous mahogany library table and many mahogany armchairs. Marla Trent, quite the Private Eyeful, greeted us smilingly.

It was quite evident that Marla Trent was acquainted with Valerie Kiss. It was just as evident, however, that Valerie Kiss was totally unacquainted with Marla Trent. I was having a strange morning. Sometimes you can blame a strange morning on a hangover, but not this morning. I had retired the night before innocent of alochol; well, somewhat innocent; let us say sufficiently innocent not to be able to blame a strange morning-after on a familiar night-before.

Slightly slack-jawed Valerie Kiss said, "Are you, er, are you Marla Trent?"

Miss Trent nodded, still brightly smiling.

Mrs. Kiss swallowed. Who could blame her?

Marla Trent was unexpected when you expected a private detective. Marla Trent, in heels, was approximately five feet nine inches tall, all curves, all woman. Marla Trent was golden-haired, white-toothed, blue-eyed, red-lipped, creamy-skinned. Marla Trent was 38-23-38 and every splendid bulge of each astonishing statistic, unsuppressed by inhibiting undergarment, was as proudly displayed as a flag. She wore simple black pumps, no stockings, a simple black skirt, and a simple white scoop-necked blouse, the sum total of which simplicity was inordinately intricate in conjunction with Marla Trent. Certainly I could understand Valerie Kiss's swallow of surprise. I was not surprised but I swallowed too before I said, "Could I talk with you alone a moment, Miss Trent?"

She was gorgeous but she was a pro. There had been no squint of askance at my presence and now there was no ruffle of discomfiture at my request. She said, "Is that all right, Mrs. Kiss?"

"Yes," said Mrs. Kiss.

There was a door at either side of the far end of the library. The door to the left opened upon Marla Trent's office, the door to the right upon the office of William Boyd Winkle, her associate. Within, the contiguous offices were connected by a heavy oak door which was closed when Miss Trent and I gathered in conclave. Quickly we grew chummy, out of earshot of the client, albeit we were separated by the bulk of her sturdy desk. Skirt up and smiling she swiveled in her swivel chair while I gaped.

"What are you doing here?" she inquired.

"Trying to earn a fee," I said.

"How much?" she said.

"I don't know yet but the lady I represent looks rich."

"She's rich. The husband is a highly rated vice president of the Corn Exchange National, Thirty-eighth Street Branch. Why does she think she needs to be represented?"

"She had an idea that your call this morning was a prelude to blackmail."

The white teeth glistened in an amiable smile. "You know, I don't blame her."

"I talked her out of *that*. But quick."

"Well, thank you. You're sweet."

"Sweet as sugar, lady, but you wouldn't know."

"I can imagine."

I had made my stab, ponderously subtle, but the retort was cryptic, subject to either interpretation: crusty or encouraging. I was not taking any chances this early in the reestablishment of business relations, so I let it lie where she had dropped it. "Blackmail is the gambit of a second-rater," I said. "Actually, my opinion is no compliment to you. Simply, you don't need it, Miss Trent."

"Why the formality, Peter? The client is in the library, remember?"

"I keep forgetting. Quite a beautiful chick, eh?" That was a second stab, even more ponderously subtle.

"A bitch." That retort was disappointing, too typical.

"Bitch?" I said trying to sound horrified.

"A cheater. A cheater is a bitch. I don't like cheaters."

"The lady is a cheater?"

"The lady is a bitch. If you're in love with a bartender, then toss up the vice president, I always say."

"A bartender?" I said. "She doesn't appear to be the type."

"The vice president is handsome, but so is the bartender. I cannot speak for the husband's bedroom proclivities, but the bartender is quite an agile performer."

"Were you there?" I said.

"I've looked at pictures," she said.

"So that's the bit?" I said.

"Frankly," she said, "I don't know what in hell the bit is. At first I thought it was the normal desire for the acquisition of evidence for divorce. Now I'm beginning to believe it's something far more complex. The vice president may even be bitchier than the bitch."

"The vice president, I take it, is your client?"

"Sorry, confidential," she said.

"He retained you to gather up the evidence, I take it."

"Sorry, confidential," she said.

"I stood up staunch for you against the blackmail."

"I repeat, you're sweet."

"I am also trying, pulled away from breakfast on a Saturday morning, to earn a fee."

"*Noblesse oblige,*" she said. "Professional courtesy can be broadened to professional confidence. You are sweet and I do believe you did stand up for me."

I beheld in awe, as she clicked a peg of her intercom and said, "Willie, would you go get the Kiss file and bring it in to me, please?"

"Your wish is my command, dearly beloved."

Hurriedly, I lit a cigarette. The blue eyes regarded me enigmatically. I smoked with all the deliberate insouciance I could muster. Natuarlly I choked, restraining a cough, but coughing enough to demolish any cigarette commercial.

"I've begun to believe that it's the husband that's the weirdo."

"Beg pardon?" I said.

"Willie agrees with me. It began as a simple matter of ob-

taining evidence for divorce, except that the client was willing to pay real good. Ten thousand bucks, the expenses
ours."

"That's good enough unless it's complicated."

"No complications. Straight adultery."

"When did it start?"

"The adultery?"

"Your being retained."

She closed her eyes, thinking, and it was restful: it was as
though Klieg lights had been turned off. Then she opened
her eyes and I was back to smoking, furiously.

"Right after New Years," she said. "January Third. The
guy called for an appointment, came into the office, and told
us his story. The old story. He had a feeling his wife was
cheating and he wanted to know. He wanted to know with all
the proof. He wanted tape recordings and he wanted pictures.
On the pictures he wanted a double-header."

"You lost me," I said.

"Tapes are tapes. Now look, Peter, don't go ingenuous
on me. You seem to be in the mood to play the little boy
this morning, but sweetie, I know how much you've been
around."

That finished the cigarette. I squeezed it out, said, "So?"

"Tapes are aural, practically secondary evidence in a
courtroom."

"Plus you have to prove the voices."

"And tapes can be faked."

"Yes," I said.

"Also, as you very well know, tapes are mostly for the
masochistic kick, to *listen,* to *hear* what's going on. If all he
would have required was tape, then we'd have known he was
a weirdo right off the bat."

"But he also wanted pictures. A double-header."

"Which made him a husband seeking evidence for divorce."

"Provided the double-header on the pictures means what I
think it means."

"You're in the business. You know. The tape and one set
of pictures for him. The second set of pictures kept right here
in the office. Dig?"

"I do," I said. "No weirdo. Straight goods. Par for the
course. It takes a lot of doing, time and expense, to obtain the
evidence, but if the wife catches up with the bit, she might

destroy tape and pictures, and the guy's got nothing to show for his trouble. And once she's wise, she also reforms, or she does her cheating more carefully, and the guy can't even get himself his divorce. With a duplicate set of pictures in the office of his operator, he's got insurance."

"Very good, dear Peter. It's nice to have you coming out of your Saturday morning fog."

"Not fog, dear Marla. Daze. Whoever isn't dazed by your dazzling presence ought to go see his doctor to check his reactions."

"Well, thank you. Not bad for Saturday morning. Not at all bad."

"Thank *you*. So let's get back to Jonathan Kiss."

"He laid ten big ones on the line, and he was a client. Actually, it was routine stuff. Willie handled it, with, of course, Willie's customary skill."

"So when did he become a weirdo?"

"Yesterday afternoon."

The door between the offices swung open and William Boyd Winkle's broad bulk filled the doorway, jamb to jamb.

FIVE

WILLIAM BOYD WINKLE was as much an anomaly in his way as Marla Trent was in hers. In a profession dominated by plug-uglies William Boyd Winkle was also a Doctor of Philosophy who had majored in abnormal psychology and whose thesis for his doctorate, like Marla's, had been concerned with criminology. Unlike Marla, however, William Boyd Winkle had been an all-American fullback at Notre Dame, an intercollegiate wrestling champion, and an undefeated wrestler three years running at the Olympic Games. He stood perfectly balanced at six feet two, massive-shouldered, flat-bellied, and homely-handsome with a broken nose. Naturally, he had been nicknamed Wee Willie Winkle. He was soft of speech and easy of manner and slow to anger but when the fuse gave out he could be dangerous. Adding anomaly to anomaly, he was a scholar of the Bible and a scholar of Shakespeare and he had turned down a full professorship at Michigan State for the dubious distinction of private detection, joining with Marla in founding the richly successful Marla Trent Enterprises. It was common knowledge that there had never been a romance between them—each had previously been married, Marla divorced and Willie widowed—and it was common knowledge that there would never be a romance between them, first because their appeal to one another was strictly cerebral, and second because they both subscribed to the pragmatic adage that sexual byplay in commercial venture tends to befoul the business nest.

"To what do we owe the pleasure?" said Willie to Marla.

"Mr. Chambers is representing Mrs. Kiss," said Marla.

"Why does she need representation?" said Willie.

"She was of the opinion she was about to be blackmailed," said Marla.

"Can you blame her?" said Willie.

"No," said Marla. "She's outside in the library."

"But Peter is inside here."

"Give him the file."

"Are we about to breach a confidence?"

"We are about to trust a fellow worker."

"Well said, dearly beloved," said Willie as he gave me the portfolio.

It contained sixty-six full-sized photos, in color yet. It was a peep-show for a pornographer, in glossy color yet. It was no wonder that Marla Trent knew Valerie Kiss and Valerie Kiss did not know Marla Trent. Valerie Kiss had never before seen Marla Trent but Marla Trent had seen all of Valerie Kiss, and in superb action. Valerie Kiss was a beautiful woman who had passed the paramount screen test: she was more beautiful unclad than clad. There were long shots, close shots, high angle shots, and very low angle shots: sexual intercourse in all its aberrations and ungraceful positions was graphically delineated in sharp, stark, sweaty, ungrained, excellent focus.

I looked at the pictures and Willie and Marla looked with me. We made comments but our comments were rigidly clinical. An amateur might have been titillated but we were professionals. We had seen many such pictures; lamentably, we had made many such pictures throughout our careers; somebody has to scrape the sewers, somebody has to mash the garbage, somebody has to clean the purple refuse in the bloody slop-pans of an operating room. There are private detectives who boast that they do not practice in divorce. They are either silly dilettantes with private incomes, or they are hypocrites giving out with the big lie. Divorce work is the backbone of the business. Sly, dirty, disgusting but perfunctory, it is the bread and butter of the profession. Ninety percent is matrimonial work, five percent is even worse, and the remainder is the glamor that the writers write about. What else would writers write about: snapping dirty pictures of dirty people at fun and games, working to prevent the alimony or aggrandize the alimony, tapping telephones, tailing miscreants, unearthing forgotten filth, digging to find where a political body is buried?

There were sixty-six photographs and the further we proceeded the more dour we became, and then silent. We were experienced professionals unremittingly exposed to the nether side of the good, gay, simple life, and our temporary silence was the loud language of our permanent shame: for Valerie, for her partner, for ourselves, for you. "Who's the guy?" I said.

"Richard Robinson Jackson known as Ritchie," said Wee Willie Winkle.

"Like how old?" I said.

"Forty-one."

"How old is the husband?"

"Forty-two."

"The husband is ugly?"

"The husband is quite as beautiful as the paramour," said Marla. "Similar type, as a matter of fact, except for the interesting color of the hair."

The hair was white. Richard Robinson Jackson known as Ritchie was tall, long-legged, broad-shouldered, blue-eyed, straight-nosed, and youthful, with an imperious well-shaped head of prematurely white hair worn close, crew-cut. Except for the neat narrow scar of an appendectomy, the body was clean, lean, long, muscular, and hairless.

I moved away from the pictures. Willie put them back into the portfolio. Marla lit a cigarette. I refused to let the silence happen again. "Come on," I said. "Let's not get melancholy again. What's the story here?"

Now Willie lit a cigarette and smiled. "Same old story. A married gal, an unmarried guy. The gal has dough, the guy has nothing. Two pretty people with a lot of sex going for them."

"What kind of guy?" I said.

"A nothing. A bartender."

"There are bartenders that aren't nothing."

"This guy was nothing."

"How do you know?"

"Preliminary research. Upon that basis, the guy was nothing. Handsome, worldly, and stupid."

"That's a lot to get out of a little preliminary research."

Willie turned down the corners of his smile to lugubrious. "Peter," he said evenly, "I need your criticisms like I need a hole in the head."

"Willie," I said, "don't go superior on me."

"Marla," said Willie, "with your permission I'll throw this oaf the hell out of here. Bodily."

"Oafully nice of you," I said, "but big as you are, I don't think you can make it."

"Gentlemen, gentlemen," said Marla, "Saturday morning is always rough. Let's try to hang on to our tempers and temperaments."

"Well, he . . ." said Willie.

"Well, he . . ." I said.

"See?" said Marla.

We laughed, all of us, uncomfortably.

"Saturday morning with the sun shining is not exactly propitious for pornography," said Marla, "especially when the lady is sitting outside in the library worried about blackmail with no idea of what we actually have in here."

"I apologize, Mr. Chambers," said Willie. "Acrimony is frequently nothing more than the rattling of guilt."

"I apologize in return, Mr. Winkle," I said. "Okay, we've rattled. So how do you know the guy is stupid?"

"In the line of my duty I listened to the tapes. The intellectual badinage was suffocating."

"What do you expect in the dialogue of lovers? Wit, wisdom, and the profundities of Plato?"

"Hear, hear," said Marla applauding by tapping out her cigarette.

Willie shrugged. "I should have stood in bed, huh? This is not my day. Once more I apologize and this time also to the handsome bartender *in absentia*."

"I'm still stuck with the preliminary research," I said.

"You're not stuck with anything," said Marla. "The preliminary research was practically nil. Jonathan Kiss came here in January with a feeling that his wife was cheating. A spouse rarely misses on that sort of feeling. I questioned him but he had no idea of the possible lover. The best he could come up with was the bartender. Seems last summer the Kisses vacationed up near Darien, Connecticut. Mrs. Kiss seemed to cotton to a bartender in a tavern called the Pink Poodle and the bartender in the Pink Poodle seemed to cotton to Mrs. Kiss. The palpable flirtation had annoyed Mr. Kiss but he had no proof that it had been anything more than a summer flirtation. In the fall the Kisses went home and that was that until the feeling of cheating crept up on friend husband."

"I'm still stuck with the preliminary research."

"The preliminary research was exactly this." Marla snapped fire to a new cigarette. "In January, the day after we were retained, I went up to Darien to the Pink Poodle. The husband had described the bartender as a good-looking guy with a white crew-cut. There was no such bartender but there had been. His name was Richard Robinson Jackson, known as Ritchie. He was a big boozer when he wasn't working. He was a hip character who was a bear with the women and he had quit the job in October. Period."

"So where did you get the line on him?"

"Willie got the line."

"Routine," said Willie. "I tailed the dame. Ritchie now had a sweet little apartment at 222 East Sixty-second Street, discreet with no doorman, and his name as big as life downstairs in the bell-bracket."

Marla took it up. "Routine established that she saw him afternoons, Monday, Tuesday, and Friday, and on sporadic evenings. She would come over at about eleven and stay until three, afternoons. Then they'd go out for some drinking at discreet little bars until five or so; then she'd go home."

"Once the routine was established," Willie said, "I dropped in while they were out and gave the joint the gander. Sweet little setup. Furnished apartment, but charmingly furnished. Three rooms. Ritchie now had a slew of new clothes, new jewelry and stuff, and lots of pocket money—all donated by my lady fair."

"And how did *you* get educated?"

"By studying my lessons—from the tapes. But that first visit, all I did was give the place a gander, and take down the number of the unlisted phone."

"And then?"

"We used Mike Rommel, Elsie Axelrod, and Artie Stouffer. Know them?"

"Very well. Aces."

"We used them to rotate as tails on her. We supplied them with his phone number. When the loving couple went out, I went in. When the loving couple would give up on one of the watering places, one of the tails would wag by calling that phone number, and I would move right out."

"Like that you set up the bugs for the tapes?"

"Correct. Then I had Manhattan Photo, Inc. set up automatic cameras for the pictures—"

"Manhattan Photo is top price."

"We could afford. Our fee was ten thousand, in case you forgot."

"I remember. How long did the deal take?"

"In six weeks we removed the equipment. The husband got the tape and one set of pictures on March 1."

Marla shrugged. Her thronged blouse shrugged with her. "After that we expected a quick call from a lawyer arranging a raid, but the call never came. Yesterday another call came."

"The husband," Willie said.

"Yesterday at four," Marla said. "Urgent, could I see him at four-thirty. That's when he came and that's when he registered as a weirdo."

"Like how?" My turn for a cigarette. I lit up.

"He wanted me to call his home at nine-fifteen this morning."

"Why nine-fifteen, did he say?"

"Yes. Because he wouldn't be there then. I was to call her and he didn't want to be there for her to ask him any questions. I was to ask her to come here at eleven."

"And you were to show her the photos."

"I was to give them to her."

I tapped ashes to the carpet. "Marla, would you mind if I broke this to her alone? Rough, this kind of deal—"

"Mind? It'll be a favor. You don't think I like this, do you? Willie, where in hell are those photos?" Willie took the photos from the portfolio and transferred them to a large yellow string-clasp envelope. "The husband laid a thousand bucks on the desk for this little deal," Marla said. "And he also laid this on the desk." She opened a drawer. "Together with the pictures, I was to give her this."

It was an ordinary envelope, letter-sized, white.

It had no writing on it and it was sealed.

SIX

SHE WAS seated at a corner of the long library table. A magazine was open before her but she was not turning any pages. When I sat down beside her she did not look at me. She said, "Bad?"

"They have intimate pictures of you and Richard Robinson Jackson."

She said, "Oh my God."

I said nothing.

She closed the magazine and opened her pocketbook.

"I have three hundred dollars—"

"They're not selling."

"Then it's for you, your fee."

"Not now. Not yet."

She closed the pocketbook. She spoke quite calmly but she bit on each word as though it had a bad taste. "How much and I hope I can afford it but you must make certain—"

"They're not selling. They're giving."

That brought her face to me. She was perspiring and her brows were contracted. "What's this all about?"

"They've been instructed to give you those photos."

"Who's the they?"

"Miss Trent has an associate, a Mr. Winkle."

"Who instructed them?"

"Your husband."

She stood up. I stood up. For a moment she leaned against me. Then she straightened. "I want to know exactly what this is all about, if you please."

"This way," I said and took her to the office.

Wee Willie, legs crossed, was submerged in an armchair out of the way. Marla was standing. She had on a loose black jacket now, buttoned, which, hanging over the prominent ledge of her breasts, made her look pregnant. Pregnant or no, loose jacket or no, she was a tax upon the libido, a surtax. She smiled gently at Valerie Kiss.

"Mrs. Kiss—my partner, Mr. Winkle."

24

Willie nodded. Valerie nodded.

Marla said, "Mr. Chambers has acquainted you with the facts?"

"I don't understand any of this."

"I shall try to be brief."

"I'd appreciate that."

"There's nothing personal involved, Mrs. Kiss."

"Would you come to the point, please."

Put two attractive women together and it is like putting two fighting cocks into a pit: at once their wattles are up. Kiss's voice was like ice and her nostrils were tight. Marla's jacket was heaving, which did me no good.

"Your husband retained us in January to obtain evidence of your adultery. We did. On March 1, we turned over a tape-recording to him which we obtained by devices installed at an apartment at 222 East Sixty-second Street. We also turned over a series of photographs obtained by other devices at that apartment. Under instruction, we kept no duplicate of the tape-recording. Under instruction, we did keep one set of duplicates of the photographs. They are in that big yellow envelope on my desk. You may examine them if you wish."

Valerie went to the desk. Willie studied the ceiling. I turned my back on Valerie Kiss and went to Marla Trent who had turned her back on Valerie Kiss. Embarrassment is the enemy of diplomacy. I heard myself say in a low confidential voice, "Marla, the Saturday morning miasma has dissipated. I think you're a beautiful woman and I've had a yen for you so long it's criminal. Saturday night is the night for squares but how's about you and me—"

In a low confidential voice she said, "I have a date for tonight."

In a low confidential voice I said, "There are other nights, like tomorrow night. As long as I've shot off my big fat mouth—"

"Thank you," said Valerie Kiss. She tied the strings to the clasp of the yellow container and laid it on the desk. "Now just what is it you want of me?"

Marla went to her. "I don't want a thing."

"Then why have you sent for me?"

"I was instructed to send for you. I'm in a business where I follow the instructions of my client."

"And just what were the instructions of your client?"

"That I give you the photographs, and that I give you this." She took up the sealed letter and handed it across without flourish. "That finishes my business with you, Mrs. Kiss."

Valerie Kiss held it as though it were contaminated. At arm's length she looked at it, turned it over and looked at it. For a moment her stringent control loosened, and her face showed emotion. Perplexity was displaced by curiosity which was displaced by frowning pique which was then displaced by the bland frigid mask which perplexity had at first displaced, as control surged back. She inserted a long red fingernail into the slit of the flap and tore open the envelope. She withdrew a sheet of paper, unfolded it and read it, and her gasp brought Willie off the ceiling and on to his feet.

Valerie handed it to Marla who read it quickly and handed it to Willie who read it quickly and handed it to me who read it quickly.

My Beloved Wife: When you read this I shall be dead. It was either you or I and I decided in my favor and against you.   *Jonathan.*

I dropped it to the desk.
I said, "Let's go."
"You bet," said Willie.

Three strangers and one wife were galvanized to action by reason of a possible emergency. Peter Chambers, who had never even heard of the guy, was running. Marla Trent, to whom the guy had been only a casual client, was running. Wee Willie Winkle, who had spied on the guy's wife, was running. The wife was running too but the wife had stopped long enough to pick up the yellow envelope because the yellow envelope contained sprightly photos in color of her off-color entertainments.

We raced through the halls, we were impatient in the elevator, and we caught a cab that was discharging passengers in front of the building. In the cab I looked at my watch as Willie urged speed and the driver grumbled about not being a magician. It was twenty-five minutes to twelve and the driver, grumbling, was not bumbling: he was accurately maneuvering along the shortest route. On Saturday before twelve New York traffic is not yet impossible glue and our pilot used the transverse through the park to Central Park

West and in ten minutes he had us spilling out of the cab in front of the Brentwood Apartments.

There was no doorman in sight.

It was a fine tall rich house on the last of the rich boulevards on the West Side. The lobby was the usual three-story tomb of marble, and the gold carpet was thick and spread wall to wall, and the self-service elevators, all glinting gilt-and-mirror, were in the rear, and one was open and waiting, and Valerie tapped the top button, and during the swift noiseless upward journey, she developed a packet of keys from her handbag.

On the twenty-fourth floor she inserted key into lock but before she could turn it the door was pulled open from within.

By a uniformed policeman.

SEVEN

THERE WERE four cops, all alert and on their feet in the living room. The one who had opened the door was a big one but young and not yet harsh. He saw the key in her hand and he said quietly, "Mrs. Kiss?"

She looked about wildly.

"I'm Petrie," he said. "Bill Petrie, ma'am."

"Please. What's wrong?"

"We're here waiting, ma'am, just expecting if you'd come along." Willie's great bulk impressed him. He said to Willie, "Just waiting. We're supposed to keep the lady here if she shows."

"Who's in charge?" Willie said.

"Detective-sergeant Wagner. We're to keep her here and inform him. Have her sit down, huh? I mean till we get the information to the sergeant."

It was bad, obviously. Cops do not stutter unless it is bad and Petrie was stuttering with all the marbles. Cops are big when it is little and little when it is big and four big brawny cops were pygmies in a spacious sumptuous living room. I could smell death and so could Willie. He moved toward Valerie and he mumbled to Valerie and he sat her down and Marla joined. I moved toward one of the other cops, another young one. I said, "Wagner is Lenny Wagner?"

"Yeah. You in the business?"

"Private. Lenny Wagner's a friend of mine."

"I'm Martino, Sal Martino." He was tall and thin with a dark face and girl's eyes.

"I'm Peter Chambers."

"I never heard of you," he said respectfully.

"What gives?"

"A jumper."

"From here?"

"Yeah."

"Bad?"

"Like disgusting." He tugged at my wrist and I went with him to a window and I looked down into a back alley. Far down, twenty-four stories down, humans like ants were crawling. "The crumb jumped. From here, it figures."

"When?"

"Eleven-twenty is the figure."

"I'll go down and talk to Wagner."

"I ought to go myself, but I won't fight you. There's a lot of pieces like smashed with guts all over. Would you do me a favor?"

"Sure."

"Tell him you talked to Martino. Tell him Martino wanted to go but you insisted. And don't forget to tell him the wife is here."

I moved away from the window and Willie's head turned and his eyes questioned me and I answered with a thumb-down motion of my right hand. Then I went out and rode down in the elevator and outside I went around to the back and there a burly cop spread a hand like a baseball mitt across my chest.

"Where the hell you think you're going?" he inquired.

"Sergeant Wagner."

"You got business?"

"I brought the wife home. Martino sent me."

"Oh." The mitt came off and he let me through.

They were scraping him together and collecting him in a canvas bag. There were six men working. The blood was all over, and the blobs of flesh, and the gleaming bone. I swallowed back gag and kept going. The sun was high in the sky, bubbling hot, but the workers looked cold. Everybody was pale.

Off to a side a couple of cops were working on a man, sick, flat on his back. I went near.

"Who is it?" I asked somebody.

"The doorman, the poor punk," somebody said.

I pushed through and they let me. I pushed through with authority and I had no uniform. Detectives push with authority and have no uniform. Nobody stopped me. I squatted over the guy and I looked up. "What's his name?" I said with authority.

"Nick," said one of the cops.

I looked down to Nick. "How are you?"

"I'm fine." His face was the color of dirty grey leather and white spit was hard at the corners of his mouth.

"What time did it happen?" I said.

"I told you guys already forty times."

"Tell again."

"Twenny after eleven. I hear this smack in back like an explosion. I run to see but before I run I look at my watch. Twenny after eleven."

"Did you see Mr. Kiss go out this morning?"

He smiled as though happy a new question had been put. The smile was hideous inside caked dry lips.

"Sure I seen him. He went out bright and early. About nine bells."

"When did he come back?"

"Around eleven. He says, 'Hi, Nickie,' and I says, 'Hi, howareya, Mr. Kiss.' And he goes in and twenny minutes later—boff! I run back here but I can't do nothing. I take one look at the mess, and I pass. I used to think I was a man but now I admit, no. I pass, and that's all I been doing, passing. Every time I sit up and take a look, pass. I ought to be ashamed, no?"

"Feel better now, Nickie?"

"Yes sir, fine," he said and fainted again.

I left him to resuscitation by cops and tried to step through splotches of blood to get to Sergeant Wagner but it was tough. They were moving the pieces, systematically, from the outer reaches toward the middle to the canvas bag into which he was being collected. I got through to Wagner and he said, "You? You another one of them morbid-type sightseers? What the hell you doing here?"

"I brought the wife home."

"Mrs. Kiss?"

"I told Martino I'd tell you myself."

"Brought her home from where?"

"She was with me."

"Mrs. Kiss was with you?"

"With me."

Wagner was a good straight cop, past middle-age but strong, and wise and weary in the trade. Wagner was tall with beefy shoulders and a gravel voice and a young wife and six kids, one of them a tot. Wagner said, "Why in hell do they jump, the bastards? And from a penthouse yet. Disgusting bastards. Who needs it?"

"Rough on you," I said.

"Rough on everybody. You think them guys sweeping him up are made of tin? They're human just like you and me with wives and kids. You think them guys are going to go home nice and normal and sit down and eat dinner tonight? Why do them bastards jump, for Chrissake? Christ, they can take pills, can't they?"

"You want to talk with the wife, don't you?"

It was as though he had not heard me. "Twenty-four floors, head first. Do you know the speed, how it accelerates? Christ, when the guy hits, it's like with bullet force. Christ, like an express train. And this guy hit head first, yet. Head first. Smashed like a rotten egg. Who needs it? You want to kill yourself, who cares? Christ, take sleeping pills. Shoot yourself. Put your head in a stove. Christ, what do you want from the people who have to pick up the pieces? I've already thrown up twice. And the wife or somebody is going to have to take a look at that garbage. That's the law. Somebody's got to identify whatever the hell there is to identify. Christ, you want to kill yourself, think of these things. How is she?"

"Who?"

"The wife."

"I don't know. I came down here for you the minute one of your cops told me what happened."

"Did they tell her?"

"That's your job, Lenny."

"Yeah." He went away from me, gave some orders to the men who were working, came back and touched my arm. "Let's go."

We walked around to the front of the building and into the lobby and he touched the button for one of the elevators. "How well do you know her?" he said.

"I just met her today."

"You're going to have to swear out a statement."

"Whatever's necessary," I said.

"He killed himself because of her."

"How do you know that?"

"He left two notes and a big envelope with pictures, none of them sealed. One note was for the authorities and that didn't say anything, just the usual bull. The other note was for her personal, and that said plenty."

"And you read them both?"

"Of course," he said. "And I also looked at the pictures. Wow!"

EIGHT

THEY HAD told her.

Petrie told us.

They had told her and she had keeled. They had brought her brandy and she had sopped up a lot of it. Then Miss Trent had taken her to the bathroom and then helped her undress and she was now in bed. Miss Trent and Mr. Winkle were in the room with her.

"Where's the notes and the pictures?" Wagner asked.

Petrie opened a drawer of a table. "Right here."

"You show her any of this?"

"Of course not, sir."

"Gimme."

Petrie took a maroon-colored folder out of the drawer. It was a legal-type folder. Wagner tucked it under his arm and he looked like a lawyer. We marched through a corridor to the bedroom. The door was closed. Wagner knocked. Willie called, "Come in."

She was seated in the bed with pillows plumped behind her. She was wearing white silk pajamas. Her face was washed, without makeup, and her hair was pulled back in a pony-tail. She held a large snifter glass of brandy in her hand. She was even more attractive without the makeup. She was flushed from the brandy and her eyes were wild.

Marla was seated near the bed. Marla also held a snifter glass of brandy. Willie was leaning against a dresser on top of which, aside from the usual toilet articles, was a tray with a bottle of brandy and one other glass. The whole damned room smelled of brandy and, somehow, smelled of woman.

"I'm in charge here," Wagner said. "Detective-sergeant Wagner. You're Mrs. Kiss, I take it?"

"Yes sir," she said.

Wagner looked from her to Marla to Willie.

I said, "Miss Marla Trent, Mr. William Boyd Winkle."

"What are they doing here?"

"Miss Trent and Mr. Winkle are the proprietors of Marla Trent Enterprises."

"Oh, *that* Marla Trent," said Wagner. "You're a private detective, no?"

"Yes," said Marla.

"You too?" he said to Willie.

"Yes," said Willie.

"What the hell is this?" he said to me. "A convention?"

"Mrs. Kiss and I had some business at Miss Trent's office," I said. "We all came back here together."

"Well, you're all going to give me statements," said Wagner.

"Only as to the externals," Marla said. "All else is confidential."

"Confidential my —" said Wagner. "You'll give me full statements."

"Just a minute, please," Valerie Kiss said.

"Yeah?" said Wagner.

"I . . . I don't want a scandal, please. I . . ."

"What in hell do you think a suicide is, lady? A PTA meeting?"

She gulped brandy. She said, "I mean . . . I'm perfectly willing to cooperate. There's no reason to hide anything, any of this, as long as it doesn't become public. I mean I don't think anything that these people can tell you is anything I'm really ashamed of—"

Wagner's tone softened. "Look, Mrs. Kiss, this is an open and shut suicide. We're just as anxious as you to close the files on it. This is a big city with a lot of crime, and we don't have the time to waste with scandals. All I want is information for the files, period. That's my job. The faster I clean this up, the better I like it. This is no federal case. Plenty of guys kick themselves off. But these people are here, and since they're here they're a part of the case, and if they're a part of the case, their statements belong in the file. Period."

She looked toward me.

I said, "Sergeant Wagner isn't one to blow up scandal." I

had my moment to warn her, and I warned her. "For instance, the Sergeant has certain notes that your husband has written. Two notes. One is general, one is personal. Your husband didn't seal them, and we certainly can understand that, in his state of mind. The sergeant has read them both, but I'm certain he'll only make public the general note. Am I right, Sergeant?"

"Damn right you're right."

Behind the sergeant's back, Willie grinned and nodded. At least Willie understood. Willie had not majored in psychology for nothing.

Valerie Kiss said, "Then all of you may tell the sergeant whatever he wishes to know." And she was back on the brandy.

"Okay, you three," Wagner said. "One of my cops will take you down to the station house, and you'll swear out your statements there."

"No," said Valerie Kiss.

Wagner said, "What's now?"

"He stays." She pointed to me.

"Why him?"

"I . . . I need somebody."

It was a small compliment but it would help with the fee.

"Look, Lenny, I mean Sergeant Wagner," I said. "We'll all go together to make our statements. As long as Mrs. Kiss wants me here, I can't see any objection to Miss Trent and Mr. Winkle also staying. We all may be able to help you, right here, right now, just in conversation, to fill in the blanks. Unless Mrs. Kiss has objection."

"No objection," she said and finished the brandy. She held the glass out to me. I took it, poured more brandy into it, and brought it back to her.

"Okay," said Wagner. "So what's the story?"

"All right, Mrs. Kiss?" I said.

"I . . . I'm depending on you," she said.

Quickly I gave him Part One, and just as quickly Willie filled him in on Part Two. Valerie lay back with her eyes closed. Marla lit a cigarette and smoked. "Okay," Wagner said, "that's the background. It explains the personal note." He opened the maroon folder and Valerie opened her eyes. He took out an envelope, seemed undecided as to what to do with it, then gave it to me. Written by hand was the scrawl: "To Whom It May Concern." I handed it to Valerie

Kiss. She handed me her glass. She opened the envelope and read the note. I drank her brandy. Then she returned the note and the envelope to me. I returned the empty glass to her and read the note:

To Whom It May Concern: I have taken my life because my life is no longer worth living. It is my wish that I be cremated at once, as soon as the authorities release what may be left of my body. I wish my ashes to be flown over the Atlantic and dropped into the sea. I wish this can be done on Sunday, a church day, a day of rest for mortals. May God forgive me and have mercy on my soul.   Jonathan Kiss.

I gave the note to Marla. She read it and handed it up to Willie. Willie read it and gave it to Wagner. Wagner put it back into the folder and drew out a second envelope. This was a larger envelope, business size, and it was bulky. The routine was now set. He handed the envelope to me. I lay back the flap and withdrew the contents. There were sixty crisp one-hundred-dollar bills, and a lengthy letter. Now I looked at the envelope. He had written: "To My Wife." I gave the envelope to Valerie, she gave it to Marla, Marla gave it to Willie, Willie gave it to Wagner, Wagner put it into the maroon folder. Then I gave the money to Valerie.

"What do I do with it?" she said.

"You keep it," Wagner said.

She placed it on the nighttable. She held out her glass to me. I took it, filled it, drank off a third, gave it to her. Her fingers touched mine as she took it. I could have sworn I felt a pressure, but I'm a morbid type. I looked at her. Her lips quivered tight together, as though in a kiss, and then they lapped at the edge of the glass.

"You keep the money," Wagner said. "The letter will explain."

Sardonically Willie said, "You mean you're not going to impound it?"

"Only the written material, and that temporary," Wagner said. "And the pictures."

Marla looked up. "There are pictures?" she inquired innocently.

"We'll come to that," Wagner said.

They were engaged with one another, as I looked toward

Valerie. The glass was away from her lips, not far, and the huge brandy-gleaming brown eyes were on me. She had a full mouth, very red. Once again the glistening lips came forward, puckered, pouting, subtly quivering and then Wagner said, "Well, read it already." I unfolded the sheet of paper and I sneaked a glance at Valerie. Her lips were back to the edge of the glass but her eyes, uptilted, were on me. I read the letter but I was not interested. I was interested in Valerie Kiss. I felt that she was interested in me. That was very sick and I knew it was very sick but it could have been healthy if she had a purpose. Maybe she had a purpose. I read the letter.

My lovely wife, you are a cheap, contemptible whore. I loved you. I no longer love you. I detest you. I had contemplated murdering you, but what sense? You would be dead but I would be alive to suffer the torment of your guilt, and the guilt of my murdering you. I have thought about it for a long time, and this way is better. I am killing myself, but you have killed me. I am leaving you everything; let's see if you can enjoy it. Let us see if you can live with horror, with the horror of knowing that you have murdered me, and let us see how long you can live with that horror. Yes, I am cruel, but no more cruel than you. I have implanted a cancer, let us see how long you can live with it. Within minutes from my writing this, I shall have flung myself out of the window. You have killed me. You live with that. I leave you torture, and I leave you my money, so that you can live with your torture. Let us see how long you can live with it. Let us see how long before you are old and ugly with guilt. Better you than me. Enjoy. I dare you. You are a cheat and a murderer now. Enjoy. I dare you. I know you. I know your mind. I am dead, but you have made me dead, and now yours will be a creeping deadness. I curse you with my last breath of life, and you will remember my curses. I know you, and the cancer is now in you. Enjoy. I dare you. Wherever I am, I await you, and when you come, I shall denounce you, and spit upon you. The money for my funeral arrangements is here contained, together with some pictures which, I trust, may amuse you more than they amused me. I remain always and forever in your memory,   Jon.

This had been a smart man, a terrible man, terribly smart. A cheating wife is entitled to knuckles if she is caught, as is a cheating husband, if he is caught. But this was not knuckles, there was no comparison: this was purgatory. A cheating wife does not deserve the curse of purgatory, nor a cheating husband. Love is not forever and love can end, love can even be divided.

She could have told him; she could have left him; but that is criticism and criticism comes easy when applied to another. Righteousness is a sturdy stick but only in the hand of the wielder. Who in life has not cheated, physically or mentally, and what circumstances have prevented the mental cheating from developing into the physical cheating? There are so many circumstances, both for cheating and for refraining from cheating. There is fear, and there is the circumstance of children, position, status, or the circumstance of residual love for the one to be cheated upon, or sympathy, or liking, or compassion. Perhaps this had been a case of divided love. Or perhaps this woman had not had the heart to hurt the man. Or perhaps it had been a case of ended love but economic ties had bound her against an open break. Certainly she had been supporting the lover and just as certainly the husband had been supporting her: to break with one might have been to lose the other. Who can unlock a heart for secrets, who has the power to peer into a soul, who knows—without knowing—what motivates a transgression, and who can presume to sit in judgment? She was a cheater, and cheating is a crime, but the punishment must fit the crime, and this punishment was way out, fiendish, too much, maniacally exquisite. For one stupid beatific moment I was overwhelmed with an impulse to be a hero; not just for this drunken woman in the white pajamas, but for all women and all men, you and me included. I had an impulse to run, get out, destroy this letter which would destroy this woman. What could they do? Sue me? So I had flipped my wig; I had popped my cork; what difference would it make: nobody here had committed a crime. What could they do? I had lots of politician friends: there wouldn't be a jail rap for this kind of idiocy. No jail rap, but they *could* lift my license. Suddenly I stopped being a hero. My license is my bread and butter, and when it comes to bread and butter, you know how it is. You damned well know how it is, *all* of you:

the muck we go through and the bastards we pretend to respect, all because of bread and butter. Disgusting, isn't it, boys and girls? Cringe, but duck it. Let it pass. Don't give it another thought. Bread and butter is bread and butter. Everybody can't be a hero, and the martyr is the hero's hero. Forget it.

I did a fast cringe and passed the letter to Valerie Kiss. Valerie Kiss passed the brandy to me and I drank thirstily. She read it. She took a long time reading it. She was either a hell of an actress or she had a lot more class than any of us had given her credit for, because she handled it perfectly. She took a long time reading, but when she was finished she passed it to Marla without comment or change in facial expression, and then she lifted her hand to me for the brandy. I gave her what was left of it and this time I *knew* her fingers caressed mine. The lady had a yen or the lady had a purpose: either way, I had nothing to lose and a lot to gain because, very obviously, the lady was a hell of a lot of woman. Suddenly I lost all interest in Marla Trent. Temporarily, of course.

NINE

AFTER THAT it went smoothly. Wagner offered the pictures to Valerie but she shook them off. Marla said, "Please," and Wagner gave them to her. Marla went through them fast and returned them. "There are sixty-six photos," she said. Marla was a pro. She did not want some wise-guy cop clipping a few for private pinups. Wagner understood. His smile was small but it was all admiration. Wagner was as much a pro in his field as Marla was in hers. "Yes ma'am," he said. "Sixty-six." He took his time packing up the maroon folder and once I saw his glance flick out, wistfully, at the brandy bottle. I knew Wagner and I knew he was troubled and I knew what he was troubled about. Somebody was going to have to identify the mess that was being scraped together downstairs: that was the law. He was now a splattered pulp and it was going to be identification by fragment and it was not going to be pretty and a woman could fall apart and Wagner was hoping that it would not have to be the woman, but it was a tough subject to get around to.

I opened it up roundabout, and Wagner took it from there. I said, "Do you know if your husband left a will, Mrs. Kiss?"

"No will," she said. "No need."

"Why not?"

"No next of kin, nobody, except me."

"No family?" I said.

"No one. His father and mother are dead, and there were no brothers or sisters. No need for a will. He had nobody except . . . except me."

"Somebody's going to have to identify him," Wagner said.

"Yes," she said faintly.

Wagner swallowed, coughed. "It's going to be rough, Mrs. Kiss. When you go down twenty-four flights you're smashed up bad, real bad."

She turned her face into the pillows.

Wagner said, "He went head first."

She made no sound.

Wagner said, "There'll be lots of time yet before we take you downtown. It's only a formality, Mrs. Kiss, but it's the law and it's got to be done. I suggest you try to get some sleep. We'll be back later."

He motioned with his thumb and Marla and Willie went out. I was at the door with him when she turned and said, "Sergeant."

"Yes ma'am?"

"I want Mr. Chambers to come back with you."

"Yes ma'am."

"I . . . I'll need somebody."

"Yes ma'am, he'll come back with me. Now do you need anything, want anything?"

"No, thank you."

"I can leave one of my men here if you want."

"No, thank you. I'll manage."

"Try to get some sleep, Mrs. Kiss."

"Thank you."

In the living room Wagner said, "Okay, we're finished here. Petrie, you'll drive these people over to the house in the squad car. They're going to swear out statements. The rest of you downstairs and help out."

Outside he put a key in the lock and turned it.

I said, "Where'd you get a key?"

"The super. Once we knew who it was from the papers in his clothes—"

"He was fully dressed?"

"Yeah. Full street wear. According to the doorman he went out at about nine, came back at about eleven, normal street clothes. He must of then wrote them notes, and then, just as he was, took the dive. Anyway once we knew who he was, we come up here, but the door was locked. We got a key from the superintendent and that's how we got in."

Downstairs Wagner went back to his work and Petrie drove us to the station house and there we were badgered by a pipsqueak cop who liked the sound of his voice and thought he was a district attorney. He took us one at a time, Marla first, and Willie and I sat around alone and jabbered. "One hell of a day," I said.

"Yeah," Willie said.

"What do you think, Willie?"

"What in hell's to think?"

"The guy was a weirdo, all right."

"All the way down the line to death."

"That suicide note, the personal one, that was something, huh?"

"Diabolical."

"Sleeping with the bartender is going to grow progressively more distasteful, I think."

"I couldn't agree more, Peter. That note will stay inside of her like a knife. Every move she makes, it will cut. The bastard left her the guilt of her adultery and now the guilt of his death, and that note made it sharp and clean. As the Bard put it, he left her 'a plague of sighing and grief.' "

"He also, it seems, left her all his dough."

"Which makes it even more diabolical. If he had cut her off with only dower rights, she could have something in the way of hate, which might give her a hinge for escape. But the weirdo left her no out. Guilt, guilt, guilt, and his money. How long can you go on that? The human mechanism is delicate, and the weirdo had the feel of it."

"Meaning?"

"On the surface, who can complain? She was cheating, so he left her free to cheat. She stayed along with him for his money, so he left her his money. On the surface, it sounds great. Inside, it all eats like acid. Cheating is guilt, and that eats. His death was her work and he made it plain, and that will eat. He bequeathed no weapon to her to lash out against him, and no balm as salve for her conscience.

He gave her no cause for wrath, for hate, for revenge, any of which might have saved her. He left her his money, and any time she spends a nickel of that on the bartender, or even on herself, it will be with the knowledge that it is money which came to her because of her cheating and his death. Unless she's strong, very strong—unless he misjudged her and I doubt that, shrewd as he has shown himself to be—then in my opinion it will be a downward spiral of guilt, self-hate, self-disgust and, in the end, destruction."

TEN

I PRESENTED myself at Valerie's apartment at eleven o'clock on Sunday morning. She was wearing a black tailored suit, a pearl grey blouse, pearl grey stockings, and pearl grey suede pumps. Her brown eyes were perfectly clear, bright and sober. The auburn hair was now in a braid on the head, every strand in place. Her makeup was discreet and subtle, her attitude casual, refined, remote. What a woman.

She went into the living room and I ambled after. She went to the bedroom and I had better sense than to amble after. She came back with six thousand dollars and said, "I think you better keep this with you."

"Yes ma'am," I said. "You want a receipt?"

"Now stop it," she said and she smiled the smile of last evening. "We'll have to attend to the arrangements."

"Arrangements?"

"Jonathan," she said.

"Oh yes," I said.

"We'll do it exactly the way he wanted it."

"Oh yes, of course of course. Well, let's go then. I've got a hunch we're going to have a busy day."

In the morgue downtown, it took two hours to get all the necessary papers taken care of before we had rights to the body. It was Sunday. On a weekday, it would have taken an hour and a half.

"Okay, he's yours," a leather-faced man said.

"Keep him," I said.

"Oh no," he said. "He's not ours any more."

"I mean temporarily," I said. "He's to be cremated. They'll pick him up."

"Arrangements already made?"

"No. I'm going to make them right now."

"It's going to be rough."

"What's rough about cremating?"

"Sunday. Everything is rough on Sunday."

He was so right. I made sixteen calls before I got somebody who would listen to me, but he did not want to listen on the telephone, so I sent Valerie home and went to the crematory.

"You're lucky," the man said. "I'm the owner. I'm here on Sunday. Why burn your man on Sunday, sir?"

"He specifically asked. I'm representing the widow."

"Our facilities are like shut down on Sunday. I'm afraid it's gonna cost you."

"How much?"

"Where do we pick him up?"

"The morgue."

"Morgue?" The grey eyes grew sympathetic and the deep voice moved up a notch, as did the price. "A thousand," he said.

"What?" I said.

"Bucks," he said.

"A thousand dollars!"

"Look, mister, even laborers get paid double time on Sunday. I'm the boss. But my people are all Union. I'm gonna hafta get a crew in here, fire up the incinerator, there's more than you think to this. Look, if you want it fancy, it'll cost you more. I mean, we have—"

"No, no. All I want is the ashes. The ashes are supposed to be dropped over the Atlantic."

"Yeah," he said somberly. "It's like a new fashion here in the east. Dropped over the Atlantic. Very thoughtless of the deceased, all these new-fangled-type deceaseds. I mean, they got folks. Folks like to visit, like to go to a cemetery. We got a special room, with niches for the urns, a real beautiful room, special designed by an interior decorator, for visiting. But when the deceased is dropped over the Atlantic. I mean what are the folks to do to go visit? Go swimming?"

"Every business has its ins and outs," I said. "You can't do better than a thousand?"

"You're getting away cheap. You're a nice, earnest young man."

"Okay," I said. "How long will it take?"

"Seven hours."

"What?"

"Now look, young man. I got to call in my crew from all over, far out as Forest Hills. There's even a special guy to drive the pickup wagon. You've got to give me seven hours."

I looked at my watch. It was three o'clock. "That means by ten you'll have the ashes at the plane."

"Yes sir, I can promise you that. Where do you want him delivered?"

That held me. "I don't know yet," I said.

"Don't know yet. Sonny, your Sunday troubles are only beginning."

"I'll call you. I'll tell you where."

"Look. Pickup, incineration, and delivery in an urn—nothing fancy, an urn—that's a thousand dollars. If we hafta keep him for you which means we'll have to stay open and ready to deliver—that's extra."

"How much extra?"

"Dunno. Depends. After ten, it'll be by the hour."

"Okay," I said.

"Just a minute," he said.

"What?" I said.

"Cash now," he said. "Or go get the cash before I start." For spite I said, "Why?" I was curious.

"Because on a quickie like this, especially on a Sunday, we don't take checks. The check bounces, what've we got for collateral? Ashes?"

"I see your point," I said.

I opened my poke and he peeked and I heard his gasp. "You're getting a bargain," he said.

I paid him and took a receipt and got out of there and went home. First I called Valerie and told her about the cremation arrangements and told her I would call her back, and then I started on the chartered planes with the Classified open. I made twenty-seven telephone calls, most of which were to Answering Services. The Answering Services, six times, were willing to give me home phone numbers, and four of them did not answer, and the fifth was a guy who was loaded and told me to talk to him on Monday, and the sixth said, "A night job! Ashes over the Atlantic at *night?*"

"Yes, sir," I said meekly.

"On Sunday? Brother, that's gonna cost you."

On Sunday, go to church. Don't try to do business on Sunday. If you wish to do business on Sunday, be prepared to pay through the nose.

"How much?" I said.

"Lemme figure."

What in hell did he have to figure? I waited.

He said, "Fifteen hunnert."

"*How* much?"

"Fifteen hunnert. A thousand down. Five hunnert when you deliver the remains."

"That's highway—"

"Goodbye, Mac."

"Hold it!"

"Yes, Mac?"

"You've got a deal."

"Okay, I'll see you in an hour."

"Where?" I said.

"Twenty-third Street and East River. Acme Airways. Ask for Stinson. No. Don't ask. I'm Stinson. I'll be the only one there."

"Okay, Stinson."

One hour later I was at Acme Airways. Stinson was skinny, tall, tow-headed, with laughing blue eyes. We made our deal. "What is it on Sunday?" I said.

"On Sunday it's for robbers, Mac. The ashes a relative of yours?"

"No. I'm handling it for his widow."

"Ten o'clock?"

"I'll be here. I'll give him a good ride. Far, wide, and handsome, and way out."

"Very good, Mr. Stinson."

"Don't forget to bring the extra five hunnert."

"I won't forget."

I went home. I called her and I told her. She thanked me. I told her I'd call her back later. I called the guy at the crematory and told him. He thanked me. I called the morgue and told them. Even they thanked me. I called Marla Trent. She wasn't at home. I called Wee Willie Winkle. He wasn't at home. I took out a bottle of Scotch, and put it away. I made coffee and drank coffee. I tried to sleep. I couldn't sleep. I tried to doze. I couldn't doze. I tried to read. I couldn't get interested. I sat down at my desk and wrote checks for my bills. That took a long time, and it made me surly. When I was finished, I stamped the envelopes, went out into the hall, and sent them down the chute. Inside I took out the bottle of Scotch again, and put it away again. I took off my clothes and got into a hot bath. I was just beginning to relax when the phone rang. I got out wet and answered it. Like that you can get electrocuted. It was Valerie Kiss.

"It's eight-thirty," she said.

"I know," I said. I didn't know. I had no idea.

"Will you be here at nine?"

"Sure," I said.

"See you at nine."

"Sure," I said.

I dressed carefully. After all I wasn't just a private richard hauling the ashes, I was a half-ass lover-boy. I got there at nine-thirty. She rushed me out. We got to Acme Airways at ten to ten. The ashes had not arrived. Promptly at ten, a black Cadillac pulled up and a bushy-haired guy got out with a package.

"Acme Airways?" he inquired.

"I'm Acme Airways," Stinson said.

"The urn is in the parcel," he said and delivered the package. "The top of the urn is removable."

"Look, Mac, you don't have to draw me no diagrams. I done this kind of job before. Everybody wants to be a master of ceremonies," Stinson said. "Okay, now's the time for the second payment, Mac."

I gave him five hundred dollars. Valerie walked with me as I walked with him to the seaplane. He looked at her. He said kindly, "I'll give him a good ride, lady." She nodded. He got into the plane and it took off. Soon, it was out of sight.

"Let's go," she said.

"Don't you want to wait?"

"What for?" she said. "I believe I've complied meticulously."

"With what?" I said.

"With my husband's directions in his letter. Haven't I?"

"You have," I said. "I'll get a cab."

"Let's walk."

It was a warm night. We walked for a long time. We didn't talk. At Thirty-fourth Street we went into a cafeteria and had coffee and English muffins. We walked more. We went all the way across town. At Times Square she said, "I'm tired."

I called a cab and we went home. In the den I went behind the bar and said, "What'll it be?"

"Nothing," she said.

The hell with her.

"It's twelve-fifteen," she said. That sounded like a hint—either way.

I took out my wallet and laid thirty-five hundred dollars on the bar. "That's your change," I said.

"That's your change," she said.

"I don't get it," I said.

"Your fee."

"You're very liberal."

She pulled up her knees and hugged them. I turned my back, pretending to seek brandy.

"Peter," she said.

I turned.

"There's the other set of pictures," she said, "and his note to me. Will we be able to get them back?"

"Sure," I said. "I'll take care of that. By the way, how well off did he leave you?"

Her eyebrows came up, and beneath the huge eyes looked unhappy. "Are you worried about the size of your fee?"

"Oh no. Please. Honey, I'd handle you for nothing." That had two meanings and I hoped both of them got through. "It's just that, well, in a sense, I'm . . . I'm interested."

She stood up, went out again, and I watched again, all the way. She came back with three bank books. They were savings accounts, husband and wife, joint. One contained $20,000; the second contained $20,000; the third contained $17,600.

"Stocks, bonds, and the like?" I said.

"None. He didn't believe in stock markets and things. He believed in saving and spending. There's also an insurance policy, in my name. Fifty thousand dollars."

"Suicide will invalidate it if it's recent."

"Not recent. He took it out when we got married."

"There'll be no trouble."

"You'll help me with everything?"

"You bet your sweet—you bet I will."

"Thank you." Now she went behind the bar and now she made her own sidecar and now she poured my brandy. We clinked glasses. We were getting cozy. I looked at my watch. It was midnight. "What about the tape?" I said.

"Tape?" she said.

"Look Valerie, let's you and I not beat the bushes. You burned the duplicate photos, and you'd like to get rid of the originals and also that letter of your husband's. Right?"

"Yes."

"I don't blame you. I'm with you. I'm on your side. Is that the way you want me?"

"I want you right alongside." If that had two meanings her face showed nothing, only interest—in the subject.

"Okay. There were two sets of photos. One set you took care of, and the other I'll be able to handle on your behalf. I'll also be able to handle the letter. But Marla Trent Enterprises also made a tape-recording along with the photos, just one tape-recording, and I'd imagine you'd want to get rid of that too, wouldn't you?"

She sipped the sidecar. Her eyes ate me. She put down the glass.

"You're a smart man," she said.

"I came well-recommended, remember?"

Softly: "You're also a very handsome man, Mr. Chambers."

"Peter." Two can play as lasciviously as one.

"Let's look, then," she said.

"You got my point," I said.

We gave that apartment as thorough a going-over as I would have liked to have given her. We put on all the lights and we looked in all the places. There were six large rooms and a terrace with wicker furniture and potted plants. There was the living room, the bedroom, the den, the kitchen, a TV and playroom with Stereo and a polished wood floor for dancing, and as completely equipped a mechanic's workroom as I had ever seen. It had everything, from power-drills to hacksaws to steel chisels to clamp-vises to electric grinders to claw hammers to files of every size to keys of every make to locks, pins, bolts, and slabs of steel, tin, silver, bronze. "That was his hobby," she said. "He worked in metals. He was a great expert. Once, long ago, he was an executive in the Harrison Safe and Lock Company."

In a drawer in the bedroom I found a gun, a Colt .45, and a silencer, and a box of cartridges. "Was this his hobby too?" I asked.

"No. He had a license." She dug in the drawer for the license and in that drawer, turned face down, there was a color picture of both of them, smiling happily at one another. I looked at it carefully. They were both suntanned and both in bathing suits. Quietly she said, "That was only a year ago." He had been a handsome, distinguished-looking man, tall and wide-shouldered, with blue eyes and a straight nose and dark hair with white temples. His chest was broad and clean and hairless, his flanks lean, his stomach flat, his body strong and muscular. "Here," she said.

"What?" I said.

She had found the license.

"Who cares?" I said.

"But you had asked."

"Skip," I said. "We're looking for a tape."

There was no tape in the apartment.

We put out the lights as we left each room, and then we were back to the fireplace, the wall-brackets, sidecar, and brandy.

"I can't understand," she said. She climbed a stool and sat knees apart. "That tape—"

"Look, he got it in March. This is June. You fool with a tape it can wipe off, it can spoil. He probably got rid of it. The pictures were enough. The pictures served his purpose. So he threw the tape away. Forget it. We gave this place as good an inspection as it can get, I'm an expert." I looked at my watch.

"You want me to stay?" I said.

"I *beg* your pardon?" Real hoity-toity.

"I mean . . . if you don't want to stay alone . . ."

"Why shouldn't I want to stay alone?"

Okay, I had no complaint. I had done my job of work. I had served her purpose. And there I stood in my fancy duds with egg on my face.

"Good night, Mr. Chambers."

"Good night, Mrs. Kiss."

Downstairs in the balmy night on Central Park West, my tail was between my legs, and without real cause, which makes it worse. My ego was in my toes and suddenly I wanted to prove myself to somebody, anybody. I walked downtown slowly. At Sixty-first I went into Henry Stampler's *Filet Mignon* and used the phone booth. It was one o'clock. I called Marla Trent. Marla Trent wasn't home. At one o'clock in the morning the bitch wasn't home. I went out and took a cab to Lorenzo's.

Lorenzo's was a supper club at Fifty-seventh and First. Lorenzo's catered to a hip crowd and the jazz was always first class, and Lorenzo was a friend. When I came in, he came up to me at once.

"Ah, Mr. Chambers," he said. You are to join a party?"

"I'm alone. And hungry."

"Very good," he said. "We have lasagna, special made tonight."

"Love it," I said.

"Shrimp cocktail first? Special sauce?"

"Love it," I said. He was catering to me and right then I needed being catered to. "This way," he said. "You would like a booth secluded?"

"Love it," I said.

He led me to the dim rosy rear and sat me into a small booth.

"Thank you," I said. "Excellent."

"A drink, Mr. Chambers?"

"Double Rob Roy, not too sweet."

"Of course." He bent to me, his mouth near my ear. "Would you like company?"

"Only gorgeous."

"It is gorgeous."

"Who is she?"

"I do not know."

I took my ear away from his mouth and looked at him. "You do not know?"

"It is a Spanish lady. She comes in alone, to listen to the music."

"Comes in often?"

"It is the first time. She comes in alone to listen to the music. You know I speak Spanish, and I am very grand with her because she is a lady."

"Who needs a lady?"

"She is exquisitely beautiful. Very rich."

"How would you know *that*?"

"Lorenzo is in the business. The gown it wears, at least four hundred. The small fur, chinchilla, at least four thousand. It drinks champagne and it knows champagne, selection Heidsieck and the year it names is the best vintage we have in the cellar."

"Then what makes you so sure you can provide this company?"

"I am not sure, but I have confidence. Lorenzo has charm. Peter Chambers has charm. And the lady is alone. So Lorenzo's charm shall detail Peter Chambers' charm, but slowly and subtly, and we shall see. It is a challenge. I will enjoy."

"Enjoy, my friend. Brother, you're a card."

"The King of Hearts. I go now. Do not be impatient. It may take time."

"I've got time. I've also got to eat, no?"

"Yes."

I had the Rob Roy, I had the shrimps, I had the lasagna— all to music. Then the table was cleared, Scotch and water appeared, the music stopped for a lull, and Lorenzo appeared —with something! But built! She looked like Marla Trent, only coffee-colored. She had a figure like Marla Trent, perhaps even bigger, but just as taut and trim. She was tall. She had jet black hair. She had jet black, deep set, luminous eyes, uptilted at the corners. She had more curves than a Picasso nude in his early period. The hips were round and proud, the waist exquisitely tiny, and a vast expanse of superb bosom topped a tight black sequined dress. The chinchilla jacket hung from the crook of a smooth round coffee-colored arm.

Lorenzo said, "Carmen Valesquez. Peter Chambers."

"It is so nice," she said. The voice was silky, soft, down-throat, husky. The accent was delightful.

"Charmed," I said. "Won't you sit down?"

She slid in. I slid in. Opposite.

She had long legs and the booth was not wide. Our knees touched.

Lorenzo said, "And now to drink?"

"Mine, the same," the lady said.

"And you, Mr. Chambers?"

"Put a bottle of J.& B. on the table, and a pitcher of ice water."

"Very good," Lorenzo said and went away.

I offered a cigarette. The lady accepted with long delicate fingers. She puffed. She said, "It is not proper, but I could not resist."

"What?"

"To meet a private detective."

"Oh, that Lorenzo with the big mouth."

"No, but serious. I did not know that such really exist. Only for the little books and the large television, I thought."

"You are very beautiful," I said.

She laughed with large, white, flashing teeth. "Just as they say on the television."

The champagne arrived, and the Scotch arrived, and the music started, and our knees jiggled to the beat, and my ego came up out of my toes. We drank, we smoked, we jiggled knees, we talked.

"How long are you here?" I said.

"In the United States? I came on June first."

"From where?"

"South America. Colombia."

"You speak English very well.

"No. Very bad. But I try."

"How long do you expect to stay?"

"One year. One year from July first."

It was conversation. Who in hell knew how much was the truth? But she was sure gorgeous to look at, and I was enjoying her knees.

"Only a year? Why only a year?" I said.

"I go to work. Now it is vacation. In June, vacation. In July, I go to work for one year."

"What kind of work?"

"In a hospital."

The manure was beginning to come through. Nobody who works in a hospital can afford to dress like that.

"You're a nurse?" I said.

"A doctor."

She was a prostitute. A semi-pro, but expensive. The semi-pro always has a crazy approach. Some of them tell you they're actresses, some are models, some are dancers, some are widows, some are misunderstood wives, some are receptionists; all are temporarily out of funds, temporarily strapped, temporarily out of a job. This one's fantasy was as bright as her lively eyes. A doctor yet.

"A surgeon, no doubt," I said.

"That's right."

The music got hotter and my knees got bolder. We talked of other subjects, and we drank up our small storm, but I couldn't make a real move because there was a table between us. At three o'clock, well-oiled, I said, "Look, sweetie, let's get out of here."

"You not like it here?"

"I like it, but I've had it. I'm restless. You seem to enjoy jazz."

"Oh yes. I love it to jazz."

"We'll go over to Eddie Condon's and listen to some real jazz."

I paid and we started our trek. At the door, Lorenzo whispered, "Success?"

"For her. She's a prostitute."

"I think you're wrong, Mr. Chambers."

"You're wrong, Lorenzo."

Condon's was crowded and smoky. We sat tight together on a wall-banquette. The heat of her thigh heated up my thighs. She stuck with champagne. She was an expensive date. Tonight I could afford her.

The music was hot. The joint was hot. I was hot.

Once she took my hand and said, "You are fine man. We are *sympatico*. I like you."

"I love you." Scotch talking in a smoky joint with wild music.

"Love is an easy word in America."

"Love isn't easy in Colombia, South America?"

"Love is a holy word in my country."

"How about *making* love in your country?"

"But to make love, one must be in love."

"I'm in love, baby."

"But I am not."

"Come off it."

"Come off—it?" The black eyes were inquiring.

"An expression. It means don't make with the phony."

"I still do not understand."

"Later, I'll demonstrate." I laughed with all the teeth.

"You are a sad man," she said.

"Oh no! What's now?"

"You laugh with the mouth, but the eyes are sad. You are my sad man."

I squeezed her hand. She squeezed my hand.

"I love you," I said.

"I like you," she said. "I like you, my sad man. Even to like for me is not quick or easy."

"Drink more champagne, baby. It'll get quicker and easier."

At four o'clock we folded the tent. We went to Reuben's for coffee and sturgeon sandwiches. Then I said, "Would you like a nightcap?"

"I would love. Order for me Drambuie."

"I could order but we would not get. In this, the biggest city in the world, there is a curfew. At four o'clock, all of a sudden you're not allowed to drink."

"Why?"

"It is a question that many people have asked. There are laws, and many laws are stupid. In this state there is a law. Up to four o'clock you can drink until you get stinking. After four o'clock it is a crime. But I know a place. Will you go?"

"With you, of course."

The place was my place, my apartment on Central Park South.

There I served her Drambuie, and I served myself Drambuie, and then I turned down the lights, and set up the soft music, and said, "Take your dress off."

"What?" she said.

"Make yourself comfortable."

"I am comfortable. Forgive me. I do not quite always understand the American sense of humor."

"Carmen, my love, the time has come." I took out my wallet and tossed hundred dollar bills into the air. They fluttered down slowly, like wet confetti, and made a rich design on the rug. "Pick out as many of those as you think you deserve, and let's go to bed."

She stood up straight and tall, and rigid. She was heaving for breath.

"Please take me home," she said.

Suddenly I was somewhat sober.

"Please take me home," she said. Her voice was controlled. "Please now."

I left the big bills on the rug. I had small bills in my pocket. I brought her jacket and she slid into it. I took her out and to a cab and took her home. Home was the Waldorf-Astoria, the Waldorf Towers. The elevator man smiled at her and said, "Good evening, Doctor." It was not evening. It was after five in the morning. "Doctor," he had called her. I was very small in the elevator. On the twenty-sixth floor she had to lead me out. She held my hand all the way to the door. She opened it, and led me in. One look and I knew it was one of the top apartments in the Towers. I got smaller. I looked about. She said, "Come, I'll show you." She had me wrong. I was looking for a hole to crawl into.

She showed me the apartment. Four sumptuous rooms. At the Waldorf Towers, that's a thousand a month, if it's a nickel. We came back to the drawing room. I sat in a corner of a couch, just sat. "I will serve the Drambuie," she said.

She did.

"Now I will get comfortable," she said.

She went away and I licked Drambuie.

She came back in red silk lounging pajamas and the frantic shape joggled in the red sheen but I hugged the Drambuie. "I forgive," she said. She smiled. "I understand."

"I'm a nothing."

"You are something. You are sweet, and very sad."

"I'm hip, super-hip, which makes me four-square like every super-hip. I'm strictly a punk from Peoria."

"I don't know what you are speaking."

"Skip."

"Skip? Now, what is?"

She came and sat near me.

I went and sat away from her.

We talked. Mostly she talked. Mostly I nodded.

She was the daughter of Jose Valesquez. I knew of Jose Valesquez. Everybody knows of Jose Valesquez. Jose Valesquez was a billionaire in Colombia, South America, who owned all sorts of things, from thousands of acres of coffee plantations to thousands of acres that had pinpoint mines of uranium. She was some sort of genius; she had been a child prodigy. She was twenty-nine years of age and she was a famous surgeon who had developed new techniques for lung cancer operations. Spanish doctors in the United States called her often for operations here in the States. Now she had accepted an invitation to serve on the staff of Harkness Pavillion for a year. She was to join the staff on July first and remain in residency until July first of next year.

I listened. I hardly spoke. It is difficult to speak when your tongue is tied up with your palate. Occasionally I lubricated with Drambuie but this was not my day, or night. Finally at seven o'clock in the morning I got up and said, "Good night, it was lovely. I'll call you sometime."

"I will be disappointed if you do not."

I went to the door and she came with me. She put her palms on my cheeks and kissed me quite simply. My hands hung limp. I went home and I collected the money from the floor and put it away. I called Lorenzo at his apartment and Lorenzo answered at once, bright and cheery.

"Hello?" he said.

"Lorenzo?"

"Ah, Peter my boy."

"You've got a quick ear."

"You have a distinctive voice. What is it you wish?"

"I wish to apologize."

"Apologize? For what?"

"The lady *is* a lady."

"Then why apologize to me? Why not apologize to the lady?"

"As my friend Sergeant Wagner would say—'I told it to you, so I apologize to you.' I told it to you, Lorenzo. I didn't tell it to her. I apologize."

"Peter, dear boy, you are the card, not I."

"Yeah," I said. "Good night, Lorenzo."

"Good morning, dear Peter."

I hung up and I called my Answering Service. I got the early morning girl, Nancy.

"Morning. Would you call my office at about ten, please?" I said.

"Certainly."

"Tell my secretary I won't be in till four o'clock."

"Yes sir. Any reason?"

"Tell her I died."

"Yes sir, Mr. Chambers."

"Good morning, Nancy."

"Good morning, Mr. Chambers," she said but the politeness was strained and the voice was pinched. Funny jokes are not for early morning.

I pulled up the covers and pulled up my knees and tried to sleep but it fought me. It had been a long day and a fruitful, fruitless day. I was tired but it was stretched out too fine. My head thumped with fragments of thoughts none of which made sense. I was in a half-trance that was almost sleep but it wasn't sleep. Once my leg shot out in a muscle twitch that almost dumped me out of bed. I thought of getting up for a pill but I was too tired to make it. I closed up my mind and forced it to black. I tried not to think, I concentrated on black, I tried hard for sleep, and finally it began to come—so the phone rang. I opened my eyes and saw the clock. It was ten minutes after nine. I took the receiver out of the cradle and laid it away and turned over and went back to sleep, but the phone continued to ring. I groaned and sat up in the bed. It was not the telephone. It was the doorbell. The hell with it. I put the receiver back on its buttons and lay out for sleep again but then I jolted up, and with a start this time. Carmen. Could it be? Could it be Carmen for company? Why not? Who knows? Who can tell? I bumbled out of bed and stumbled through the apartment and opened the door.

My company was not Carmen.

My company was cops.

ELEVEN

THEY WERE detectives, in plain clothes, but cops are cops, and even a layman can tell, and I am no layman when it comes to cops. One was blond and the other was bald and both were beefy and both were brusk and one was nasty and the other was grim and that is about par for the course.

The blond was the nasty one.

"Get your clothes on, buster," he said. "Hurry up! Move!"

"What cooks?" I said.

"You heard me," he said and he shoved me but not too hard.

"What the hell is this all about?"

"We were sent to pick you up," the blond one said, slightly politely.

"By whom?" I said.

"Lieutenant Parker."

"Lieutenant Parker is a friend of mine."

"That's what he said."

"This is the way you treat a friend of the lieutenant?"

"What the hell is it with you, Jack?" said the bald one. "You sensitive or something? You been treated bad or something? We tell you to get a move on in a hurry. So what's bad?"

The cops began to act human.

"Can you tell me where we're going?" I said.

"Corn Exchange National on Thirty-eighth Street."

I thought fast. Corn Exchange National. Thirty-eighth Street Branch. It was at Thirty-eighth and Seventh. Jonathan Kiss had been a vice president at the Corn Exchange National, Thirty-eighth Street Branch. But Lieutenant Parker was Homicide. Detective-lieutenant Louis Parker, Homicide West, was an old, dear, and respected friend, and a bright and honorable cop.

It didn't make sense. Kiss was a suicide. Parker was Homicide. Suicide wasn't homicide. And where was I mixed up in this?

We drove faster than hell all the way downtown with the siren wide open. In the bank everything was normal and quiet. The cops slowed down and strolled and I strolled with them to the elevator which took us to the third floor, where the executive offices were. My cops led me to a big oak door and the bald one knocked.

"Yeah? Who is it?" came from inside.

"O'Malley. We got Chambers here."

"Well, come in for Chrissake."

It was a large room with a beige carpet and fancy drapes and carved desks. It contained four detectives, two uniformed cops, one pale bank executive, one Medical Examiner, Detective-lieutenant Parker, and three stiffs.

Three!

They lay face down and fully dressed on the beige carpet.

Parker glanced at me and smiled without humor. He pointed toward the three prone stiffs. "Take a look at them, Pete."

I bent and I looked. They were very dead, very cold: no rigor mortis, they had come unstuck and they were beginning to smell. Each one had a blast in back of the head, one bullet but from up close. I unbent, fought off nausea, and looked toward Parker. He beckoned and we went together through a doorway into an anteroom. "Sorry I had to yank you out of bed," he said.

"You could have sent more gentle emissaries."

"It wasn't an invitation to tea."

He sat down behind a big desk. He put a cigar into his mouth and lit it. He was a thick, short, black-haired man. He was a cop with compassion and brains. He was brilliant and efficient. He wasn't a time-killer. He knew his job and he did his job and when his job was finished he went on to his next job. He wasn't a glory-seeker and he wasn't a grandstander. He was a good cop, the best. There aren't enough good cops. There aren't enough good doctors, for that matter, or enough good accountants, actors, bricklayers, architects, writers, dentists, comedians, scientists, researchers, statesmen, lawyers, even private detectives; there aren't enough good people in any profession. There are always the top-people, and beneath them a gap, and then a vast plateau of the usual crumbs. In his profession, Detective-lieutenant Louis Parker was the best.

He waved to me to sit down, and I sat in a chair alongside the desk, and he smoked his cigar, and we looked like *tete-a-tete* for a home-owner's loan.

"The three dead guys are bank guards," he said.

"Yes sir," I said.

"You may be able to help," he said.

"Yes sir," I said.

He leaned back and puffed hard. Blue smoke rose up toward the ceiling. "They were killed on Friday night. One bullet each in back of the head. The slugs were .45's."

A bell rang. "Yes, sir," I said.

"This is the set-up. When the bank closes on Friday night, these three guys stay here. They stay till Monday morning. During Friday night, Saturday, Sunday, they take turns going out for a bite, coffee, a meal, you know. There's a small side-door on Thirty-eighth and that's the one they use. Monday morning, they check out and the new guards come in. They get two days off, and they rotate regular till the weekend. Got it?"

"Yes sir."

"On Monday, one of the executives opens up shop at eight o'clock. That's the guy you saw outside here, Mr. Franklin, an executive vice president. By eight-thirty, most of the rest of the crew shows up. By a quarter to nine, they're all here. At nine the bank is open for business. Got that?"

"Yes sir."

"Okay, today Franklin comes in at eight o'clock. He finds one of the guards in an office downstairs. This guard is sitting in a chair, dead. He calls the cops. We come right away. I'm in charge. We find another guard on the second floor, also in an office; and the third guard on the third floor, in another office. Each one got it close up. Which figures each one was approached by somebody he knew and trusted. Also, a gunshot in a bank that's empty can make plenty of noise, and each one of these guys was no dope, each one was a retired cop. So we figure a silencer."

That rang another bell. I did not interrupt.

"Yes sir," I said.

"We bring them up here and we lay them out and by then the eight-thirty crew arrives and we order a check. Nothing. Nothing has been taken. Not a nickel has been lifted out of this bank. A pointless crime. It figures for a nut, but a nut who was known around here. Then from Sergeant Wagner I get info that Jonathan Kiss, an executive here, committed suicide Saturday morning. A suicide is a nut. If he's a nut on Saturday morning, he can be nutty Friday night. I got Marla Trent, I got William Winkle, and I got Mrs. Kiss, all sitting in my office waiting till I get back. I wanted you here because I know you, I respect you, and we're old friends. That's the story. Now what have you got for me, if anything?" He kept the cigar in his mouth. He leaned forward and clasped his hands on the desk.

"The guy *was* a nut," I said.

"How do you know?"

"The notes he left, and the whole story on the suicide. Wagner will tell you when you have the time."

"Anything else, Pete?"

"Yes, I'm sure."

"*Sure?*" Now he sat upright and the cigar was between his fingers.

I sighed. "I gave the joint an inspection."

"What joint?"

"Kiss's apartment."

"Why?"

"The wife and I were looking for a tape."

"Tape? What kind of tape?"

"It doesn't apply here. Proof of adultery—which was the basis of knocking him off his rocker. We didn't find the tape, and that has no bearing."

"What *has* bearing, please, Pete?"

"In a drawer of the bedroom dresser, there's a .45 Colt revolver, and a silencer."

Parker stood up. He smiled with one corner of his mouth. "I played a hunch to get you here right away, and my hunch paid off. Next hunch is that this'll clear it up. Now, Pete, I'm going to have O'Malley take you down to my office. You'll stick around with the rest of them. I'll give orders that you people can go out, eat, have drinks, do what you like—as long as you'll all be available when I need you."

"And how long will that be?"

"Long, I'm afraid. We've got to go through this joint with a fine comb before we can know that nothing has been taken. It's a banking day now, and we can't close the joint down. There'll be other work in the meantime for us—autopsies, checking that gun and silencer you mentioned—but once the banking hours are finished, we can put on extra people for a real thorough sift-job. That's gonna hold you people up. I wish I could let you all go back to business, but I can't, because I don't know when I'll need any one of you. Get the bit?"

"I think so."

"You folks will have all the freedom you want, but you'll just have to be near, so we can talk to any one of you if we have to."

"With your charming cops on our necks all the way."

"No, no. You people can be on your own. I'm depending on you. Explain it to them. Then all of you—go where you want to relax, but leave word where we can pick you up if we need you. Okay, Pete?"

"I can't deny you when you're making a reasonable request."

He grinned around the cigar. "It's reasonable?"

"Yes," I said.

TWELVE

IT DEVELOPED into a curious day, mostly boring, but with some crossfire. A polite young man, Lieutenant Cassidy, was in charge of us. "Ladies and gentlemen," he said pleasantly, "these are my instructions. You may go where you wish, but not too far away, and you may do as you wish, as long as you do it all together. You must leave word here where you are, and if you go anywhere else, you must call in and tell us where you are, so that we may be able to reach you. Mr. Chambers is responsible."

"How long does this figure?" I said.

"According to Lieutenant Parker, until about six o'clock."

"That's a full day."

We ate downstairs in the rathskeller of Longchamps at Thirty-fourth and Fifth. We were a peculiar foursome. Valerie paid a good deal of attention to Willie because she paid no attention at all to me, and Marla paid a good deal of attention to me because she paid no attention at all to Valerie. After luncheon we strolled up Fifth Avenue, and then we went to the cocktail lounge of the Four Seasons and there, actually, we were seated separately; near, but separately. The maitre d' had mistaken us for two individual couples, and nobody corrected him. I was peeved at the kiss-off I was getting from the Kiss, Marla appeared relieved to be away from her, and Willie was engrossed in her: so everybody was happy.

Over a brandy stinger Marla said, "What is it between you and that broad?"

"Nothing between us."

"Don't kid me, baby."

"I'm not kidding, baby."

"Not much you're not. Why, she's been avoiding you like you have leaping tuberculosis. Did you make a pass?"

"Me?" I said innocently.

"A forward pass that missed the receiver."

"Not me."

"Not much. On Saturday she was clinging to you like a burr. Sunday you did the job for her with the husband's remains."

"How do you know?"

"She told us. Monday, she's all wrapped up in Willie and all unwrapped from you."

"Maybe it's because she can't use me any more."

"Or maybe because you tried to use her."

Be a gentleman. Be chivalrous. Don't kiss Kiss and tell, or vice versa. Nuts. "Not me, honey. I'm a one-woman man."

"That'll be the day."

Bleakly I said, "Men will never understand women."

"See? You learned something today."

"I learned that a long time ago."

"Then I've underlined it for you."

"You underlined it before you mentioned it."

Now the blue eyes squinted. "When?"

"All day."

"You're being cryptic, Peter."

"All day," I said. "Your reaction to Valerie Kiss. You detest her."

"You're so right."

"But I don't understand."

"You wouldn't."

"Who would?"

"Perhaps another woman."

"Would you explain it to a mere man?"

"Sure. Order up fresh drinks, would you?"

"A bitch," she said when the new drink had been deposited on the table. She sipped. "Pure bitch."

I sipped. "This is like intuitive?"

She shrugged. "Perhaps a bit but not really, I don't think. Intuition is an elusive term. Many small things may affect you consciously or unconsciously and the sum total produces a reaction and *that* reaction we may choose to call intuitive. Perhaps it is. Perhaps a small reaction, somehow magnified, is intuition."

"Don't get too far out, sweetie, or you'll lose me. I'm a simple fellow."

"At first, in a way, I was sorry for her. No question the husband was a weirdo. I think I was sorriest for her *before* I met her. Right from the start, she rubbed me the wrong way—I mean when we showed her the pictures and told her all about the deal."

"But why she rubbed you—"

"Too contained. Too assured. Too much in control. Did you notice that when we left my office, she made certain that she took the photos with her?"

"I noticed."

"I bet she burnt every one of them in that lovely fireplace of hers."

My shrug was admiration. "Every one. I watched. But that doesn't make her a bitch. That makes her a smart woman protecting her flanks."

"Peter, I'm no moralist. But this chick handled it cool, too cool for my liking. The way she flirted with you, the way she hung on to you . . ."

I grinned, kidding. "Jealous?"

She was serious. "Perhaps, in the broadest sense of the word. But I won't go philosophical on you. She hung on to you because she needed you.

"Then on Sunday, with your help, she attended to all the rites. She told us all about it, even about giving you thirty-five hundred dollars as a fee, every dollar of which, if you ask me, you deserved."

"Want a cut?"

"Don't be funny. And today, in Lieutenant Parker's office, she was the coolest of all. We'd been told about the killing of the three bank guards, and the possibility that the husband, in his madness, might have done it, but nothing shakes that baby. Willie says the guilt will get her in the end. Maybe. Willie's a man. Men don't understand women. I don't think anything will get her. She's got it all. All she's wanted. Money, a dead husband, and a live bartender."

"That bartender interests me," I said.

"Tell you a secret," she said. "Me too."

That was fraught with meaning, all sorts of meaning. She had seen those action photos. Her interest might have been far different from my interest. She had said it and said it well: men will never understand women.

We came back in high happy humor to Parker's office at five-thirty, all of us slightly smashed, but it dribbled away and we were moody and morose by six-thirty, and so was Parker when he arrived. At six-thirty.

Grey-black bristles showed in his beard, he was perspiring, his clothes were wrinkled, but his voice was clear, and his manners, as always, were unsoiled.

"I beg your pardon for having had to keep you so long," he said. Parker drew a handkerchief and wiped it across his face. He put the handkerchief away and rubbed the middle finger of each hand against each temple. Then he straightened his elbows, stretched the fingers of both hands, and then clenched the hands except for one finger which remained pointing at the paper that Cassidy had laid upon the desk.

"That's for you, Mrs. Kiss," he said.

"Me?" she said.

"A receipt. My people were at your apartment and took a .45 Colt, licensed in your husband's name, and a silencer. That is the receipt for same. Please take it."

She stood up, strong and shapely. She took the paper, folded it, placed it into her handbag, and sat down. No fuss, no flicker, no tremor, no nothing.

Marla looked at me.

I looked at Parker.

"That's the gun what done the job." He grinned, badly. It fell off his mouth and he sighed. "That's about it, Mrs. Kiss. There's no further reason for you to be inconvenienced. I'll have you driven home."

She stood up.

He poked the intercom. "Cassidy."

"Yes sir?"

"Mrs. Kiss is going home now."

Cassidy came in and took Mrs. Kiss away.

Parker pulled a drawer of his desk. "Look," he said.

We stood up and looked. Inside a tape recorder was turning slowly. "You're all professionals," Parker said wearily. "You understand that there must be a record of these proceedings, such as they may be." He sighed. "I just wanted to acquaint you with the fact."

He closed the drawer.

We sat down again.

Parker pressed his fingers against his temples. The poor guy had had a rough day and it showed. "Nothing was taken from the bank," he said. "Nothing. Three guys dead because one crazy nut went off his rocker. Small satisfaction to their families that the murderer is also dead. Now please, for the record, I'd like to know all about this thing, exactly how you people were involved with Kiss, all of it, in detail."

Marla told him, Willie added some, and I closed it out.

Parker grunted. "These guys were killed Friday night. Kiss was in your office Friday afternoon. How did he look? Did he act, you know, wacky?"

"Didn't act wacky," Marla said. "But he was tense, nervous, obviously under strain."

"Which is the way wacky people are," I said. "Tense, nervous, obviously under strain."

Willie lit a cigarette. "Lieutenant, if I may."

"Sure."

"I have a theory on this."

"So have I, Mr. Winkle. Let's hear yours."

"Well." Willie took a long puff and dragged it in deep. "To begin with, any person contemplating suicide, seriously contemplating suicide, is not well."

"Wacky," said Parker.

"As good a word as any. Unbalanced."

"Have it your way," Parker said.

"This man, in my opinion, was seriously unbalanced."

"Why, doctor?" Parker said but he was not being sarcastic.

"He planned and plotted this to make it as horrible as possible—for the wife. He had a gun, but he didn't use it on himself, did he? He chose a much more horrible way.

He had plotted revenge, with himself as a sacrifice, and he made sure that it would last, that it would be indelible. The note he wrote, the pictures he left, even the money for the funeral which she would have to attend to at once, and the method of the suicide—the total effect is of a diseased mind, a sick man, very sick."

I said, "Yes, doctor." I was getting impatient.

Willie moved his massive shoulders unconcernedly. "Now here's my theory, and remember we're dealing with a psycho, at least temporarily deranged."

"Go, man, already," I said.

It would take more than my sarcasm to move Willie. He took two more puffs on the cigarette, stood up, dumped it into an ashtray on the desk, went back to his chair and sat down. "The pictures," he said. "I'm pretty certain he kept them at the bank. He could not keep them at home. If she'd discover them, there would go the whole carefully conceived kooky plan."

"Maybe that's where the tape is," I said.

"What tape?" Marla said.

"Your tape of Valerie and the good Ritchie. It wasn't at the apartment. I figured he'd destroyed it. But it could be it's at the bank."

"No," Parker said. "No tape. We scraped that bank with a fine-tooth comb."

"Okay, he destroyed it. Back to the pictures, William."

Willie finally picked up the tempo. "He kept them at the bank. Late Friday night, he went for them. He already had it arranged for us to get her out of the apartment Saturday morning. So if he brought them in late and put them away —all would be clear for Saturday morning. Now at the bank I'd imagine he'd have to sign in . . ."

"You're doing very well, Mr. Winkle," Parker said. "He signed into the bank at twenty minutes after ten Friday night."

"But he had to take a package out, and from what I've heard in banks—"

"Right again, Mr. Winkle. After closing, any package going in or any package going out must be inspected by one of the guards. Rule of the bank."

"So he brought his gun and the silencer."

There was a long silence.

Parker lit a cigar.

Willie said, "To a demented mind, life is cheap, the balance is screwy. He couldn't let the guard see pictures of his wife in *flagrante delicto* with another man—"

I said, "How would the guard know it was the vice president's wife?"

"He may have known Mrs. Kiss or he may not—that *we'll* never know," Willie said. "Either way, he couldn't let the guard see what was in the package. If the guard knew the wife, it was food for juicy scandal. If not, then the vice president had sixty-six pornographic photos in color, and that was scandal in its own way. Scandal travels fast. Phones can be used at night. Gossip grows and mushrooms and if it got out of hand it could interfere with Saturday morning, and he could not permit that to happen. An official of the bank might learn during the night and might call to inquire, or might call a conference for the morning, or might—anything. The demented mind with a fixed idea will brook no possibility of interference, and will go to any length to prevent it. Life is meaningless. Life is cheap. The perspective is completely out of focus. He was giving up his own life, wasn't he? To hell with any other life. Nothing must interfere with the grand plan, there must be no possibility of interference, he had worked on it too long and too carefully."

"But all three?" Parker said and closed his eyes against the answer, because he knew the answer.

"With one dead, either of the other two could find him, and the furor would commence. Jonathan Kiss wanted no furor, none whatever, not until after Saturday morning. It is also quite possible that one, or both, of the other guards had seen him when he had come upon whatever pretext he pretended."

Willie was finished. He was in good shape. He was always in good shape. He wasn't even breathing heavily.

Marla said, "What about your theory, Lieutenant?"

Parker's eyes were open, wide open. "Mr. Winkle expressed my theory precisely, and far better than I could have. As a police matter, there's nothing further to do. A guy killed three guys, but the guy is dead, and our job is therefore finished. The explanation—with which I concur—is now part of the record. Do you disagree with any of it, Miss Trent?"

"I'm afraid not. It's the only logical explanation, if the word logic can be applied to such illogical behavior."

"The logic *traces* the behavior," Willie said meticulously. "It does not *apply* to the behavior."

"Peter?" said Parker.

"I've got to go along with it," I said.

Parker chomped down on the cigar. "That's it, then. Case closed. I thank you very much for your cooperation."

THIRTEEN

FOR THE next three weeks there was a lull, in everything, including my love life. The weather turned hot and stayed hot without relief. So did I.

I had called Marla Trent but Marla Trent had gone to Europe on vacation and Marla Trent was not due back until after Labor Day. William Boyd Winkle functioned as factotum of Marla Trent Enterprises but the enterprise I desired with Marla could not function with William.

I did not call Carmen Valesquez.

I wanted to, but I did not call Carmen Valesquez.

I kept remembering my evening with her—I could not forget it, or her—but I could not forget my blithering bungle and the enormity of it grew progressively more clear with the passing of each day. This was a fine, decent woman, and I had mistaken her for a prostitute. This was a woman of breeding and wealth and I had harried at her like a harlot. This was a physician (I had checked Harkness), a famous surgeon, and I had spewed vile passion in vile manner as though she were a common strumpet. I remembered, and whenever I remembered, my mouth got dry. I remembered that afterward, at her apartment, she had been polite, kind, and good—because she was a fine woman who knew in advance the shame and remorse which would overtake me. She had even kissed me, but I understood that too; it had not been a carnal kiss; no kiss of passion: it had been a kiss of comfort, comfort for me, in advance; she had known, womanlike and wisely, the self-denigration and humiliation that, later, would attack me like a disease, and she had tried, in advance, to make it easier for me—but it made it worse. I was ashamed: it lay heavy and searing in my psyche like a malignant growth and I could not extirpate it.

I wanted her. I wanted to see her. I wanted to be with her. Throughout the heat, the work, the humdrum activities of business of those three weeks, she was always with me in back of my mind; I could not get rid of my guilt but neither could I get rid of her. On occasion—too damned many occasions—I tried to call her, but each time my finger got stuck in the hole, each time I could not continue to dial, and each time as, abortively, I hung up, so the shame got bigger and the self-respect got smaller. Somehow she was connected with the other two, with Marla Trent and Valerie Kiss, and somehow I felt, as I vaguely groped for an antidote, that the rescue of my pride lay with one or the other of them: but Trent was in Europe and Kiss had her bartender and so Chambers remained sick with a malaise that was a combination of conscience and gaucherie, and then on July seventh at ten-thirty of a burning hot morning the office phone rang and the cool voice on the other end was that of Valerie Kiss.

"Valerie Kiss here," she said.

"Uh-oh?" It was part pleasure, part surprise, but mostly just plain grunt.

"Will you be able to come here, please?" she said.

"Where?"

"My place."

"When?"

"I don't want to inconvenience you, but whenever you're free."

"I'm free now."

"Splendid," she said. "Eleven o'clock?"

At eleven o'clock, at her place, she was something to see, and I kept looking. She wore a pale pink peignoir that was not transparent but neither was it opaque: translucent would be the best word. The long ripe lines of her body were exposed in outline but without the detail of flesh: it was as though she were nude behind pale pink frosted glass. She greeted me with a bright smile and a warm handshake and she led me toward the den and I followed behind her admiring the structure behind the frosted-glass peignoir. At the ebony bar she said, "What would you like?"

"Nothing to drink, thank you."

The brown eyes were amused. "Wagon?" she said.

"So far today."

"Would you be subject to coaxing?"

"Not to drink."

She dug, but she pretended that she didn't. The amused expression clung to the corners of her eyes, but the eyes seemed to grow darker, and wider. The full mouth quivered as though she could not restrain it, and then she smiled, almost a shy smile. She was flirting—she wanted something. I wondered how far I could stretch that. She looked well, very well; her face was fuller, as though she had gained a bit of weight, and it was unlined and untroubled: there was no trace of strain. Except for the audacious peignoir all else was prim and conservative: she wore no makeup except pink lip-rouge on the curved, glistening, avaricious mouth, and the glinting auburn hair was in a new do, severe, Grecian style. She said, "Not even sherry? Please have some sherry. I'm drinking sherry."

"No, thank you."

She shrugged and seated herself upon one of the tall ebony bar stools. She crossed her knees and the peignoir parted revealing one long graceful leg. She twisted her body, leaning toward the bar, as she extended her hand for her long-stemmed glass of sherry. More of the peignoir fell away, and now I had all of her legs and a part of her thighs. I stiffened but I did not move. I was standing with my back to one of the leather couches. As I tightened I could feel my calves touching the edge of the seat of the couch. I was tempted to go to her but I restrained myself. My ego was way down, close to nadir: a rebuff at this time and I would spit at myself in every mirror I saw, and like that you can go crazy. I was in a bad period, at a bad time; my pride was bruised, my confidence undermined, my self-respect at ebb. I could use uplift but further denigration could blow me apart. Who needs a breakdown? I had been brooding too long about Carmen Valesquez and the significance of that episode: had I become so rotten, so hip, so would-be sophisticated, that I could no longer distinguish between good and evil, that I accepted all as evil, including myself? Fervently, I hoped not.

I was cynical; of course I was cynical; in my racket, in a short time, you are either cynical or you are no longer in the racket; but there is a difference between cynical and rotten; and I had seen too many in my profession who had grown rotten without hope of redemption; and I had prided myself that I had always recognized the line between the one and the other and that I had never crossed the line; but now, at this period, at this time, the doubts had been gnawing and I was in bad shape. So I stood there like a schoolboy with my calves tight against the edge of the seat of the couch, trying not to tremble. I wanted to make a move but I did not dare.

And now she turned back to me, the glass in her hand. She sipped the sherry reflectively, the brown eyes studying me, and I saw the contempt in the eyes, and the contempt did me no good. She drained the glass and set it back on the bar and turned back to face me again, the pink quivering mouth now red-wet with sherry, and then, as though suddenly aware of the nakedness of her limbs, she drew the peignoir closed, but her eyes stayed on mine, as she slid off the stool and walked toward me on cork-bottomed, open-toed, high-heeled, pink lounging pumps. When she came to me, she pushed hard at my chest with the five stiff fingers of her right hand, open like a claw, consciously upsetting my balance, waiting, as suddenly I sat, abruptly, ungracefully, knees apart, upon the black leather couch, and then she moved away from me, her left hand pulling the peignoir tight about her. All was contempt, even her rigid back, even the exaggerated strut as the elliptical mounds of her buttocks, smooth-pink and bulbous in the tightened peignoir, swayed rhythmically as though in a slow seductive dance to silent music. The female had extended an invitation and the male had stood awkward and motionless with his calves against the couch. Now the male sat, awkward and motionless, as the female strutted, swaying, slowly, decisively, from window to window, lowering each venetian blind and closing the slats, until at last all were lowered and all were closed, and the room was clouded in a blue dimness of night inside and sunshine outside, and then in the middle of the room, she shrugged out of the pink peignoir and stood tall and naked and contemptuous and haughty, and then she kicked out of the cork-bottomed pumps, and came forward swiftly, as though driven, impelled, she sought me.

FOURTEEN

"I WANT you to help me," she said.
"Naturally," I said.

"There are loose ends to tie up, and you know about these things. I don't. Will you help me? Please, will you help me?"

"I'll be happy to help you."

Why not? *She* had helped *me*. She had not known she had helped me, but she had helped me. In some cockeyed, peculiar, inexplicable manner, she had helped restore a part of my self-esteem. I was on the other side of the hill, on the good side; I was healing. Whatever had been my crisis, I was over it. In time, Carmen Valesquez (in conjunction with Marla Trent) would complete the cure; the cure would be restoration; I would recognize myself: cynical but not rotten and not evil and quite capable of genuine surprise, even bewilderment. Now we were seated in the living room, Valerie Kiss and I, drinking. I was drinking Scotch and she was drinking sherry, and I was dressed as I had been when I had come, and she was wearing a grey plaid suit and a black blouse and black pumps.

"Most of this nightmare is over," she said.

"Yes ma'am," I said.

"Most of it has gone well, or as well as could be expected."

"Yes ma'am," I said.

"The insurance people were most sympathetic. They talked with me, talked with the police, and then the man came with the check."

"For fifty big ones?"

"Fifty thousand dollars. The man came several times, and we talked, and he had drinks with me, and he talked with the police, and then he came again, and we had drinks, and then he came with the check. You'll help me, Peter?"

"Sure." The man from the insurance company must have had an unexpected ball, if he was young enough to enjoy. "A young man?" I said.

"Oh yes. Young and charming and most cooperative."

The man from the insurance company had had a ball.

"I'm glad," I said.

"For what?"

"That he was cooperative. Now what do you want with me?"

"I want you to make it finished," she said. "Everything is taken care of. The apartment is sold—"

"Sold?"

"It's a co-op. I got a good price—for the apartment, the furniture, everything. The new people take possession August first. By then I expect to be far away from here, with all of this finished and over with."

"Yes ma'am. What do you want with me?"

"Those pictures that the police still have. Will you get them for me? Can you? And his notes too, if possible. I want to destroy them. It's the last chore that I must do here, before I can go away, before I can begin to . . . to forget . . . all of it . . ."

"I'm sure it can be managed."

"Please. Will you try?"

"Sure."

"When?"

"Now." She may have thought it was a big deal but it was no more than ordinary routine, and I only served to implement it. I went to the phone and made the necessary calls and then I came back to her and said, "All right, let's go."

"Must I?"

"Yes, and take along identification, just in case we run up against one of the more stupid bully-boys."

"But must I go? It's so terribly unpleasant. Can't you . . .?"

"I could, but I'd have to have a power of attorney from you, so that I can sign receipts in your behalf, and there can be all sorts of other hitches. With you personally present, I don't think it'll take more than an hour . . ."

It took two hours and there were no hitches. Most of the time was spent in waiting and in being shuttled from one bully-boy to another. Clerical cops are the worst. Their chief characteristics, in common with all other bureaucratic civil employees, are a great show of being busy with other matters, and an eagerness to pass you on to another employee. (If ever you wish to file a simple paper in the Office of the County Clerk, or if ever you wish to see a will already on file—get a lawyer!)

I knew the ropes, and I knew some of the people, and so it only took two hours, and then she had her bundle nicely packed—the photos and both suicide notes—and I took her home and she opened her door but she blocked the entrance and lamely I said, "Is there anything else I can do for you?"

"Nothing, thank you, you've been most efficient." My job was done and she was dismissing me. Her actress's voice was chilly and clipped. Suddenly it had British overtones. "Well, goodbye. There's so much I must do now."

Cop a walk. Just like that. I've used you, now beat it.

I hung on to my temper. Sweetly I said, "Will I be seeing you again?"

"I doubt it. I intend to be getting out of this city as quickly as I can manage it. Well, goodbye again."

I was burning but I held it. "Any forwarding address?"

"None."

"Any special place you're going to?"

"I don't think that's any of your business."

So I threw the zinger. "Taking the bartender with you?"

So she threw the right hand. Wide open and with force. She slapped me and she slammed the door and there I stood, lonely in the hallway, the sting of her fingers warming my left cheek. By the time I got downstairs, both cheeks were burning, and suddenly I was on the bartender's side. Suddenly we were brothers, Richard Robinson Jackson and I. This was a dame who would use a man and then cast him off. I had found that out now, twice, in minor matters. I wondered about the other guy. He was involved in a major matter, a love affair. If she had been using him, the thud would hurt when she dropped him. Somehow, roundabout, casually, without insinuating myself into his personal business, I wanted to warn him.

I walked to Columbus Avenue and used a public phone booth. I called my office for messages. There were none. I called Marla Trent Enterprises and got through to William Boyd Winkle.

"That Jackson's address is 222 East Sixty-second. Right?" I said.

"Yes," Willie said. "Why?"

"What's his phone number?"

"Why?" Willie said.

"I'm stepping out of character. I'm playing Samaritan." There was a silence. Willie was too polite to probe.

I said, "Well?"

"I'm checking it," he said.

He gave me the number.

"Thank you," I said and I hung up and I called the number and I got the operator and she asked me to repeat the number and I did and she informed me that it was disconnected.

"Temporarily or permanently?" I said.

"Permanently."

"Could you tell me when it was disconnected?"

"I'll let you talk to the supervisor."

The supervisor asked nosey questions in a nasal voice. She learned that I was Mr. Jackson's brother, that I had just returned from London, that I could not understand why the phone was disconnected, and that I wished to know when it had been disconnected.

"Just one moment, please," she said.

I waited five minutes in the steaming booth.

Then she said, "I have the records right here before me."

"I'm thrilled to the core," I said.

"Beg pardon?"

"I couldn't ask for anything more," I said.

"Yes sir," she said. Pause. "Now let me see." Pause. "Ah." Pause. Then: "The telephone was disconnected upon Mr. Richard Robinson Jackson's request at 4:05 P.M. of June 17. The request was made personally from the telephone which was requested to be disconnected. There is due at this time an unpaid—"

"Thank you."

"But—"

I hung up. I got out of the steamy cubicle and walked in the hot sun which felt cool in comparison on Columbus Avenue. June 17, the lady had said. On June 17, at eleven-twenty, Jonathan Kiss had committed suicide. At four o'clock the bartender had closed up shop. Had he done so in order to avoid being involved in the scandal? Or had he done so upon orders of his mistress? Or had he not closed up shop? Had he disconnected the phone and ducked in order to avoid the possible pryings of reporters? But the operator had said—permanently. Why permanently, if he were temporarily ducking? And this was now July 7. The heat was off and the matter had cooled: there was no longer need to duck. Perhaps he had installed a new number, disconnected one and taken on another—but the supervisor had said something about unpaid . . .

I flagged a cab and went to Sixty-second Street. Number 222 was a neat, narrow, white-faced house, four stories high. The lobby was small and square, separated from the inner hallway by a clean glass door. Jackson's name was on a bell-bracket alongside the apartment number: 2B. There was a little black button, which I pressed. No answer.

To one side there was a large white button. Above it was a small plaque stating: ALL DELIVERIES THROUGH

REAR ENTRANCE. Beneath it, upon a plastic strip, was indented, MARIA MIRA. I put my thumb on the large white button and I could hear a ringing in the rear. Then there was a buzz at the glass door and I went through into a narrow hallway. To my left was a small elevator. To my right was a steep staircase. To the rear, all the way in back, there was one door, painted red. I stood in the hallway and waited. The red door opened and a small woman came out.

"Yes?" she said.

"Miss Mira?"

"Mrs. Mira." She approached me. She was swarthy, neatly dressed, smiling.

"Are you the caretaker?" I said.

The smile was pleasant. "I am the owner." She had a faint foreign accent. "We do not have any vacancies at the present."

"I'm not looking for an apartment, Mrs. Mira."

"No? What then?"

"I am looking for Mr. Jackson."

"It is apartment 2B."

"I know. He doesn't answer."

"Oh. You wish to leave a message with me?"

"No, not exactly. I'm a little worried."

Thin dark eyebrows contracted. "I do not understand."

"I've been trying to get in touch with Mr. Jackson for several days. He doesn't answer the phone when I call. He doesn't buzz back when I come here."

"So? Perhaps he is away."

"Could be, except that he's been expecting me."

"Expecting you?" She looked at me keenly with small dark eyes.

"I'm from Canada. I'm a cousin of Ritchie's—Mr. Jackson. He knows I'm here in New York. He knows I'm coming to see him. He wouldn't be away. I mean, not for so long. I've been trying for five days now."

"Oh." Alarm came into the dark eyes.

"My cousin is a bachelor. Lives alone, you know."

"Yes, I know."

"There's always the possibility that something may have happened, a seizure . . ."

"Yes." We were silent, staring upon one another. Then she said, tentatively, "Perhaps . . . do you think we should go look?"

"I'd appreciate that, Mrs. Mira."

"Yes. Would you please wait, Mr. . . . Mr. . . . "

"Chambers. Peter Chambers."

"I will only be a moment, Mr. Chambers."

She went back into her apartment, and returned with a key.

"This one opens for the second floor," she said. "Except if the bolt is closed inside. Each apartment has a slide-bolt inside."

"All we can do is try."

"Yes," she said and took me to the elevator and we had a short ride and then she rang the bell of 2B and there was no answer. She put the key into the lock and the door opened but she lingered, hesitant. I went in first and she followed me. I could hear her breathing behind me, rapid and shallow. No question she was apprehensive. So was I.

The apartment was empty.

A thin patina of dust covered everything.

Empty. The closets were empty, the drawers were empty, even the medicine cabinet in the bathroom was empty.

"He must have moved out," I said.

"Yes, it seems." She was smiling again, her relief manifest. A bachelor in a furnished apartment can always turn up as an unexpected corpse and an unexpected corpse is always unpleasant even in an unfurnished apartment. "Yes," she said. "Seems he has moved out."

"So now you have an apartment for rent."

"No, I have not, for it is paid until August first. He has the right to come back till August first. After that, I have the right to rent. We will go out now, please. We do not belong."

"Of course."

Downstairs in the narrow hallway she said, "If he comes, you wish I should give him a message?"

"Doesn't look like he'll be coming."

"You cannot tell. Yes, he has gone away, seems for some time, but he might come back."

"Just tell him his cousin from Canada, please."

"I am sorry you are disappointed."

"So it goes. It must have been something urgent, and a cousin from Canada isn't the most important thing in the world. I'm sure he'll be in touch with me and explain. I thank you very much for your trouble, Mrs. Mira."

"No trouble at all, you are welcome."

I went out into the hot July afternoon. My bird had popped the coop, probably on orders from Central Park West. If the lady still burned, then they had arranged a rendezvous, but if the lady no longer yearned, then our Ritchie would be back to tending bar, and if the bar was a good bar, there would be new ladies, rich and pretty and bored and vulnerable. I shrugged as I walked. I had tried. I felt good. And hungry. I went into an air-conditioned restaurant and had a large lunch. I felt even better. I had failed in my mission but my intention had been pure. Good intentions are a tonic. I came back to my office in a pleasant frame of mind and it instantly grew more pleasant. There was a reward awaiting me. Poetic justice. Cast thy bread upon the waters. The reward lay flat and simple in the middle of my desk. It was a small square sheet of memo paper upon which my secretary had typed: *Dr. Valesquez called. You are to call back the Waldorf Towers at six o'clock.*

FIFTEEN

I CALLED from my apartment, at six-fifteen. I had been trying to call since six but each time I froze. For fifteen minutes I fought the phone and fought myself. I realized, each time I hit the phone and began to dial and stopped, just how much she had been on my mind and how seriously I had thought about her. I remembered her graciousness, her sweetness, her kindness all through that one night when we had been together. My jibes had been vicious but until the end she had not understood and her reactions had been charming and warm and humorous; and when at end I had finally made myself despicably clear, even then she had sensed that I was not as rotten as I had thought it hip-chic to pretend. She was a wise and lovely woman, and a beautiful woman, and a little bit, I was in love. More than a little bit.

At six-fifteen I put through the call, mouth-dry and tense, and my heart pounded like the heart of a boy making his first call for his first date.

She answered quickly.

"Hello?"

"Carmen?"

"It is Carmen. Who?"

"Peter Chambers."

"Ah, Peter. So good for you to call. How is it all?"

"It is all fine."

"And you? Yourself?

"Fine." Peter Chambers, the laconic. Peter Chambers, the man of the world, making with the scintillating conversation. Phooey. "And you, Carmen? How are you?"

"Oh, well indeed. Why have you not called me in so long?"

"I . . . I think you know why."

"You are wrong. It is wrong. I have waited. I have expected. It is not the lady who should call. It is?"

"No."

"That night, silly, over, foolish, forgotten, understood and finished. Did you not know?"

"Not really I didn't know. I knew you were being kind . . ."

"I do not like to chase the man."

"Honey, you're not chasing . . ."

"You would like to take me to a play tonight? I have tickets given to me by a patient. *Nothing Succeeds Like Failure.* You would like . . .?"

"I would love."

"It is opening night."

"So I've heard."

"It is formal," she said. "I hope it is not too much to ask you to wear the tuxedo."

"It is not too much," I said. What in hell *could* I say?

"Seven o'clock, all right?" she said. "I shall be awaiting you."

I showered, I shaved, I dabbed, I doused, I powdered, perfumed, patted, primped, donned my most expensive clothes, but nothing helped: my ego remained at half mast.

It was a good show, a great show, but I didn't enjoy because I wasn't with it—I was with her; nor did I enjoy the party afterward, for the same reason. All the bloods of the town were at the private room upstairs at Sardi's, and the gleam of diamonds vied with the gleam of the decolletage, and there were speeches by famous orators and jokes by famous comedians, and the food was superb and the drinks copious, and I ate and I got tanked, but I couldn't loosen up. I couldn't get gay, because I was in love, and love is damned serious.

One time I had her alone and I said, "Carmen, I want to apologize, I have to say this clear and clean—"

"No, dear Peter, dear sad man, there is nothing to say."

"It's been on my mind for weeks. I want you to forgive—"

"Of course. It is forgiven. It is forgotten."

"I haven't forgotten."

"Then do, please do. I understand, believe me.

"Are we still . . . *sympatico?*"

"Oh but yes, of course."

"I want to see you, often . . . very often."

"As often as it is possible but you must remember I am very busy."

I was in love.

I saw her often, but not often enough, sometimes once a week, sometimes twice a week, sometimes not for two weeks. We went to plays, restaurants, ballet, jazz, opera, even the museums. I was in love, and I was a different man. For the first time in my life I wanted to get married, and that in itself presented many problems. She lived in Colombia, I lived in the United States. She was enormously wealthy, the daughter of a billionaire; I was a guy earning a living, a good living, but a living. She was a famous surgeon, I was a lowly richard. She was high society, I was a guy from nowhere. She intended to be in the United States for a year and then go home—what about me? I couldn't go to Colombia to live and work: I didn't even know the language, and even if I did, what could I do there, and certainly I couldn't live off her, no matter her wealth. Could I persuade her to stay in the United States? I didn't dare ask, I didn't dare broach it: I wanted to get married but I didn't dare talk about it. And *she* had other dates (which I didn't). Frequently a guy from South America came up to see her and he stayed in New York for days at a time, and although she mentioned it, she didn't elaborate, and I didn't press. It was none of my business, I had no right to inquire.

I had made one faux pas, I did not intend to make another. I was a suitor, a swain. I was in there pitching, trying to make points; and I was a different man. I saw no other girls; she was my one date and that all too infrequently; and I did not make a pass, I didn't even try to kiss her. I was a swain, not a lover-boy. A swain is not a lover-boy (don't you know)? A lover-boy—or lover-gal—takes liberties and enjoys. A swain sweats it out. I was afraid to make a move, I was afraid to upset the balance. And so I plodded along swinelike—pardon, swainlike—hoping against hope, waiting for her to take the initiative. Business stank, business was slow, and so I had time to nurse my madness along, and love is madness. The months marched; summer died and autumn blossomed; the heat waned and the cold grew; hot July drifted to cold November; and I was true and I was faithful; I was a plumping swain with nothing else to do because business was nowhere and I had nothing else to think about, and then on a bright cold day in November, Thanksgiving Day, suddenly, I was with Marla Trent.

She did not call me. I did not call her. We were called.
I saw her, but not alone.
I was in a bad way.
Alone, she might have helped.
She was not alone.
She was in the presence of seven presidents.

SIXTEEN

THE CALL came at ten o'clock on Thanksgiving Day, and it was from Victor Mason, himself. It was not from one of his many secretaries (female) nor from his executive secretary (male), it was from Victor Mason, in person. Mason was president of International Guarantee, but Mason was much more. Vic Mason had been a United States Senator, and before that he had been a successful criminal lawyer, and before that he had been graduated from Princeton *summa cum laude*, and before that he had been a three-year all-American fullback—the famous Old Vic. Mason was now fifty and at the peak of a remarkable career. He had been an idol of mine, and he still was, and I was Mason's boy for confidential work for International Guarantee.

"Peter?" said the booming voice. "Vic Mason here."
"Hi, Vic."
"Can you be down at my office at noon?"
"On Thanksgiving Day?"
"That's the way it has to be," he said, "and it's important."
"See you at noon," I said.
"Good boy," he said. "The doors will be open. Go right through to the conference room."

The offices of International Guarantee comprised the entire fifty-sixth floor of the Empire State Building. It was a legal holiday and the building had a skeleton staff. I had to ring a loud clang-bell for the elevator and I was deposited on the fifty-sixth floor at seven minutes after twelve. I opened a thick mahogany door and I walked through empty corridors to the conference room, and that door was locked. I knocked. Victor Mason opened the door.

"Hi," he said.

I entered and he locked the door behind me.

Then he went back and seated himself at the head of a long conference table.

It was a shiny-topped rectangular table. Vic Mason was seated at the narrow end, the head of the table. To his right, up-table, sat three men; to his left, up-table, sat three more men. Far down-table, to his right, sat Marla Trent. Far down-table, to his left, sat William Boyd Winkle.

I seated myself at the narrow end of the rectangle, at the foot of the table.

Blue smoke hung in the air. The table-top was fitted with ashtrays, pads, pencils, cigarettes, cigars, lighters, and leather-covered boxes for memoranda. I knew one of the men, and nodded to him. He was Saul Durnell, president of Universal Insurance, and Universal was a client of Marla Trent Enterprises. Insurance companies have investigators of their own but on occasion, for special matters, they retain private investigators. For such special matters, Universal retained Marla Trent Enterprises. For such special matters, International Guarantee retained me.

I looked toward Marla. She shrugged, beautifully. I looked toward Willie. He barely lifted his eyebrows but the gesture was an eloquent I-don't-know-what-this-is-all-about-either. I folded my hands on the table and looked all the way up-table to Victor Mason.

He was a big man with large grey eyes, black hair, a high forehead, a wide mouth, and a square steel-blue jaw. He was an intense but affable man, quick to smile with strong teeth, but today he was not smiling. Neither were any of the others.

Mason plucked a cigar from a box, lit it carefully, puffed, then laid it away on the edge of his ashtray. "Miss Trent and Mr. Winkle have already met my colleagues here. I'd like to introduce you now, Peter."

"I know Mr. Chambers," Durnell said.

I smiled. He did not smile. Nobody else smiled. I stopped smiling. Mason introduced me to the other five. They were Adam Gable, president of Oceanic Insurance; Clyde Powers, president of North Atlantic Insurance; Simon Hellman, president of Commercial Insurance; John Martin, president of Metro Insurance; and Stanley Podell, president of Empire Insurance. Each acknowledged me in turn, and I acknowledged each.

Mason said, "Thanksgiving Day is a hell of a day to get you people down here, I mean you, Miss Trent, and you, Mr. Winkle, and you, Peter. The rest of us know why we're here today." He had a deep, thick, booming voice.

"Why?" Willie said. His voice was as thick and deep as Mason's.

"We are here to discuss a matter of extreme importance in the strictest confidence. *There must be no leak nor possibility of leak.* We had decided, therefore, that when we were ready, we would have this conference on a legal holiday when there would be no employees—no one—in the office. We are ready now, so we chose this day. If any of you couldn't make it today, we would have postponed to next Sunday or the first Sunday when you were all available. Clear, Mr. Winkle?"

"As far as it goes," Willie said.

"It goes much farther, and much deeper." Mason smiled grimly. "We needed people whom we could trust and you people, in particular, as you shall learn, fit this job. I've been doing business with Peter Chambers for fifteen years and I trust him implicitly. Saul Durnell has been doing business with Marla Trent Enterprises for ten years and he trusts them implicitly. Clear, Mr. Winkle?" he said and added somewhat sarcastically, "As far as it goes?"

"Take it easy, Vic," I said.

"Sorry, Mr. Winkle." Mason smiled a real smile, warm and engaging. "I'm upset—we all are—and presently you'll understand why." He took up his cigar, puffed it back to life, then sighed and laid it away. "What I'm about to tell you is so incredible, it's almost beyond belief. I'm about to tell you about the most unique crime ever perpetrated in this country. I'm about to tell you about the most skillful robbery I've ever heard about in my entire career. I'm about to tell you of the Big Heist—the biggest. Eight million six hundred thousand dollars! *In cash!*"

"Wow," I said and my hands came off the table.

"And I'm about to tell you the reason for the murders of the three bank guards at the Corn Exchange National."

Wee Willie Winkle sat bolt upright.

Marla Trent, her face impassive, lit a cigarette, but her fingers were trembling.

Victor Mason pursed his mouth and watched us. He seemed pleased that at last he had broken through, that he had impressed us.

"All right, ready?" he asked.

"Go," I said.

"First I'll give it to you off the cuff, straight, in full. Then we'll work out details by your asking questions, whatever may occur to you. All right?"

The question was rhetorical and the answer was tacit: we made no answer.

Mason said slowly: "Eight million six hundred thousand dollars, in cash, has been stolen from certain of the vaults of the Corn Exchange National Bank on West Thirty-eighth Street." Then he took up his cigar, leaned back, puffed, and waited.

Marla asked the first question. Womanlike, it was oblique. "Why are all these gentlemen here?"

Durnell replied. "We here represent insurers, co-insurers, underwriters, and indemnifiers. We have made good the claims, and we have sustained the loss. All the private individuals have been paid. Our aggregate loss is eight million six hundred thousand dollars. We are here because we are interested in trying to effect a return of all or some of that money—which is why, in fact, you people are here."

Marla propounded the second question and that too was oblique. "Why all the hush-hush secrecy?"

Mason fielded that one. He laid his cigar away and rubbed his big hands together nervously. "There are two answers to that question, one specific, one general."

"Let's have the specific first," I said.

"I happen to be Chairman of the Board of Directors of the Corn Exchange National and I'm also probably the largest individual stockholder, so I can speak for the bank, specifically." He drew a deep breath. "If this thing ever got out—if this thing ever became public knowledge—that more than eight and a half million dollars, in cash, was stolen out of our vaults—we might just as well fold up. Every vault-owner would cancel and every big depositor would simply withdraw, and I wouldn't blame any one of them. Concisely, I believe the bank would fail. I also believe we would be subject to harrassment and possibly dissolution by reason of State and Federal authorities who have a right to inquiry. A bank is a quasi-public corporate body, you know."

"And the general?" I said.

Simon Hellman smiled. "I'd like to answer that, please." He was a sallow, thin-lipped, horse-faced man, with clicking false teeth. "I am a member of quite a number of interlocking directorates of various banks—more than anyone else in this room—and I believe I am most qualified to answer that question." He laid his palms together as though he were praying. "You see, Mr. Chambers, there are certain accepted institutions which must remain inviolate or else suffer total disintegration. There is a public picture, a public image, *that must not be disturbed on penalty of anarchy*. I mean, the President of the United States is not subject to bribery. God's church is not the house of the devil. The medical profession is not made up of quacks. The decisions of the Supreme Court cannot be influenced by cheap politicians. Do you understand, sir?"

"Yes, of course," I said.

"Banks have their place in the stability of the system. Bank vaults are invulnerable, and the public believes that, and must believe that, and *should* believe that. Billions—in cash, jewelry, securities, and personal private papers—are kept in vaults with full confidence and full security and full reliance. Undermine public faith in such inviolability and you destroy, for all time, one of the basic institutions of our democracy. Do you understand *that*, sir?"

"Yes," I said.

"It does not happen, it has never before happened! It probably will not happen again in a hundred years—even more! We are dealing here with a most unusual case, most unusual circumstances. A peculiar, gifted, genius-type psychopath—in the right place at the right time with the right knowledge and the right skills—and when I say right, I mean wrong, all wrong, terribly wrong. None of this must ever become public knowledge, and it is our duty to see to it that it doesn't. For that reason we cannot go to the police; and we cannot let this leak to our own people. It might create a public scandal, and it is just this type of public scandal which we *must* avoid, even if we do lose the entire sum of eight million six hundred thousand dollars. Have I answered your question, Mr. Chambers?"

"Yes," I said.

Now Willie popped up, point blank. "Just what happened?" he said.

Victor Mason said, "On the twenty-second day of July, Jay Whitney Sylvester went up to the office of the president of Corn Exchange National, Michael Kohany, and Jay Whitney said to Mike: 'You owe me seven hundred thousand dollars.' I expect you people know who Jay Whitney Sylvester is."

"He's reputed to be one of the twenty richest men in the world," Willie said.

"Correct. He used to be in oil, and then in electronics, and now in textiles. The Corn Exchange National is located in the heart of the textile industry in New York which is the heart of the textile industry of the world, and some of the richest men in the world are our depositors and safe deposit box holders. Rich people, as you know, for reasons of their own, keep fabulous amounts of cash in their safe deposit boxes. I myself, for instance. And I am one of those whose box was rifled for four hundred thousand."

"I hope the insurance company paid you," I said.

"I was paid," he said.

"What happened, just what happened?" Willie stuck with it.

"Jay Whitney Sylvester is not a man to get excited, even about seven hundred thousand dollars. Quite calmly he told Mike Kohany that he had gone to his vault to withdraw some cash, and that there was no cash. Jewelry, securities, papers, were all intact. The cash was gone. He had a record of that cash. Seven hundred thousand dollars. Kohany isn't an excitable guy either. Kohany went down to the vaults with Sylvester, checked the box again with him, but Sylvester insisted that the cash had been there *and that the cash was no longer there.* The box had not been tampered with, there was no such sign. You know how these things work?"

"The bank has a key to the outside lock, and the customer has his own private personal key to the inside lock," I said.

"Correct. Kohany didn't get excited, but Kohany remembered about the death of the three bank guards, remembered about the suicide of Jonathan Kiss, and remembered that Kiss was a vice president in charge of the Safe Deposit Vault Department."

"Kiss was in charge?" Willie said.

"That was his job," Mason said.

"So?" I said.

"Jay Whitney Sylvester is no little punk putting in with some sort of phony claim," Mason said. "Kohany soothed him, told him he would do a check, and told him he wanted a few days for investigation. I was then in Israel, on vacation. Kohany called me on the phone, and immediately I flew home. Kohany gave me the facts and I did a bit of a check of my own—on Jay Whitney Sylvester. He was financially sound. He was worth four hundred million bucks, and he wouldn't stoop to swindle. That box had been robbed, period. We were sure it was Kiss, but what in hell could we do about it? We paid Sylvester every penny of his claim, but nonetheless he withdrew from the bank. Right then I checked my own box. The cash, four hundred thousand, was missing. We knew we were in trouble, big trouble."

"How did you handle it?" Marla said.

"We understood the job had been done that Friday night when the guards had been killed. Kiss had come to the bank at twenty after ten Friday night. He had to kill the guards, each one separately, that would take some time, so he went to work on the boxes at, say, eleven. He knew, routine—the bank would be open at eight. He had to give himself at least an hour's leeway, probably more, to be able to take the stuff out in the dark rather than in daylight. We figured he put in about six hours work—eleven to about five. If you hit the right boxes—and Kiss would know the right boxes—you can do a lot of damage in six hours, even carrying out the loot in small packages, in installments as it were. He did eight million six hundred thousand dollars worth of damages."

"How did you work it?" I said. "How did you ascertain, I mean without blowing it up to scandal?"

Mason drew on his cigar again. "There are different sizes of vault boxes. The great general run are small boxes. Then there are the medium-sized boxes. And then there are the large, the really large-sized boxes—only sixty of them in the vault tomb. The big boxes are owned by the big boys. With a limited time to work, Kiss would naturally hit the big boxes. How about that, detective?" he said to me.

"Reasonable," I said.

"Well, we had the owners of those boxes in one at a time. We gave each one a song and dance that we were shifting up the entire vault system and that we'd like them to check their boxes before we made the transferences, with their consent of course. Of the sixty, most of it was normal routine. But sixteen—aside from Sylvester and myself—had had their cash lifted, sixteen of the real big ones: Kiss had excellent judgment. Well, each one of those sixteen sat in with us in private conference, we told each one the Kiss story, we told each one that this sort of thing could happen once in a million years, we requested secrecy on the same basis as Simon's admirable lecture to you, and we paid each one the amount of their alleged loss without question or quibble. We did, if I must say so myself, a good job. We lost four customers—with Sylvester, that made five—and we got no scandal. Here and there a small rumor flitted about, but hell, that we expected. Rumors always pop up and then die down without real hurt to an institution. There was no scandal, no newspaper stuff, no wide-open big deal, *and there must not be any, remember!* It's over now, cooled down and flattened away, and that's why, now, we've called you people in."

"You sure it's over?" Willie said.

"Oh yes. It's two months now since we've put in an entire new vault system down there. Not a peep, all quiet, and that's the way it must remain. Aside from our loss of eight million six hundred thousand dollars, we're all back to normal now."

I hit with a practical question. "How much of that do you figure is kosher?" I said.

That brought smiles all around the table.

Mason said, "They had us over a barrel, but these were all enormously wealthy people. We figure we paid out about a million over—that they padded for about a million."

That brought more smiles.

"That makes the actual loss about seven and a half million," I said.

John Martin said, "Our loss is eight million six hundred thousand dollars."

Marla Trent, womanlike, switched from the quixotic, and struck at the vitals. "Just what, Mr. Mason, do you want from us?"

The cigar was dead. The lighter flashed. Blue smoke curled. "We want eight million six hundred thousand dollars or as close to it as possible—without scandal, without publicity, private and utterly confidential."

Stanley Podell, fat, wrinkled, rumpled, said in a high squeak-voice: "We are business men. We have taken a loss but we do not believe it to be irretrievable. No loss is ever entirely irretrievable. We have decided to make an investment, a large investment, but small in comparison. You people are highly regarded in your profession, the highest. We wish to employ you, discreetly of course, most discreetly, to endeavor to get back our money."

"For how much?" Oh, that Marla.

Mason lifted the leather cover of the box nearest him. He took out two checks. He did not display them. He held them in his fingertips as he spoke. "You people have a bit of a head start. You were in on Kiss's suicide and the events that led to it. We have no interest in any of that. We are interested in the possible return of our money. This will not be an easy job nor one that can be done in a hurry."

"You bet," Willie said.

"We want your services exclusively applied to this project for a period of at least one year. If you are successful before that, fine. If nothing happens in a year, then we'll take it up again. But we want you—Peter Chambers and Marla Trent Enterprises—for one year."

"For how much?" Marla said.

"I have a check here to your outfit for fifty thousand dollars, and a check to Peter Chambers for fifty thousand dollars. Those are for your exclusive services for one year. And there's a bonus."

I spoke up. "Like what?"

"Two percent of whatever you recover, one percent for you, one percent for Marla Trent Enterprises. Do we have a deal?"

I didn't have to think twice. "You have a deal with me," I said.

"You have a deal," Marla said.

"There are papers to sign before I turn over these checks," Mason said.

"What about expenses?" I said.

"You have unlimited expenses," Mason said. "You can

also call on us for any help in investigation. We all have large staffs of investigators. One proviso, though. Our investigators cannot have any idea as to the *basis* of what they're investigating; blind investigation for specific purposes, if you know what I mean."

"Yes," I said.

"And you must understand the urgency of the discretion involved here. This entire project must be completely amongst us; no other, no agency, not even the police, can be involved; except, as our own investigators, piecemeal, for specific little purposes, but without knowledge of the real basis or the real need."

"But the guy's dead," Marla said.

"Who in hell cares?" Mason said. "There's approximately eight million dollars around, very live. Nobody can spend eight million dollars in this short a time, can they?"

"Money has no earmarks," Marla said.

"That's your job," Mason said. "That's what we're paying you for. We're investing a hundred thousand dollars, plus expenses, for you people to try to find that money and find it earmarked as *our* money. Nobody says it's an easy job—it may be an impossible job—but we're paying you people a hundred thousand dollars for a year, or less, of your time and your expert services to *try*, and to go all out trying. Now I have contracts here . . ."

We signed. We took the money.

Willie said, "Our first job is to check the background of Jonathan Kiss."

Mason said, "That's been done for you already. Part of our own routine involving his suicide and the death of the bank guards."

"I'm dying to hear," Marla said.

"There's no need to keep my colleagues," Mason said. "Once this initial situation has been settled, let's let them go home to their families and their Thanksgiving dinners. Oh, just one more thing. On your end, Peter Chambers is in charge, he's the boss, he's the general. On this end, I'm in charge. You take your orders from Chambers, he takes his orders from me. And he, and only he, reports to me. Okay, that's it."

Everybody stood up. The presidents looked happy about throwing away an additional hundred thousand dollars. They knew, as we knew, that they had catapulted us upon a fool's errand, but throwing good money after bad is a sound business principle: you just cannot let the bad money go down the river without trying to fish some of it back. The fishing equipment was expensive and any reasonable prognosis was all bad, but hell, they had to try. A hundred thousand dollars (and expenses) is a lot of money but it is a pittance when divided among seven insurance companies, and it is certainly a pittance when compared to eight million six hundred thousand dollars.

All seven presidents were smiling as though they had accomplished a good day's work, and all three private richards were smiling because they *had* accomplished a good day's work, and then everybody shook hands and Mason unlocked the door and the other six presidents filed out and went home and Mason turned to us and said, "How about a fine sumptuous Thanksgiving dinner to start you off right—on the expense account?"

SEVENTEEN

HIS CAR and chauffeur were waiting outside the Empire State Building and we drove down to Luchow's and there he was greeted with all of the grandeur naturally devolving upon big executives with big expense accounts. We took a small private room and we had cocktails and a festive dinner with all the stuffing and white wine and then champagne and we did not talk about our job until the cigarettes and the cigars and the coffee and then Victor Mason said, "I don't care about the suicide or the charming widow or anything else except the dough. I know all about all of that. Part of routine, I saw his notes and I saw those photos and I don't give a hoot in hell one way or another. If you people want to work from that angle, that's your business; any angle from which you work, that's your business, and I'm too good an executive to attempt to advise you in the operation of your business. However, I've done some spade work for you on Jonathan Kiss, and also I knew him personally, quite well, as a matter of fact, and if you'd like to discuss that, I'm ready. After that, I'll butt out, I promise you."

"Spade work?" I said.

"That also went under the heading of routine. A bank

officer is a suicide, so I want full information on him for our files."

"Who got you the information?" I said.

"Our own investigators. Of course I only got interested after the bank was robbed, but our investigators know nothing of that. The guy hadn't only been a suicide. In his madness, he had also killed three bank guards."

"Where'd he stem from?" Willie said.

"Born in New York City."

"Family?" Marla said.

"Only child, comparatively poor family. But they made all kinds of sacrifices to educate him well."

"How well?" Marla said.

"Harvard, all the way up to his Masters. A truly brilliant student all the way. It's interesting to note that his thesis had to do with locks and keys and safety devices and vaults and their history all the way from their beginnings. He was an expert, probably as expert in the field as any one in the world."

"Explains the workshop in his apartment," I said.

"I didn't see that," Mason said. "By the time I got around to it, the widow had already moved out. But both Sergeant Wagner and Lieutenant Parker told me about it, and I read their reports on it with quite a good deal of interest, naturally."

"According to the wife," I said, "he was once an executive with the Harrison Safe and Lock Company. How about that?"

"In a way, that's how he got the job at the bank," Mason said.

"Would you do that slowly, please?" said Marla.

"Upon his graduation from Harvard, the Dean of Men there recommended him to Harrison Safe and Lock, and that outfit grabbed him because, simply, he knew more about locks and stuff than anybody they had there. He was only twenty-four at that time but they regarded him as the boy-wonder, and they groomed him carefully but quickly. He invented a couple of new devices—which the company owned, since that was part of his work—but he was upped, in appreciation, and soon he was on the executive level. He remained with the company for twelve years. When I met him, he was thirty-six years of age, and he was earning thirty thousand dollars a year."

"Pretty good for a guy thirty-six," Marla said.

"You met him," I said. "How?"

"Six years ago, we were setting up new locking devices in our various branches—we have six of them you know—six branches of the Corn Exchange National. We were setting up new locking devices, and putting in safety cameras which would go into operation at the touch of a foot-button in case of holdups and such. It was a big job—new locks for the vaults and the cameras for all our branches—and Harrison Safe and Lock had the contract. Jonathan Kiss was in charge, and that's how I met him."

"What was he like?" Marla said.

"Tall, handsome, charming, learned, and at that time a bachelor. We got rather well acquainted."

"Were you a bachelor too?" Marla said.

"I was, and am a widower, which is the same in sum as far as outside interests are concerned."

"And you and he had similar interests?" Marla said.

"Mostly women." Mason grinned. "Oh, there was more, of course. He was a brilliant, intelligent, intellectual man, and excellent company." He rolled his cigar around in his mouth. "Of course, now in retrospect I realize that *he* was cultivating *me* and cultivating me quite assiduously. Now in retrospect I know it was all a part of his plan, a grand plan, a long-range plan, a brilliant plan."

I said, "And the first step in that plan was to get a job with the bank."

"And I'm responsible for that," Mason said.

"Oh?" said Willie.

"He had told me he was bored with his work at Harrison, that he had settled into a rut, that it no longer presented any challenge. Any large organization, and Corn Exchange National is no exception, is always in the market for really good top-level executive people. Kiss *was* tops, brilliant. I sounded him out on the possibilities of coming with us, and he appeared interested. Later on, when one of our older executives retired, I propositioned Kiss."

"What sort of proposition?" I said.

"Oh, let me add that on quite a number of occasions he hinted, quite broadly, that he would be very much interested in going in with us, with the bank."

"What sort of proposition?" I said.

"First, he would have to take a cut in salary. He was earning thirty thousand with Harrison, we could offer him twenty-five to start."

"And he was willing?" Willie said.

"We told him that in time we would bring him up to par, and that eventually he would go above that, and so he was willing. Then, there would have to be a breaking-in period of anywhere from six months to a year. He understood that necessity, and he went along with that too. At first his job was not with the vault department, he maneuvered himself into that later on, that is, there at the Thirty-eighth Street Branch. Acually, we wanted him as a sort of roving overseer for all of our banks for the installation of protective devices and for the implementation of any protective ideas that he could come up with—and he came up with plenty.

"You may remember that at about that time—six years ago—there was a wave of bank robberies, people slipping a note to a teller demanding money on penalty of dropping nitro and such. Oh, he was good. In his time he set up new and impregnable systems in all of our vaults, he devised extra little gimmicks for the cameras and had them installed, the cameras, in the most advantageous positions, including one giant camera that plays right out into the street and could catch shots of a guy running away. He also devised a system of sliding doors that could lock when the button was pushed for the cameras, so that the guy with a gun could be locked in. Actually we didn't use that because we felt that in panic a criminal might start shooting, or might have the nitro and drop it, and that too many innocent people could get killed. But we advertised it big, and it served to discourage would-be bank robbers. In point of fact, since Kiss came with us, Corn Exchange National has had the lowest rate of robbery attempts of any other bank. There have been only five attempts in all our banks over the last six-year period. Four were aborted right there at the banks, and the fifth guy was caught because of the perfect photos, from every angle, that we had of him.

"I repeat, the guy was good, great. He saw to it that only limited amounts of money were kept in the drawers of the normal bank tellers. Those who dealt in big money had specially devised cubicles with thick, plate-glass, bullet-proof windows that could drop down and seal them in and divide them from the would-be robber. That device in itself frightened off two attempts, the guys panicked and ran, and our own guards apprehended them. He devised a system of toots, alarms, and whistles—"

"Okay, okay," I said, "the guy was great."

Mason poured coffee, sipped, smiled. "Lost my head," he said.

"When was he put in charge of the vaults at Thirty-eighth Street?" I said.

"Four years ago. By then he knew everything about the banking business, he was already upped to thirty thousand, and he sat in on all top-level executive meetings. It was at one of those meetings, while we were in the process of shifting personnel, that he suggested himself for that job. It was, of course, a natural for him. We had kept him in various positions at various of the branches, while he attended also to his other duties. This would continue, but home base would be vice president in charge of the safety deposit vaults, Thirty-eighth Street Branch. His salary went up to thirty-two thousand."

"Had he been bonded?" I said.

"Well, naturally. Bonded, fingerprinted, all of that, when he came with us. That's routine with every employee."

"How much was he earning when he died?" Marla said.

"Thirty-five thousand dollars a year."

Marla sighed. "Why should a guy risk a robbery and make a fugitive of himself when he's doing that well?"

"Is that a rhetorical question," Mason said, "or do you mean it?"

"Well, both," Marla said and giggled prettily.

Mason said, "Thirty-five thousand a year is a lot or a little depending upon what you want and how you live. This guy lived big, real big. The best in clothes, the best in entertainment, the best in women, the best in clubs, and he himself entertained lavishly, especially after he married."

"Did you know the wife?" I said.

"Of course," he said.

I looked at him. "Know her well?"

He looked right back at me. "Not *that* well."

"Thirty-five thousand dollars a year," Willie said, "minus income tax could be very little for a guy who wants to live very big."

"Plus," said Mason, "you've got to work. Five days a week you work for your income. With eight million dollars, if you can shift your identity so that you can escape being a fugitive, and this guy was smart enough, you can live royally, and with proper investments, you can augment your fortune while still living like a king."

"He shifted his identity, all right," Marla said. "He killed himself."

"There's no answering for the psychopathic mind," Willie said. "Certainly it's not stable."

"And the wife is still alive," I said. "Who knows what the hell went on?"

"There's approximately eight million dollars in cash around somewhere," Mason said.

"Mr. Mason," Willie said, "you knew the man. How long do you think he planned this deal?"

"I think he planned it all his life," Mason said. "How do you like that?"

"I like it," Willie said.

"This was a poor boy from a poor background. In college he knew rich boys from rich backgrounds. He visited at palatial estates. He saw how the truly rich live. I'd say he wanted that, and with his peculiar, brilliant mind, he planned for that."

"Including his interest in locks and stuff?" Marla said.

"Yes," said Mason.

"Of course," Willie said. "Where is money? I mean, where is money, *per se*, kept? Somewhere behind lock and key. And if you know all about locks and all about keys—all!—then already you have a jump to get close to money, real money."

Mason applauded lightly and his grey eyes shrewdly regarded Willie with new approval. "Any time you'd like a job with a bank or an insurance company, Mr. Winkle . . ."

"I'm happy with the job I have," said Mr. Winkle.

"I think he planned it all of his adult life," Mason said. "Planned it broadly at first and then narrowed it in scope. I agree with Mr. Winkle about his interest in locks and keys and such. And I believe that when he accepted the job with Harrison Safe and Lock, it was still a part of the long-range, overall plan. Harrison did an immense amount of work with banks and banks are where the money is kept. He worked for twelve long years with Harrison—of course, he was well paid—but I believe even that was part of the plan: establishing a reputation, giving himself bulk and body, making himself ready to be accepted in high financial circles. He was young and he was building toward the *coup*. If, at about age forty, he could really pull off the big one, then he had a great deal of his life left to live—like a king. And in the meanwhile, he certainly wasn't starving."

"Lived well all the way, didn't he?" Willie said.

"Look," Mason said, "with all he earned at Harrison and with all he earned at Corn Exchange National—" He leaned back and closed his eyes while the inside cash register worked. "I'd say that would be about a half million." The grey eyes opened smilingly. "I bet he died comparatively broke, aside from the eight million somewhere stashed."

I said, "Approximately fifty-eight thousand dollars in cash, and a life insurance policy for fifty gees, period."

"How do *you* know?" Marla said.

"I'm a detective," I said.

"If Peter says, Peter knows," Mason said. "Yes, I'd say he was planning for the big one all of his adult life."

"What took him so long—six years—after he got to the bank?" I said.

"For a year or so he was breaking in, and it took another year before he was in charge of the vaults on Thirty-eighth Street," Mason said. "And all that time he was establishing character."

"And the next four years?"

"You know that answer as well as I do."

"Sure," I said.

"He must have been working to establish some outside identity, possibly—probably—in a foreign country. Once he hit it big, he would have to retire to that. That's what I'm hoping, that you people will discover that, and in that way, get a line on the money. Also, on the inside, he was getting a line on the big people, the ones with the big vaults, the ones that in the most likelihood would have large amounts of cash in their vaults. It was a big, important operation, and it is the planning that takes all the time. The actual work, always, once the plan is perfect, is simple."

"In this case," Willie said, "the *modus operandi* was nothing more than having duplicate keys to the outside locks and duplicate keys to the inside locks of those safety deposit vaults and that, for our man, in his position, was utterly simple."

Mason smiled again. "Any time you want a job, Mr. Winkle . . ."

Willie shrugged it off.

I stood up. "I think that's about it," I said.

"You're the general," Mason said. "I'm sorry I held you people up so long. Thanksgiving Day."

"You coming?" I said.

"No," he said. "There's a date meeting me here."

"Leave it to the executive," I said. "He covers everything."

"Champagne, coffee, something?" he said.

"Nothing," Marla said, "and thank you, Mr. Mason."

Downstairs, we stopped at the big bar for a drink. I said, "That's about it for today. Enjoy your Thanksgiving. Also give thanks for the fifty thousand dollar fee. I've got a hunch we're going to have a hell of a lot of work, but there's no hurry, we've got a year. Get yourselves shaped up, your office, routine, all of it. Suppose we meet for dinner tomorrow at six? That all right?"

"Yes," Willie said.

"I'll call you during the day and tell you where."

"You're the general," Willie said.

"*Achtung!*" said Marla and flipped up a palm in a Hitler-type salute. That brought laughter from the Thanksgiving cheerers around the crowded bar and embarrassment to me.

"Cut it out," I said.

"You're the general, General," she said.

"Let's get out of here," I said.

"My sentiments," Willie said.

We got out of there.

That night I had a date with Carmen Valesquez. We went to the opera and sat thigh by thigh at *La Boheme.* Then I took her to Goldie's for supper, and then I took her home, and we had coffee together. I made with the charm, and the jokes, and the wit, and she laughed, and that satisfied me. Then I went home and I went to sleep. What the hell, I was a swain, remember, and not a lover-boy, and I was faithful, remember, which made it worse.

EIGHTEEN

NEXT DAY, Friday, I hustled to the bank and deposited fifty thousand dollars and withdrew three thousand dollars in cash—for expenses. Then I went to the Brentwood Apartments on Central Park West and rode up to the twenty-fourth floor and rang the bell of what had been the Kiss apartment. A white-haired elderly lady opened the door and I said, "Is Mrs. Kiss in?"

"Mrs. Kiss doesn't live here any more."

"Oh," I said, "I'm sorry, I didn't know."

"It's been quite some time now."

"Oh, I'm sorry, I've been away. Can you tell me where I can reach her?"

"I have no idea, none whatever."

"Thank you. Sorry to have troubled you."

"No trouble at all."

Then I took a cab across town to 222 East Sixty-second and talked with Mrs. Mira. Richard Robinson Jackson had never shown up again, and the apartment was now rented to a very nice young lady.

Then I went to the neighborhood post office on the east side and checked: Richard Robinson Jackson had filed no forwarding address for the rerouting of mail. Then I went back across town to another neighborhood post office: there was no forwarding address on file for a Mrs. Jonathan Kiss or a Mrs. Valerie Kiss or a Miss Valerie Dayton.

Then I went back to the office and cleaned up as much routine as I could until five o'clock. Then I called Marla Trent and said, "We'll eat at Lorenzo's. Okay?"

"Fine," she said. "Six o'clock?"

I arrived at five-thirty and Lorenzo's was bright and cheery and airy, with a smattering of glowing customers engrossed in menus, a warm odor of good cooking, many idle waiters still alert and perky, and Lorenzo himself, neat and natty, having a drink at the bar.

"Ah, Mr. Chambers," he said, "always so good to see you, you are looking very well. You will join Lorenzo for an aperitif?"

"Thank you, Lorenzo. A Rob Roy, not too sweet."

"Ah, yes," he said and gave the bartender the order and then he said, "If it is a Rob Roy, which is a cocktail, then you are here for dinner, yes, no?"

"Yes. Yes."

"Alone?"

"No. There will be two people joining me at six o'clock."

He snapped his fingers at a maitre d'. "Table six," he said, "for Mr. Chambers. It will be a party of three, for six o'clock. And the best of service for my friend Mr. Chambers."

The maitre d' smiled, nodded, and went away.

Lorenzo said, "The dinner is for six o'clock, and it is now five-thirty and you are here alone. It has a reason, I suspect."

"You're a shrewd old fox, my friend."

"Shrewd, I take. Fox, I take. Old, no."

He was fifty, slim, dapper, thin-nosed, smiling, notoriously virile, bright-eyed dark-eyed, with black hair, far too black: he dyed it. He had been in the racket for thirty years and saloon keepers are a close clique in the east; one knows the other in a wide radius with Manhattan as the nucleus: Jersey, Connecticut, Long Island, Pennsylvania, and then a long skip south to Florida, and then a diagonal cut west to Nevada and California.

"There's a joint up in Darien, the Pink Poodle," I said.

"Oh no, not a joint, Mr. Chambers. The Pink Poodle is an excellent establishment, one of the finest in the country. Not a joint. Please!"

"Lorenzo, my fine Italian apologist, do not wax excited."

"Who is excited?" he said excitedly. "Lorenzo is never excited!"

"You know who owns the Pink Poodle?"

"Of course, my friend."

"Who?"

"Bernard Momserla. Bernie is an old friend. Once, long ago, he was a bartender in Bleek's. A fine man, good, kind, simple, friendly—very rich now in Connecticut."

"Could you call him for me, Lorenzo?"

"On the telephone?"

"I don't expect you to holler all the way up to Connecticut."

"Hah, hah, always with the *bon mot*. I should call him, why?"

"I've got to go up there tonight, on business. I want, sort of, a recommendation. You know?"

"Of course I know, my friend. Enjoy. I will be back soon."

I drank my Rob Roy and ordered another and drank that and paid for my drinks and the drink Lorenzo had had, although the bartender protested, and when Lorenzo came back, he protested, but that is the way of a guy at a bar, and protest or no, the boss appreciates.

"I have spoke," he said. "You will receive a fine welcome from Bernie."

"Thank you, Lorenzo."

"Oh no, you are entitled. And now, please, a drink *on* the house."

We drank, we chatted, and then Lorenzo's eyes lifted over my shoulder, and rounded, and he murmured, "Oh *Mama mia*, this is my type; oh, so beauty."

I did not turn but then Lorenzo straightened and scurried off to play host and then I turned and he was playing host to my guests, checking their coats at the checkroom. Marla, fluff-blonde and red-lipped, was in blue velvet, light blue velvet that matched her eyes. I scurried after Lorenzo to prevent his enthusiasm from earning him a bop from Willie and I said quickly, "My party for table six."

"Oh? So?" breathed Lorenzo as the maitre d' took over, and we trailed, and Lorenzo whispered to me, "So blonde, so white, so soft, so beautiful—*this* one I envy you."

"It's not mine," I said. "It's the big guy's and he can hit like hell."

"Oh, so, I understand, it is too bad," Lorenzo said.

Later, over leisurely coffee and exquisite pastry, I said, "We'll start by doing a rundown on the parties we know about. Marla, you'll take Mrs. Jonathan Kiss who once was an actress under her maiden name, Valerie Dayton. Willie, you take Kiss himself. See what you can dig up other than what Mason told us. I'll take Richard Robinson Jackson, known as Ritchie."

"Any reason for this division in the assignments?" Willie said.

"Valerie's a woman, and so I set a woman upon a woman. Ritchie is a bartender and I like to work saloons and I know a good many saloon-type people. That leaves Kiss for you. Any objections?"

"Achtung!" said Marla and grinned with all the shining white teeth.

"I'm starting now, tonight," I said. "If you kiddies don't want to work the weekend, that's up to you."

"Why not?" Marla said. "Hell, we're being paid enough."

NINETEEN

I ARRIVED at the Pink Poodle in Darien, Connecticut, at ten o'clock on Friday night of a cool November, the day after Thanksgiving. It was a refined-type saloon, not at all like its name: there was nothing pink or poodly about it. It was rough-hewn, woodsy, oak-beamed, spacious, and well lighted. One room was a bar and cocktail lounge; the main room was high-ceilinged and wood-walled with sturdy booths and sturdy tables. There were stuffed animal heads on the walls, crossed rifles, and shelves with golf trophies. It was not a youngsters' juke-box joint. It was a substantial restaurant that obviously catered to substantial citizens with substantial pocketbooks. The piano music in the main room was unremitting, uninspired, uninspiring, but, best of all, unobtrusive. I did not know Bernard Momserla but without knowing him I respected him; he ran his racket with a resolute constancy; and when I did meet him, he himself was characteristic.

He was small, round, plump, chubby-faced, and slow-talking. He was expensively but tweedily dressed all the way up to a stylish grey wool shirt and narrow black knit tie. We sat in a far booth away from the customers.

"Lorenzo spoke very good of you," he said. "Tells me you're one of them eyeballs, but with class. I like people with class. Just what can I do for you, Mr. Chambers?"

I gave him a load of glockenspiel about that I'd been retained by a lady to learn all about Richard Robinson Jackson who had been a bartender of his.

"A lady, it figures," he said and his small muddy eyes got lost in fat as he smiled. "That Ritchie was a ladies man, all the way."

"Could you give me a bit of his background?"

"I do not know any background. I met him as a customer. He used to come in here, a couple of years ago, with some rich chick from Westport. Then he started coming in alone, so I figured they broke up. Then one day he propositioned me about a job as a bartender, told me that was his work, and that he was running out of dough. He had a real nice appearance and a very charming manner and I was not happy with one of my bartenders at that time, so I gave it a whirl. I put

intricate nonsense of all private clubs, and then there came
the return click, and he opened the door for me and I walked
into another wide carpeted lobby, this one more like a hotel
lobby, and this one policed by *four* dinner-jacketed well-
muscled young minions.

To my left was a checkroom presided over by three long-
legged red-headed opera-hosed girls in red costumes that
clung like bathing suits. To my right was a long narrow desk,
like a hotel desk, behind which was another opera-hosed red-
head who smiled at me encouragingly.

I checked my coat and went across to the desk, one of the
dinner-jacket boys quietly alongside me. "I'm Peter Chambers," I said. "Mr. Farragut is expecting me."

"Oh yes," said the girl behind the desk and turned a register to me and said, "Will you please sign in?"

I signed, and the dinner-jacket took me to another door
where he went through the cabalistic rigmarole with another
button and now the door was opened from the inside by still
another red-hosed red-costumed red-haired tall young gal
who said, "Good evening! Welcome!" and then I was taken
in tow by the captain and he was something.

He was Chinese, in impeccable tails. I am over six feet
tall, but I was small in comparison. The guy was at least
six-six and with bulk to match and he walked strong and
lithe. He spoke without accent.

"You are not a member, sir. I presume you are a guest of a
member. Which party do you wish to join?"

"No party. I'm a guest of Mr. Farragut. Name's Chambers."

"Oh yes sir. This way, please. Table twelve."

The room was vast, rectangular, and crowded. The clien-
tele was sporty, wealthy, noisy. At least half of the customers were in evening wear and diamonds were a dime-a-dozen
all over the place including the pinky-fingers of the men.
There was a dance floor in the middle, and people were dancing, and a large stage at one end, but there was no one on-
stage except the orchestra. Table twelve was right up front.
The captain seated me and said, "If you wish me, sir, my
name is John Chong. I will tell Mr. Farragut you're here."

The service was by waitress: all red-headed, all red hosed,
all red-costumed. First my waitress brought a bottle of Haig
& Haig, Pinch, with glasses, ice, water, and soda, and then
she brought Eli Farragut.

"Ah, dear Peter, so good, so good," he said and sat down and poured and we drank and we chatted.

Eli Farragut was no Bernard Momserla. Farragut, in splendidly tailored dinner clothes, was suave, polished, soft-spoken. He looked somewhat like Carmen Valesquez's father except taller, thinner, and younger. Farragut was one of the top men in his racket—very rich, very wise, very worldly, with solid connections both in the upper and underworld. You could get killed if you crossed up Eli Farragut.

He was apparently glad to see an old friend and happy to talk, and he did most of the talking. He had opened the Club Farragut as a theater-cabaret eight years ago, but with only minor success. He found, however, that he attracted many stay-up-laters who consistently complained about the curfew, so he switched it to a private club. A private club is a dodge that can get around the state laws pertaining to public clubs and is thus a legitimate after-hours spot. The drinkers can drink as early in the morning as they like or as late at night as they like. His entertainment had grown looser as his political connections had grown firmer, and Club Farragut was now a fixture, paying off plenty of ice, but a howling sucess. Eli giggled about it.

"I keep switching the entertainment policy," he said. "You know these people aren't yokels. They're mostly New York business men, Wall Street boys, Madison Avenue people, that stuff, with homes up here. You've got to titillate the bastards. Recently, as you know, there's been big interest in strippers and belly-dancers. Well, sir, here they strip, but all the way, and the belly-dancers really give you the belly, man. Funny thing, it's attracted the women. The *women* go for it. Ah, women, the mad creatures. Did I say recently? I've been giving them strippers and belly workers—call them art dancers —for four years now, and they eat it up. Of course, I've got the best, and I've lost a lot of them to the Broadway shows. Why, my best customers are the New York producers. Okay, Peter, enjoy. I've got to toddle now. You're a guest of the house."

"Absolutely not."

He didn't fight me. "Okay, then you pay. But this I can do for you. From here on in, you're a member. You signed the register, didn't you?"

"Yes."

"I'll leave instructions. You'll always be able to come in. You're a life member. And I *am* doing something for you. Membership fee is $1000 per year. For you, it's nothing. Compliments of Eli Farragut."

That was Eli Farragut. Whatever he did, he did big. He went away and I didn't see him again the rest of the night. That was fine by me. There was plenty to see without Eli Farragut, and it began, for me, with the last show, at one o'clock.

The peelers really peeled, but all the way, and the belly dancers were without pelvic peer. Midway through the show, my person was introduced. Momserla had slurred the name. It was not Anna Estherwing. It was Anna Esther Wing. She was an Oriental and she was absolutely exquisite.

She was petite, perhaps five feet, with a waist that you could encompass within your two hands. She wore a tight orange gown that embraced a figure that was built for embraces. Shining black hair was piled tall on her head; she had a tiny, perky, delicate nose; a heart-shaped face with a pointed chin; a curved red mouth, small, like an unopened rosebud—and blue eyes! I was up close. I could see. She had gleaming, almond-shaped, smoke-blue eyes ringed within long black lashes. Something? An exquisite Oriental with a body like a fragile goddess and blue eyes!

And she could dance! This was no peeler with a lecherous wiggle! This was a consummate artist! A dancer!

Soon enough, of course, the orange gown came off, and she was in orange satin brief-and-bra and now you could see the body and that body was something to see all the way from the slender ankles to the long curve of the calves to the full glistening thighs to the protruding pear-shaped breasts and the firm out-thrust wriggling rump. And the music got hotter and the dance got wilder and then she turned her back to the audience and stood legs apart, the body shimmering and quivering to the rhythm, and you knew she was going to strip naked, and you wondered how she would work it.

First her hands went up to her hair. She plucked out pins and flung them away and then the hair fell down covering her to the base of her buttocks like a black-gleaming shade. The hair was shiny and thick, long but not extraordinarily long, because she herself was petite, and then she bent backward, the hair hiding her, the music throbbing, and then the bra was flung away, and then the panties were flung away, and still she was hidden by the screen of hair, and the music got wilder and the drums were crazy, and she went into a whirling dance that was a tease to end all stripteases: she used her hair as others have used fans or whatever their props; it was the best I had ever seen and I had thought I had seen them all; she was a trained artist, a skilled dancer, a talent; she whirled and whisked and quivered and twisted but not once was she exposed where you expected it would have to happen: not the pubis, not the nipples, not the crevice of the buttocks; and you wondered, with all the rest of the audience, how she could manage so precisely in all the abandon of the dance; and then it was over as she sank down cross-legged, the hair covering all of her, and then, as the music stopped, there was the compliment of total silence before the applause broke deafeningly, and the stage went dark. When the lights came on, she was gone, and she did not return, not even for a bow.

All the rest, of course, was anticlimax.

I hardly looked. When my waitress came, I asked for a pencil, notepaper, and envelope, and it must have been a common request, because she understood at once, and complied within minutes. I wrote: *Miss Wing, Please join me at Table twelve, Peter Chambers.* I folded the paper, put it into the envelope, and asked my waitress for John Chong. When he came I gave him the envelope and said, "This is for Miss Wing, please."

He smiled and went away.

The show ended and the dancing began and I nibbled on Haig & Haig Pinch and then I asked for John Chong again and he came and I said, "Did you give Miss Wing my note?"

"Yes, sir."

"I asked her to join me."

He shrugged his powerful shoulders. "I figured."

"She hasn't joined me."

"So I see." His eyes were inscrutable.

"Do you know where she is?"

"She went home."

I asked for my check and I got it, I sure did. For a few shots of Haig & Haig Pinch, bottle on the table, the tab was fifty-seven dollars. Well, why not? Unfair is fair, where it fits. Here it fit.

Saturday I lay long and had afternoon breakfast in bed and thought about a vault heist of eight million dollars and got a few ideas which I kept in the hopper for simmering.

At twelve o'clock midnight I was back at Club Farragut and I repeated the routine with one small exception—I put a hundred-dollar bill into the envelope with my note—but it availed me the same fat zero as the night before.

"She went home," said John Chong.

There had been one slight difference, though. I had sent the note before the one o'clock show went on. During the early portions of her dance, the slower portions, she had looked directly down at Table twelve, and I could have sworn that the rosebud mouth smiled a small special smile in my direction. Nothing else, though, had changed. Although I had ordered my own brand of Scotch, J. & B. was my preference at that period, the tab was similar, fifty-five dollars for about seven drinks, although the bottle was on the table. I kept it even up: the tip to the waitress was fifteen instead of thirteen but John Chong got a smile, less cheery this trip, more dour.

On Sunday my ideas about the vault heist bubbled up to good focus, but I gave more attention to the Wing ding. Anna Esther was the star of the show, no question. She was a talent, an artist, as different from the peelers and the shakers as a creative architect is different from a highly skilled bricklayer. According to Momserla and the grapevine, Richard Robinson Jackson had been in there pitching but he hadn't pitched any strikes; well, neither had I, and I was not in Connecticut to try to pitch like Ritchie or to play handball against a putty wall. This section of the deal needed a new approach and I *was* on an expense account.

Sunday night I changed it all up. The brand of whiskey became Bell's Twenty (and the tab became seventy-four bucks). The operation became more lavish and I snapped my fingers at the help. I skipped the waitress for the pencil, the paper, the envelope: I ordered them from John Chong and I ordered them early. I wrote my note while he stood over me, same note: *Miss Wing, Please join me at Table twelve, Peter Chambers.* But then I went dramatic with all the furbelows. First I displayed my well-stuffed poke and I made sure that John Chong got an eyeful. Then I put a thousand bucks into the envelope with the note—a thousand bucks—and I said to John Chong, "Be sure Miss Wing gets this, Pappy."

"She'll get it, Pappy," he said and there was grit at the base of his throat, and twenty minutes later, before the show went on, he was back, and he laid the envelope on the table in front of me. I picked it up without fuss and handled it casually. It was heavy but the thousand bucks were not weighing it down. The thousand bucks were gone. Instead, there was a key.

On the reverse side of my note, an excellent hand had written: *I have noticed you. You are an extremely attractive man and I am not one to flatter. The rules of the house do not permit my accepting your invitation to join you at your table but they do not prevent me from inviting you to join me at my convenience. The key is the key to my house. The address is 2 Nelson Street. Please go there at once and wait for me. I shall come.   Anna.*

I got up, got out, got directions, and went to Nelson Street. It was a small cottage near the ocean where it was windy and cold but inside the cottage the oil-burner was going full blast and it was hot. There were three neatly furnished rooms, living room, bedroom, and kitchen, and the living room had a well-stocked liquor cabinet and a well-stocked bookcase. I took off my coat, my jacket, my tie, opened my collar and made myself comfortable. I checked the bookcase and if the books were hers, she was not only a talent, she was also an intellectual. I made a highball and took out a book. I drank a little, read a little, then lay out on the couch and erected plans about the vault heist and erected fantasies about Anna Esther Wing, and then I dozed.

She came at one-thirty. I had left the door unlocked, her key on the table. She came in without knocking, smiled, and locked the door. Neither of us said a word. I swung my legs off the couch, sat and watched. She placed her pocketbook on the table, hung her coat in a closet, and then she said in a lovely voice in beautiful diction, "If you please, I'll change."

"I please," I said.

She went to the bedroom and when she came back her hair was down, caught behind her in a long pony tail, and she was wearing a tight white lounging gown and tiny white high-heeled scuffs. She smiled again but the smoky blue eyes were frightened.

"Are you afraid of me?" I said.

"No. Why should I be afraid of you?"

"You speak so beautifully, Miss Wing."

"People always say that. They're surprised at my English. Well, I don't know any other language. I'm an American, born in Baltimore."

"And the blue eyes, the beautiful blue eyes?" They were blue and beautiful but they were awfully damned frightened and so I kept talking to ease whatever tension there was. "Most unusual. Striking."

"My mother was Irish, my father Chinese. My mother had blue eyes."

"From whom did you inherit the talent, because you sure are talented."

"I don't believe that talent is an inherited trait."

I wasn't making a move. I was just sitting. But the eyes stayed frightened.

I said, "I've got a drink sitting on the table there. May I make one for you?"

"No, thank you," she said quickly. "I'll do it myself."

For a little gal she sure made a big drink and she drank it in a hurry as though she needed it. She didn't sit down. She kept standing, moving as she talked.

I said, "What is one like you doing in the Club Farragut?"

"Making a living," she said. "I have a two-year contract with Mr. Farragut. I earn three-fifty a week. I'm saving my money. In the spring, I'll have enough saved up so that I can make the rounds again for a Broadway play. I'll have enough to live for a year, seeking the kind of work I want. I'm not only a dancer, I'm an actress, and that is my life. I have a great career planned for myself. This is an interlude, a period in my life."

"I hope you make it."

"Thank you."

"But what do you want with me?"

"I'm a private detective. I'm investigating Richard Robinson Jackson. You're supposed to know about him. What about him?"

"A dolt, a boor. Handsome but empty."

"Did you make it with him?"

"No, please. Oh, I'm not a saint. But I pick my people."

"Tell me about Ritchie, all you know."

She knew plenty. He was born in Mexico of American parents. His father was killed in a brawl when he was twelve and his mother took him to New Orleans. She died there of tuberculosis when he was thirteen, and from then

on he drifted all over the country. Somewhere as he grew up
he learned to be a bartender. He was handsome and he lived
off women. In between affairs, he tended bar. Chance had
brought him to Club Farragut and he had fallen in love with
Anna Esther Wing. He had become a nuisance. That was
her story.

"Thank you," I said.

She dimmed the lights. She slipped out of the gown. She
came to me and slid her arms around my neck. Her body
quivered against mine. "Please stay," she whispered. "Please
stay with me."

"I can't."

"Please, why?"

"I've got a girl and for the first time in my life I'm trying
to be faithful. Pretty sick, huh?"

"I admire you," she said while the quivering body drove me
crazy.

"Sick," I said and broke free and got out of there.

I had a bad night that night: the worst night since I'd
met Carmen Valesquez.

TWENTY

MONDAY IN Manhattan I put the car back into the garage,
walked home, and drew a bath. My mind was back on the
vault heist, and in the middle of undressing, I went to the
phone. I called my travel agent about a flight to Hollywood,
and he offered a reservation on a jet leaving at one ayem,
and I accepted it. Then I bathed, shaved, dressed, packed
a bag and left it at the ready, and went to Quo Vadis and
arrived there at seven o'clock to find my trio already eating
but obviously disgruntled, all three. I could understand Marla
and I could understand Willie: they had been ordered to go
to dinner, and nobody likes to go to dinner on order. Mason's
discomfiture was more subtle, but I dug that too.

Marla had dressed. She was in a cocktail gown with
gorgeous cleavage and with her figure that was enough to
upset the most spartan of hosts. It might have been pure spite,
but even that was all woman. She had responded to an order
but she was a soldier who had a choice of uniform and what
she had chosen was gnawing at the commander. She was a

ravishingly beautiful woman and she had made a point, in make-up, hair-do, and attire, to highlight her beauty, and the commander was having trouble adhering to his business principles.

I was tired but I belted away at my duty. I was nauseatingly cheerful. "Okay," I said, "How're we doing on our investigations?"

I ordered and I ate and they gave me the business.

First Willie. "Jonathan Kiss was all that Mr. Mason had said."

"Well, great," I said.

Willie was quick. "When there's nothing to investigate, investigation avails nothing."

"Worthy of the Bard," I said. "Are you through?"

"From some of his Harvard associates, and from some of the old professors up there I can verify that Kiss had a taste for wealth and ran with the wealthiest. He was highly regarded academically, was rated near genius in I.Q., was Phi Beta Kappa, and *summa cum laude*."

"So what's new?" I said.

"He was also an excellent actor with a great interest in the theater. At Harvard he was president of the Drama Club and as undergraduate he was the star of every show the club or the school put on."

"Seems he maintained this interest in the theater after he was graduated," Marla said. "That's how he met and married Valerie Dayton."

"How?" I said.

"He had invested some money in a show for which she auditioned. They met, they flipped, they got married. When they met and they flipped, she was still married to another guy, but she got divorced."

"Did you get background on her?"

"Aside from a mutual interest in the theater and a mutual interest in each other, they had one other mutual interest. Money."

"Come on, now. Let's not pull teeth. Let's have it."

She gave it.

Valerie Dayton had been born in Miami, Florida, and had been graduated from the University of Miami. One year after her graduation, her father had died leaving her a bequest of thirty thousand dollars which she spent within two years in New York. Then she married a successful actor, an older man, one Felix Davenport. Her mother had moved to Washington and there she had met a member of the Russian embassy. She had renounced her American citizenship, had married the diplomat, had returned with him to Russia, and they had both been swallowed up behind the iron curtain. As for Valerie, one month after her meeting with Kiss, she had instituted divorce proceedings against Davenport, in Reno, and one year later she and Kiss had been married.

"Davenport's in Hollywood now," she said. "I'm arranging to check that through."

"Skip it," I said. "I'm leaving for Hollywood tonight. For that purpose."

Victor Mason had been taking out his frustration on a huge parfait loaded with cholesterol. Now he went to work on me. "Peter," he said blandly enough but there was gravel in the baritone, "all of this may be intensely interesting to you but it's dull as dishwater to me, and a hell of a waste of my time. I have no intention of sitting in on all of your preliminary conferences, or on *any* of your conferences, for that matter. You people have been retained to do a job of work, or to try to do a job of work, and that's your business, and none of my business.

"Once and for all, I'd like to lay it out for you explicitly. I'm a busy man who believes in the delegation of authority, and in this case full authority has been delegated to you in conjunction with Miss Trent and Mr. Winkle. I am not to be called into consultation unless the matter is at a head or unless there are other matters of extreme urgency or importance. Candidly, I'm surprised at this manifestation of exceedingly bad judgment . . ."

Marla and Willie, busily keeping their eyes averted, were nonetheless obviously enjoying my castigation, and in a way I couldn't blame them. They were a couple of big shots with their own agency but I had been set up as their superior and that didn't rub right with them, and when the general gets chewed out by the commander-in-chief, the lesser officers enjoy, and they were enjoying. As for the commander-in-chief, Marla's creamy bosom had put him out of sorts and out of bounds. But I had a trump, and I am not taking too much credit for it. Sooner or later Marla or Willie would have thought of it; they probably would have thought of it by now except for the fact that their roles had been established: they were taking orders, not plotting policy.

"I wanted you to finish your dinner," I said, "before I laid out a plan that I think is a good one. After I'm through, if you don't think you should have been consulted on this, then I'll resign."

He said nothing but already the grey eyes were remorseful. That Marla was enough to upset anyone, even as seasoned a campaigner as Vic Mason.

"I've been giving this thing a hell of a lot of thought," I said. "Now please listen." I lit a cigarette. "Kiss pulled this heist the Friday night-Saturday morning of June 17. I think we're all agreed on that."

"Yes," Mason said.

"Okay, he killed the guards, all of that, no sense to do the recap. But there *is* sense in trying to work out the actual *modus operandi*, and I think I've done that. There's only one method possible and any one of you would easily have come up with it had you thought it important enough to give it some thought."

"And you think the *modus operandi* is important?" Mason said.

"Yes, and I'll try to explain that if you won't interrupt."

He grinned and he shook his head. He loved me again.

"Eight million bucks represents a hell of a lot of paper, I mean in weight and in volume," I said. "It would require a number of trips." I squeezed out my cigarette. "Now I say he came to the bank in his car and parked it at the side entrance." I looked to Willie. "He had a car, I take it?"

"Late model Caddy," Willie said. "In the wife's name."

"What happened to it, by the way?"

"The wife sold it to a used car dealer."

"Tore all the ties, didn't she?"

"Yes sir," Willie said.

"Okay. He had a couple of bags in the car. He knocked off the guards, brought in the bags, filled them, brought them out to the car, carted them somewhere, emptied them, came back, filled them, carted them off, until the job was finished."

"Carted them where?" Marla said.

"Ah, now we're beginning to get to the importance of the *modus operandi*. He had to cart that loot somewhere, didn't he? And once it was all carted, he'd have to load it up into something. Something like a good big sturdy trunk." Willie was fidgeting. "How'm I doing, Willie?"

"I think you're doing beautifully, Peter."

"And where would this base of operations be?" Marla said.

"Not too far away from the bank. I think we've all accepted the idea that the guy had planned this truly amazing heist all of his adult life. Oh, I've got some other thoughts, but they'll have to wait their turn."

"The base of operations," Marla insisted.

"I'd say he'd taken an apartment somewhere, not too far away from the bank, taken it far in advance. I'd say it was a ground-floor apartment in a fairly good building, sort of a professional apartment with a private outside entrance. I'd say there were some excellent bars on the windows and that he'd installed some fine locks on the door, the best, and if this guy didn't know about locks, nobody did."

"You mean the locks and stuff would be to protect the trunk full of money," Marla said. "What purpose? Once he had that trunk full of money, he could have stayed with it himself, until *that* was carted away."

"No ma'am," I said. "This was a guy who had done his planning for years, and he covered any possible eventuality. He had to be home on Saturday morning, just in case the dead bank guards were found. Then if any officials called him, he was home, or he had been at home. It wouldn't do if he were out all night and not at home in the morning. He left his own apartment on Central Park West at nine o'clock in the morning, and the doorman saw him, and he came back at about eleven, and the doorman saw him again."

"All right, so what are you trying to prove?" Marla said. "That now, five months later, we're seeking a ground-floor apartment with bars on the windows and special locks on the doors? And if we find it, what have we found?"

Mason finally surmounted Marla's boobs. "Quiet," he growled. "Let him talk. He's cooking." He smiled at me, he wrinkled his eyes at me, he loved me, I was his boy. I could have held him up for more dough right then and there and it would have served him right. I didn't because he had paid me enough dough, and because his eyes were apologetic, and because he was cottoning up to me like a penitent tomcat—make that a lion.

"This is where you come in, Vic," I said.

"Yes, Peter," he said respectfully.

"That guy shipped that trunk somewhere, arrangements made in advance. Yes?"

"Go on," he said.

"Let's give that apartment a wide range. Ten blocks north from Thirty-eighth Street and ten blocks south, river to river. Let's give it an extra ten blocks, north and south, for safety's sake, river to river. That means from Fifty-eighth Street to Eighteenth Street, all the way east and all the way west. Okay?"

"Yes."

"The guy was away from his home between nine and eleven that Saturday morning. Let's give it that entire span. Okay?"

"Yes."

"There aren't too many top-flight express companies, and for that trunk, wherever it was going, he'd want the best, wouldn't he?"

"Yes, Peter," Mason purred.

"All right. You've got plenty of investigators that you can stick on to this. The express companies have records. Not too many trunks could possibly have been picked up between Fifty-eighth Street and Eighteenth Street on Saturday, June 17, between nine and eleven o'clock. Each one had a destination and Miss Trent and Mr. Winkle will follow up on such destinations. I'd suggest the top express companies, I repeat, because that cargo was very valuable. I'd also suggest that they can narrow it down by limiting themselves as to point of pickup."

"Point of pickup?" Mason said.

"A ground floor apartment with a private entrance, bars on the windows, and solid locks on the door."

"Look," Willie said, "I don't know about Mr. Mason, but you've got my apology, at least for my attitude which up to now has been lousy."

"Welcome," I said.

Marla also, finally, joined the team. She bent over and lightly kissed my temple. Not so lightly her bosom rested on my arm. Maybe that got to Mason because he was gruff again, saying, "Why can't you head up this deal, Peter?"

"I want to talk to Felix Davenport."

"Don't you think this thing is more important? I'll have my investigators all out on it first thing in the morning."

"Davenport is important."

"Hell, why?"

"I've got another idea I'm working on."

"Go," he said. "I won't cross you any more and certainly

I won't criticize. Go, kid, but go in style. For you the expense
account is unlimited. Make it big, make it good, and make it
hurt. You're entitled."

He had voiced his apology.

TWENTY-ONE

I ARRIVED at the sunny side of the nation, after the usual de-
lays of a non-stop (but stoppable) haul, at eleven-thirty
Tuesday morning, and at twelve o'clock I was ensconced in
an excellent suite at the Beverly Hilton on the expense account. I had two expansive and expensive rooms, thickly
carpeted: a sitting room with a wide-screen television and
a bedroom with a wide inviting bed. I accepted the invitation,
wearing all my clothes, for a momentary nap, and I woke
up at seven o'clock in the evening, too late to check the
agencies for Felix Davenport. I unpacked my bag, showered, shaved, and went out for a solitary dinner. Then I
attended some of the strip joints on the Strip, got loaded,
flirted, but stayed faithful, and went back to bed, this time
with my clothes off, and at nine o'clock in the morning I
was ready for business but business was not ready for me.
I called some of the big agencies, and the second one, for
spite, was MCA, and MCA handled Felix Davenport, and
the girl was very polite but it didn't help. She gave me his
home address and his home phone number and told me he
was not at home. He was in Mexico on a picture, but he
would be back on Friday. I called Marla Trent Enterprises—
neither Marla nor Willie was in—and I left word that I could
be reached at the Beverly Hilton. Then I called Carmen
Valesquez at Harkness and we had a long, friendly, trans-
continental chat on the expense account. Then I went out
shopping, bought lightweight sports clothes, hired a car,
packed a bag, and drove out to Palm Springs. There, for two
days, I rested and baked the booze out of the old bones, and
on Friday I was back at the Beverly, rosy, ruddy, and ready
for business.

Friday evening I took Felix Davenport to Romanoff's for
an elaborate dinner. Felix was sixty-seven years of age with
a round face, twinkling humorous eyes, bushy white eyebrows, and a nimbus of white hair sitting like a crown on a

glowing pink pate. After dinner he had brandy and bene-
dictine and smoked a long thin cigar and said in his deep
rolling voice, "All right, Peter, I've been polite, but I'm
dying of curiosity. To what do I owe this pleasure?"

I hit him square because Felix was not one for cavorting
around bushes. "I've been retained to do a complete check on
Valerie Dayton. You're one of the checkpoints."

"Well," he said, "is she coming into a fortune or something?"

"If it works out the way I want it to work out, she'll be
losing a fortune. Maybe."

"I'd say, right off, that you'll have a difficult problem
there. Trying to pry money out of Valerie is like trying to pry
open a closed can with your bare fingers."

"Likes money?"

"Loves money."

"What else does she love?"

"Money first. Now that sounds like a rap but actually it
isn't. There are many people who love money, although with
Valerie I'd say it's a passion. On the other hand, there are
many fine things about her. She is a true intellectual, utterly
bored with anything mediocre. She has excellent taste, excellent manners, excellent judgment. She has courage and a
high order of intelligence. She has a deep inner core of
strength and she can be depended upon in an emergency.
She has quality and—"

"Okay, let's lower the body."

He chuckled. "I admit that sounded like a eulogy."

"Let's try the other side of the coin. Would you say she
married you for money?"

"Of course. I'm not a wealthy man but I have solid investments and I'm comfortable. At that time, she was broke,
struggling as an actress. I'd say she married me for two reasons. She wouldn't have to worry about money and I could
help her in her career, which I did. She could have been a
great actress if she'd had the drive."

"You don't seem to resent her, Felix."

"Man, why should I? I was old enough to be her father.
She wasn't in love with me and that didn't bother me in the
least. I wanted her and I paid to get her and I think I got the
best of the bargain as long as it lasted."

"Do you think she was faithful to you?"

"Of course not. Valerie couldn't be faithful to anyone.

But she's not one to be judged by normal criteria of morality. In that sense, Valerie is entirely amoral. She uses sex like an instrument."

"Does she enjoy?"

"Certainly. She simply doesn't limit herself."

"And it didn't bother you?"

"I'm not a boy now and I wasn't a boy then. I understood her. We had an excellent relationship, if I must say so myself."

"So what happened to the excellent relationship?"

"She fell in love."

"Jonathan Kiss?"

"I see you've worked on some other checkpoints."

"Naturally."

"For the first time in her life, she fell deeply, truly in love."

"She told you?"

"As soon as she was sure, and she introduced me to him too. She told me she wanted to marry him, and of course I released her."

"What kind of a guy, Felix? I mean, did you see him often enough to come to any conclusions?"

"Oh yes. We were all rather good friends for a while. A hell of a nice man, young enough and just her type."

"What's her type?"

"He was. Handsome, cultured, suave, interesting, highly intelligent, and, best of all, a banker. With money."

"Do you think she's been faithful to him?"

"If you mean sexually, of course not."

"You mean sexually she just *can't* be faithful."

"That's what I mean, although I don't think faithful is the proper word. In her way, she isn't being faithless; that just isn't important enough to her; and, in her own way, she *is* being faithful—to herself, to her innate promiscuity, to her nature."

"How about any other way. Do you think she's been faithful to him?"

"Absolutely. She had found the guy for her. She adored him. Nothing else would have broken her out of the comfortable marriage with me. She cared for me and I took care of her and I gave her every freedom she desired. She loves the guy, I'd take an oath on that, and she'd do anything for him, go to any length, die for him. Oh, I know that gal and I tell you she loves this man."

He talked of Kiss in the present tense, so he did not know of the suicide, which was perfectly natural. A suicide in New York—unless it is the suicide of some one in the theatrical field—has very little repercussion in Hollywood, and Felix was now too far removed from Valerie for any personal communication.

I let it lie, shifted the conversation, and we rambled on to other matters. Later we did a bit of the town, then I dropped him off at his home and went back to the hotel.

I slept until noon and began to pack, desultorily, for the trip back east, when I saw the yellow envelope that had been slipped under my door. I went to it sleepily, sleepily opened it, and sleepily read:

CONGRATULATIONS ON RATIOCINATIONS. THANKS TO YOU WE HIT THE JACKPOT FIRST CRACK. GET IN TOUCH WITH US WHEN YOU HAVE THE TIME AT THE BEVERLY HILTON. CONGRATULATIONS AGAIN FOR YOUR SKILLFUL THINKING. WILLIAM AND MARLA.

I let the telegram flutter to the floor and went to the bathroom for a shower and then, in the longest double-take on record, I ran out, wet and naked, and picked up the telegram and read it again. *Get in touch with us when you have the time at the Beverly Hilton.* That could mean that I, at the Beverly Hilton, when I had the time, could get in touch with them. It could also mean that when I had the time I could get in touch with *them* at the Beverly Hilton. The telegram was signed William and Marla, William first, which meant that he had sent it. Willie had a sense of humor and Willie could write English far less ambiguously. I glanced at the top of the telegram and sure enough it had been sent from a Beverly Hills office only an hour before.

I grabbed the phone and said, "This is Chambers in 605. Do we have a William Boyd Winkle registered here? And a Marla Trent?"

"Just one moment, Mr. Chambers." Then the voice said, "Mr. Winkle is in suite 403. Miss Trent in 407."

"Connect me with 403, please."

"Yes sir."

I got the clicks in the ear and then I got Willie.

"Son of a bitch," I said.

"Good morning," he said pleasantly.

"Big joke," I said.

"No joke," he said. "I didn't want to wake you. I told them to slip the thing under the door."

"Suppose I'd have checked out before that?"

"You couldn't have. I left instructions at the desk."

"When did you get into town?"

"Yesterday morning."

"Why didn't you get in touch with me?"

"We had work to do during the day. In the evening, you were out. So we went out too."

Half hour later, in my sporty west coast sport clothes I was in Willie's suite, and Willie was in sporty west coast sport clothes, and Marla was in tight toreador pants which is enough to knock you right on the part that stuck out best on her. I gobbled breakfast while they talked, but Marla's great big blue eyes shot a lot of respect at me and that slowed the gobble down to gulps while I ogled right back at her.

"Victor Mason put his boys and his influence to work with the express companies," Willie said, "and by Thursday morning we had the list. On Saturday, June 17, between nine and eleven in the morning, within the area you described, only eight trunks were picked up. We checked the pick-up addresses and sure enough on Thirty-third right off Park, there was the ground-floor private-entrance apartment, practically as you described it, bars on the windows and *three* lovely locks on the door. It was now a dentist's office but the dentist had only been there since September. The prior tenant—we learned from the landlord—had been somewhat of an eccentric, the guy who had put all the locks on the door and locks and bolts on the inside doors too—a traveling man, quite rarely at the apartment—name, John Keith. Funny how they always stay with their initials."

"Um," I said gulping bacon and ogling Marla.

"Point of destination: 109 Marble Drive, Pacific Palisades, right here on the West Coast. Name of consignee, Mr. and Mrs. Sam Casey. So, Thursday night we lit out for the Coast."

"And Friday you arrived."

"And on Friday you were proven to be one hell of a good man," Marla said.

"You ought to try me some time," I said. Talk is cheap. I was still faithful to Carmen.

"On Friday," said Willie, "we did some discreet checking. The house on Marble Drive was a rented house. It's an area, actually a vacation area, with many houses for rent. It was rented last February for a period of eighteen months. And it was rented in the name of—*Mrs. Richard Robinson Jackson.*"

That lifted me right out of my breakfast. "Already," I said, "way back there in February—Mrs. Richard Robinson Jackson?" I shoved away the plates, pulled a cup and poured coffee.

"The lady came alone," Willie said, "and rented alone and paid alone. Eighteen months in advance for a furnished house."

"Who's Mr. and Mrs. Sam Casey?"

"An elderly couple she retained as caretakers."

"And they got fired when the man of the house arrived on June 18."

"Wrong, I'm pleased to say." Willie's grin went all the way to the ears. "A guy's got to miss once in a while."

"So they were fired when the *lady* of the house arrived."

"And the couple was fired ten days after Mrs. Jackson arrived," Willie said.

"The alleged Mrs. Jackson," I said.

"That alleged became kosher ten days after," Willie said. "The records show that on August 7 Mrs. Valerie Dayton Kiss, a widow, was married to Mr. Richard Robinson Jackson, first marriage for him. The ceremony was at the house, and the Caseys were witnesses, and then, probably with a good piece of severance pay, they were disengaged from service."

"Nice work, you two."

"We accomplished one more thing before we checked in here last evening."

"You found the eight million bucks and you closed the case."

"Not quite. We found a house in a perfect location to observe the Jackson house on Marble Drive."

"You sound like you accomplished a feat, pal."

"In a way it is. You see, Peter, in that area the houses

are set far apart, isolated from one another, a quarter of a mile, half a mile, sometimes a mile, and it's a wooded area, trees and stuff. We did a hell of a lot of exploring." ,

"So?"

"We found this house, this one house for our purpose. It's a big damned rambling house, and it's going to be awfully expensive, but it is for rent. It's the only house in the entire area that can give us an unobstructed view of the house on Marble Drive."

"Where, exactly, is it?"

"On a rutty road called Laurel Drive. Uphill from the Jackson house, about a half mile."

"And from there you can observe?"

"We did. With these." He took a pair of powerful binoculars from a drawer. "From up the hill there, near the house I'm talking about, through these, we saw dear Valerie and we saw dear old Ritchie."

"You saw Jackson?"

"Big as life."

"I doubt it."

"*Now* what?" said Marla.

"How'd he look?" I said to Willie.

"Fat," Willie said. "He's put on forty pounds, I'd say. Fat and sunburned, but still good-looking, still white-haired crew-cut."

"I doubt it," I said.

"What the hell?" Willie said. "What? What do you doubt? I tell you it's a clear view. I tell you, half mile or no, through good binoculars, it's as though you're right on top of them. We saw them, both of them, big as life, you could make out a pimple on the nose. What in hell do you doubt, Pappy?"

"I doubt you saw Richard Robinson Jackson."

"But I'm *telling* you—"

"And I'm telling *you*. You saw Jonathan Kiss."

"Kiss? You're out of your mind," Marla said.

"It's my one *other* big idea," I said.

"Like this they flip," Marla said. She shrugged toward Willie. The way Marla was built, her shrug could be disconcerting. I was disconcerted. "A guy gets a genius-type idea, one genius-type idea—which I admit he did—and he wants to try to top himself." To me she said, "Peter, that bit with the trunk, point of pick-up to point of destination, was a sheer stroke of genius. If we track down that loot, you did it, Victor Mason can thank you. But, baby, you can rest on your laurels, don't try to top yourself, settle back to normal."

"The killer's Kiss," I said.

"Pardon?" Willie said.

"Killer's Kiss," I said.

"Killer's kiss—*what?*" Willie said.

"I had *two* big ideas, if you please," I said. "One of them has shaped up. I'd like to discuss the other one. Nobody ever got pregnant discussing. Okay if we discuss?"

"Okay, discuss," said Marla.

"Have some coffee," I said.

TWENTY-TWO

WE SAT and we had coffee, all around.

We smoked cigarettes, all around.

Willie fiddled with the binoculars, and Marla fiddled with nothing, but every now and then she drew a deep breath, and that had me fiddling. So I talked and I talked fast in the aroma of the coffee and in the blue smoke of the cigarettes.

"Here's a guy, admittedly a brilliant man, who, we have decided, devoted most of his adult life to planning a big one, the biggest, a super-heist. Each step, as we follow it and as it develops, was masterfully plotted and masterfully executed. Even now that we're onto it, we don't know if he left a hole big enough for any of us to stick a finger into. He may still get away with it, a heist of about eight million dollars. Consequently, my dear colleagues, we must not underestimate him."

"Who in hell," said Marla, "is underestimating?"

"We must *over*estimate, if that is possible. We must work from the top and give *him* every benefit of our doubts. This baby is entitled."

"He's dead," Marla said.

"He's alive," I said.

"He's dead," Marla said. "Genius is a hair's-breadth away from nuttiness. In his genius he plotted a big one, the biggest; in his nuttiness, he knocked himself off because of jealousy, to spite the wife."

"You're underestimating."

"How would it be—*over*estimating?"

"That he planned even that."

"Even what?"

"That if we ever got this close, we would believe in the nuttiness."

"Now *you're* nutty."

Quietly Willie said, "Let him talk."

"Thank you," I said.

"Talk," said Willie.

"Let's start with us, the investigators. The first you ever heard of the guy is when he came to you in January to adduce proof that his wife was indulging in adultery. In March, you delivered the proof. He did nothing until June. That's strange enough but what he did in June is even stranger. He came to you on Friday, June 16, to instruct you to call his wife on the morning of Saturday, June 17. You were to deliver the duplicate set of photos to her. You were also to deliver the sealed letter informing her that he was already a suicide. Nutty? A diseased mind attempting an elaborate system of torture for the erring wife? Maybe. I doubt it."

"Why?" Marla said.

"He gave you the sealed note on Friday afternoon. It was to be delivered to the wife. You were to call the wife Saturday morning at nine-fifteen and deliver the photos and the note at eleven. Correct?"

"The note stated that when she read it he'd be dead, a suicide."

"Correct," Marla said.

"Now follow this. On Friday afternoon he delivers a note that he'll be a suicide Saturday morning. Nonetheless, *that* Friday night he kills three men at the bank, he steals approximately eight million dollars in cash, he transfers it to a trunk at that apartment on Thirty-third Street, and on Saturday morning he leaves his own apartment, goes to the one on Thirty-third, waits for the express company to pick up the trunk, and then—then returns to his apartment and kills himself. Nonsense."

"He didn't kill himself," Willie said.

"Then you agree . . . ?"

"No."

"But you just said . . ."

"One at a time," Willie said. "You complete your theory."

"Sure," I said. "Remember when we were talking with

Victor Mason at Luchow's? We decided that the only way to enjoy that kind of stolen money was to be able to shift your identity so that you wouldn't be a fugitive. Well, our boy shifted."

"Did he?" Marla said. "Or did—"

"Please listen," I said seriously. "Please listen attentively. This was a big crime, the biggest I've ever worked on. I haven't once stopped thinking about it—I've applied all my energies to it—and I believe my conclusions make sense and can help us."

"I'll try not to interrupt," Marla said.

"A crime like this, plotted by a brilliant mind, *must* fall into four phases. Phase One: preparation. Phase Two: perpetration. Phase Three: establishing a new identity so as not to be a fugitive. Phase Four: establishing a new residence and a new life where one can properly enjoy the new fortune under the new identity. Any disagreement on that?"

"None," said Willie.

"We know a good deal about Phase One, probably not all. We know all about Phase Two. We got into the case during Phase Three. And, with luck, we might break the thing wide open during Phase Four."

"Let's first finish Phase Three," Marla said.

"I say Kiss knew all about Richard Robinson Jackson, probably helped pick him out as a likely subject. Later on he retained you people so that proof would exist to give reason, however convoluted, for his suicide. She retained me that morning so that she would have some one to help her clean up after the suicide; after all, she would be alone then, without Kiss *or* Jackson. The date was set at your office for eleven o'clock because that would keep her away from her apartment at that time, and so she wouldn't be involved, and three witnesses—us—could swear to that. Also, she would be able to pick up those photos, so there wouldn't be any dirty loose ends around. She destroyed those."

"What about the ones he had?" Marla said.

"He got them way back in March, and so he had a good chance to study them, to have closeups of Jackson, to know just what Jackson looked like. He knew, after the alleged suicide, that she'd be able to get them back from the police—I did that for her—and destroy those also."

"And what do you think *did* happen that Saturday morning?" Marla said.

"I'd say Jackson came there by appointment at eleven o'clock, probably to discuss a divorce, man to man, that sort of crap, something she was able to talk him into. Kiss was charming, suave, cordial, then bopped him on the head, changed clothes with him, and dropped him out of the window, head first. He left the notes and the photos and during all of the excitement slipped out. The cremation took place the next day, and that was that. Kiss had his new identity. He took a crew-cut, dyed his hair white, and came out here to the house that had been *rented in February by Mrs. Richard Robinson Jackson."*

Marla said softly, "Baby, you're all right."

Willie said, "Maybe."

"Do you disagree?" I said.

"The guy I saw through the binoculars certainly *looked* like Jackson."

"Those two looked somewhat alike to begin with. That's the reason Jackson was chosen. You say he's fat now, put on maybe forty pounds. With the addition of forty pounds, sunburned, crew-cut, and with white hair, who in hell could tell one from the other? Where do you disagree with me, Willie?"

"Pappy, I agree all the way, except that I think the door should be left open to the possibility that Jackson is Jackson, not Kiss."

"What does that mean?" I said.

"That Jackson killed Kiss, rather than Kiss killed Jackson. I won't be adamant on it but I certainly don't think we should shut the door on that possibility."

"But why, how?"

"Suppose the lady fell in love—with Jackson. Everything works all the way as you expressed it, except she tips Jackson as to what's going to happen Saturday morning at Kiss's apartment. So Jackson bops Kiss and dumps him out the window, puts out the prepared notes and photos, and goes his merry way. Then the lady and the gentleman live happily ever after on the fruits of Kiss's years of planning and work."

"No good," I said.

"Why not?" I said.

"I know from the former husband that Valerie was crazy about Jonathan."

"That can change. Ladies are variable."

"Also she went for vital, vibrant, intellectual men."

"How do you know?"

"From the former husband—Felix Davenport. Also I know from the owner of the Pink Poodle that Jackson was a boozer who lived off women. And I know from an Oriental young lady whom he was chasing that he was a dolt, a boor, a guy with nothing, empty. He wasn't Valerie's type, not by a long shot."

Nothing ruffled Willie. Quietly he said, "All hearsay, my friend. The *opinions* of Davenport and the proprietor of the Pink Poodle and the Oriental lady. You're too long in the game to accept hearsay. The lady may have tired of Kiss, who knows? And Jackson was, or is, a beautiful man and he's one hell of an athlete in the hay, and that's not hearsay."

"All right," Marla said, "so he's either Kiss or Jackson and let's leave *both* doors open. What about Phase Four?"

"There I think we're in good shape," I said. "I believe the guy is Kiss and I'm going to refer to him as Kiss. I don't think Jonathan Kiss stole eight million dollars to live in a rented house in Pacific Palisades. The very fact that they're still there shows us that Phase Four is still in the opening stages, and that's a good break for us."

"Do that easy, please," Marla said.

"The house on Marble Drive is the base of operations. The guy got here on June 18, and the trunk with the dough was here, and I don't think he'd make a move out of the house until his lady arrived. The lady arrived on July 28, they got married in the house on August 7, then they got rid of the caretakers, and then, I'd say, gradually, they began to get the money out. I'd say they took turns, one remaining, one taking a valise full of dough. They wouldn't leave that house alone, unprotected, I'm sure. Since they're still here, I'd say that operation is continuing. Planting money in many banks, vaults, in and out of the country, takes time, and they have time. The first time we see them going out together, leaving the house alone—"

"We'll see them?" Marla said.

"You bet. The first time we see them going out together, leaving the house alone, we'll know that the money is out. After that, I believe, they'll begin arranging for a new residence, a permanent residence, probably out of the country, where Mr. and Mrs. Richard Robinson Jackson, slowly and discreetly, will become a part of the new community."

"So now it's a matter of surveillance," Marla said.

"The closest, but none of us is going to be involved. If the guy is Kiss, he knows both of you. She, certainly, knows all three of us. We're going to have to put on a staff, a big staff, that will keep rotating and shifting, but we'll need the best. We'll also take that house on Laurel Drive and that'll be *our* base of operations."

"How big a staff?" said Willie.

"Big," I said. "We'll have to have somebody on them all the time, and there'll probably be trips out of the country, and the faces can't show. Now right here in Los Angeles I know four really good people and I'm going to put them on salary right now."

"Oh, that Peter Chambers!" said Marla.

The way she said it, I was beginning to feel unfaithful to Carmen Valesquez.

TWENTY-THREE

FROM THEN we went into action, big action. I called Adam Wembley, Charles Wilson, Amy Hamilton, and Sol Bennett —top private operators—and I put them to work at once, for an indefinite period, as tails on the occupants of the house on Marble Drive. I informed them that they were the advance guard, that they would have reinforcements and that, at least temporarily, they would deliver their reports to the Beverly Hilton, Suite 403; Willie's suite.

I went out, that afternoon, with Willie and Marla, to see the house on Laurel Drive. It was massive, with wide rolling grounds, and a swimming pool, and a high iron fence around the entire property. The agent for the property was in Beverly Hills but it was owned by a corporation in San Francisco and that day I flew up to San Francisco to work a deal.

Within two days the deal was closed and I had rented a house, full payment made on Victor Mason's expense account. I remained an extra day rounding up a select group of private investigators, all of whom I knew. When I returned to Beverly Hills I brought with me Alice Hastings, Ralph

Nolan, Betty Shulman, Doris Mann, George Winters, and Harry Grant—top people all—and that day we took up residence in the old mansion on Laurel Drive.

The house was in perfect shape, clean, furnished, and in excellent repair. The grounds were in superb condition.

I called Chicago and we augmented the staff by Ben Wolf, Irv Burns, Ken Swanson, and Claire Keeley. I called New York and we further augmented the staff with Artie Stouffer and Elsie Axelrod. We got several extra sets of binoculars, and a small telescope which we installed so that it pointed directly at the house on Marble Drive. Through the telescope we were able to observe them as closely as though we were standing alongside them. They did a lot of pottering around in their garden and a lot of sunbathing on their patio. The house itself was a modest one of perhaps seven or eight rooms. Valerie was more beautiful than ever, and we saw a good deal of her in shorts and bandana in the sun. She appeared rested and radiant. Kiss was Kiss, or maybe he was Jackson. I had never seen either in person, only pictures, and the guy down there could have been either one, nut-brown, crew-cut, white-haired, and somewhat plump now, but tall enough to carry the extra weight with grace. On the fourth day of our residence at The Mansion—Marla had dubbed it The Mansion—I was at the telescope and Willie was beside me with the binoculars. Our couple were in bathing suits on the patio taking the sun on chaise lounges and drinking tall collinses. Suddenly I said, "Look, Willie, his right hand! Do you see?"

"Yes!"

The guy had the frosty Tom Collins to his lips and his hand was clear to us.

The first two fingers of his right hand were stumps to the second knuckle!

I got off the telescope and Willie laid away the binoculars.

I said, "Was Kiss mutilated like that?"

"No sir," Willie said. "The guy had all his marbles and all his fingers."

"What about Jackson? I seem to remember—"

"He had all his fingers."

"Is this a *third* guy?"

"It's Jackson or it's Kiss with a couple of joints off his first two fingers."

The next day, for the first time since we took up surveillance, the guy left the house. He took off at noon in the beat-up Chevvie that was their only car. They were playing it cool and conservative down there on Marble Drive: they were not inviting attention or burglars. They didn't dress richly, they didn't entertain, they had no neighbors, no friends, no company. He took off at noon and he came back at four and at four-ten Sol Bennett reported to us.

"On Friday he's going to Zurich, Switzerland," Sol told us. "A two-hop jump. First hop New York, next hop Switzerland."

"You'll go with him," I said, "on the same flight. Ralph, Harry, Doris—you'll take off for Zurich tomorrow. You'll let us know where you're staying. Sol, once you know where he's staying in Zurich, you'll turn him over to Ralph and Harry and Doris and you'll come home. You three will do the tail-job."

On Friday morning at ten o'clock our pigeon, carrying two bags, was carted off in a cab, but Sol Bennett had preceded him. On Friday at three o'clock I took off for New York and on Saturday afternoon I was in conference with Victor Mason in his office at the Empire State Building. I brought him up to date on all of the facts and all of the theories.

"Nice work," he said. "Beautiful."

"And expensive."

"Hell, that figures." Then he creased his eyes at me. "But do you actually need a staff of *sixteen?*"

"That Kiss and his wife—"

"Or Jackson and his wife."

"They've got to lead us to the dough—and we've got to follow. My people are experts, but it's got to be a shift-operation; that couple can't see the same faces. We've got to have it all shaped up, all ready, before we dare make a move. It's going to take months, many months, and there are going to be more expenses—bribes, angles, you know. But now, basically, it's a tail-operation. Whether it's Kiss or Jackson or Valerie working angles of her own; we've first got to learn where the loot is being stashed."

"You're so damned right."

"After that—"

"After that, we'll be able to get the court orders, quietly. Don't worry that pretty head of yours about those details, Peter, not yet. I think you've done wonderfully well so far."

"Thank you, Victor."

He wrote a check and handed it to me. I looked. It was for a mere fifty thousand dollars.

"First payment on expenses," he said. "Hell, kid, we're trying to recoup about eight million dollars, and you've got to invest if you're trying to recoup. We paid out a hundred thousand plus a promise of bonus to you and Trent and Winkle, didn't we? We'll go for another couple of hundred thousand without any strain. You can't get unless you put out, that's a basic axiom in any business."

"You're the boss, boss."

Strong teeth gleamed in a wide smile. "While your troop of sixteen is traipsing about the world, and you're enjoying with the svelte Marla at your mansion, just remember to do some bookkeeping. Send along the bills and the statements so that I can justify the expenses with my people back here."

"Will do."

"A prima donna like you, I expected a complaint about the paper work."

"No complaint."

"And I have no complaint either." The grey eyes narrowed. "Is it Kiss or is it Jackson?"

"I told you, I lean to Kiss, all the way."

"I go along with you, but Winkle doesn't, does he?"

"Winkle is a brain, aside from brawn, and Winkle is not as emotional as I am, or perhaps you are. Willie keeps all the doors open."

"Good for Winkle." He took out a cigar and lit it. "I'm impatient, of course, but we cannot make our moves yet, I know that."

"Not for months, in my opinion."

"Work it your own way, Peter, I have full confidence in you."

"Thank you, boss."

That night I had a date with Carmen Valesquez. We went to the ballet and then we had supper and listened to jazz at Lorenzo's. I told her, sketchily, of the work in which I was involved, which would keep me out of New York, to my regret, because I loved her.

"I believe you, sad man," she said.

"Believe me, what?" I said.

"That you are beginning to have the emotion, the true emotion."

We went back, late, to the Waldorf Towers, and we had nightcaps, and then she changed into what she called comfortable, which made me most uncomfortable—mauve silk lounging pajamas—and then she told me that she had a week's vacation, which was jake by me, nobody needed me on the West Coast for a week, and that night for the first time she kissed me, just before I left, standing up, but really kissed me, the hot body tight against me, the soft mouth pressing, but I played it like a swain—hell, I wanted to get married—and my lips went to her ear and I said, "I love you."

"I believe you," she said.

"Tomorrow night?" I breathed.

"Yes," she whispered and took me to her again and I could have knocked her over right then on the floor but I was a swain and so I broke it up and stumbled out of there, and the next day when I called her she told me that the chump from South America had come up for a ten-day stay, and it was required that she give him her attention, but that she could give me Thursday evening, and in a lover's pique I told her I had to go back to the Coast on Thursday, which was not true, but I lit out at once for the Pacific Palisades and The Mansion and Wee Willie and Marla Trent.

I stayed on my job for months. I wrote silly letters to Carmen, and I called her often, but I stayed on the job. Love is love, but ethics are ethics, and work is work. Victor Mason had contributed reliance aside from dough and I was in charge, so I stayed on tap.

The Mansion was home base and the reports kept filtering in. The reports began to fit together and a mosaic of knowledge was developed, but neither Marla nor Willie nor I was deployed upon the gathering of facts. We had a good deal of free time and we went out often: Marla and I alone, Marla and I and Willie, Marla and I and Willie and a girl he had found in one of the peel-joints. And one night in the Spanish section of Los Angeles, in a smoky little Mexican club, Marla ordered a Black Russian and the waiter had never heard of it (nor had I).

"Champagne, vodka, and creme de cocoa," Marla said. "The bartender'll know."

"It's a new one on me," I said when the waiter went away.

We were sitting thigh by thigh on a wall bench with a square little table in front of us.

"It's a drink that releases my inhibitions," she said.

"You releasing tonight?"

"A little."

"How much is little?"

"Enough to talk."

"Like intimately?"

"Like about two Black Russians' worth."

"What happens on two Black Russians."

"I loosen up."

"What happens on more?"

"I fly."

"Fly, baby."

"Not tonight, baby." And a Black Russian came and another came after that and she said, "You're winning your battle, baby."

"I'm not fighting anyone."

"You're winning anyway."

"What am I winning?"

"Me."

That brought us closer at the little table.

"Another Black Russian?" I suggested.

She giggled. Sweetly. It set my prickles to goosefleshing.

"No more," she said and then she said, "Peter, I've gotten to know you rather well in our enforced togetherness, and you're not at all the man that rumor has made you out."

"Disappointed?"

"Delighted. You're a doll. You've stayed in line; you haven't been snide, offensive, forward; you haven't made a pass. Dear man, if that's your system—"

"No system."

"It's working."

"No system. Just afraid."

"Seems when you don't try to live up to that rather unsavory reputation of yours, you're a fine, decent kind of guy, and most attractive. When this case is over, when we're no longer working together . . ."

It was a promise and I didn't push it. I was learning. Not pushing pushes you further than pushing. Aggressiveness had almost toppled me with Carmen; passivity had practically toppled the delectable Anna Esther Wing; and now the gorgeous Marla was shaking loose.

"When this case is over . . ."

It was taking a hell of a long time, but no longer than we had expected. As the months merged to more months our quarry bounced all over the world—one out, one at home— and our mosaic of information took firm outline. Our operatives were top performers and our pigeons had no notion that they were continuously follcwed, observed and inquired about, with money flowing freely in discreet bribes that pricked all privacy. Mr. and Mrs. Richard Robinson Jackson had joint bank accounts and joint vaults under their own names and under fictitious names and even under numbers in banks in Beverly Hills, Las Vegas, Denver, Zurich, Geneva, Antwerp, Surrey, London, Rome, Paris, Munich, Lisbon, Madrid, Mexico City, Rio de Janeiro, and Buenos Aires, and they maintained a small apartment in London which led us to believe that in the end they expected to settle in England.

The first change in pattern occurred on a warm morning in May: May 3 at eleven o'clock. We were in the Observation Room—the room with the telescope—Marla, Willie, and I. The Los Angeles newspapers being what they are, we subscribed to the New York papers (sometimes receiving them two days late but late news is better than no news). Willie, reading, was sprawled on a couch; I, reading, was sprawled on another couch; and Marla, splendidly seated, was idling at the telescope. I was reading the *Times* and I was enthralled in a squib on the drama page:

The highly-touted Leland Logan musical, MAID IN JAPAN, two years in the writing, is finally in rehearsal. As is usual with a Logan show—even after the writing —it shall be long in preparation. Scheduled for Broadway in October, it will have, before opening, three months of rehearsal in New York and then a two-month tour on the road. Although it abounds with name stars, the lead is an unknown, another Logan discovery assuredly headed for stardom. Daughter of slain missionaries in China, recommended by an elderly clergyman with an unerring eye for major talent, auditioned by Logan in the quiet convent-school which she attended in Connecticut, Anna Esther Wing is the most unusual of ingenues: unspoiled, innocent, a hot-

*house flower protectively reared. Of poignant fragile
beauty and enormous talent, Miss Anna Esther Wing . . .*

I threw the paper into the air.
"Hooray!" I said.
Dryly Marla said, "Are you psychic or something?"
"When you strive you should succeed," I said. "I'm an
advocate of Zen and Horatio Alger."
"The hell with Alger," Marla said. "Look!"
Marla was standing, taut, at the telescope. Marla, taut, was
enough to have anybody leap off a couch. Marla taut at the
telescope was doubly propulsive. I leaped off my couch faster
than a patient suddenly disabused by his analyst. Willie leaped
even faster, as though goosed by an analyst epicenely berserk.
We grabbed at binoculars and ranged up against Marla.
Mr. and Mrs. Richard Robinson Jackson were packing
bags into the trunk of their ancient Chevvie.
And then Mr. and Mrs. Richard Robinson Jackson climbed
into the ancient Chevvie and drove off.
"Together at last," said Marla.
"Which means the dough is out," said Willie.
"Wembley's here, I hope," I said.
"Of course he's here," Willie said. "And he'll be *here* in
a minute."
"The initial stage is over," said Marla.
We had prepared for a long time. Four teams were ready,
and since the Jacksons were using their car, four cars, linked
by short-wave, would take turns following. None of the
teams would contain Adam Wembley because Adam Wemb-
ley had been born and reared in Los Angeles and Adam
Wembley was in contact with certain trusted experts in Los
Angeles—a glazier and a locksmith.
Within minutes Adam Wembley was in the Observation
Room.
"Should I bring in my people?" Wembley said.
"Have them ready," I said, "and stay with them. I'll call
you."
Wembley went away and we sat around impatiently, growing more peevish by the minute. Finally Marla burst out,
"Will somebody tell me why in hell we've waited all these
months? Maybe all the money wasn't in that house, but a
hell of a lot of it *was* there. I've had all sorts of hints at ex-
planations, and I've pretended to be very clever, but I wish

somebody would explain it to me once and for all. Jackson may be Kiss or the other way around, but Valerie is Valerie and Valerie was the wife of Kiss and Kiss had killed three people and had stolen millions of dollars. Why didn't we get court orders and move in legally and impound that money? Hell, how could they explain millions, *literally millions of dollars in cash,* lying around in that little house on Marble Drive?"

"Because legally means a lawsuit," Willie said, "and for a lawsuit there must be a plaintiff and the bank would have to be the plaintiff and the bank—as you remember from Simon Hellman's admirable lecture, simply cannot publicly admit a robbery of more than eight million dollars from its vaults. Remember, please, this robbery has not even been reported to the police. Rather than open it up to public scandal the bank, and the insurance companies, are willing to swallow the loss. It's a tough swallow, it's choking them, as witness our being retained."

"But what, actually, can we do? What—"

"We flounder about," I said, "but we flounder with a purpose."

"Purpose? But—"

"We stay with it, we learn whatever we can, we play the soft underbelly, the human being. If we find a breach, a hole, we shove through."

"Shove through—what?"

"We're working impromptu," Willie said. "We don't know. It could develop, if propitious, into a ransom deal."

"Ransom!"

"Either the tropical climate is getting to you, Marla, or you're pretending this girlish ingenuousness for the benefit of Peter."

"Ransom without kidnapping?"

"Come off it," he said sharply.

He was irritable. We were all irritable.

"There've been jewel robberies with that specific purpose," I said. "You know that. And paintings stolen, masterpieces."

"Of course she knows." Willie frowned at her. "She knows damn well that insurance companies have paid twenty percent, more, as ransom for hot ice, no questions asked. The same for valuable paintings. The same for—"

"Cash? I don't know anything of the sort. I've never heard of cash being paid to ransom cash. Have you?"

"There are special cases."

"Do you consider this such a case?"

"Who in hell knows *what* kind of case this is?"

"Okay now, easy; easy does it," I said. "Simmer down, both of you. Lay off. This case we play by ear, and it may turn out to be a ransom deal—cash for cash. Possible. The insurance companies are stuck for eight million six hundred thousand dollars. They'd like to keep a closed book on it, simple and neat. I bet they'd be happy to settle for a net return of a clean six million. Personally I don't know whether Kiss would go for it."

Pointedly Willie said, "Would Jackson?"

"So we have no set course," Marla said.

"By ear," I said, "looking for holes, for breaks, for psychological angles."

The phone rang.

It was a member of our cavalcade of cars. The cavalcade was no longer a cavalcade. "I'm calling from the airport," Amy Hamilton informed me. "They've taken off for Las Vegas. Charlie Wilson managed a seat on the same plane. The rest of us are following. Okay?"

"Yes," I said. "Keep in close touch."

"Will do," she said and hung up.

I called Adam Wembley.

"Bring in your people," I said.

TWENTY-FOUR

THE HOUSE on Marble Drive had a faded red roof and dull grey shingles. It was narrow, which made its two stories look tall. It had a solid oak front door and a solid oak back door, but we did not use either.

We used a back window.

The glazier expertly cut out the pane and Willie and I and the locksmith (with all his equipment) stepped through. At once the glazier went to work replacing the pane.

The purpose of the locksmith was to make us a key to the front door so that we would not have to cut out window panes every time we wanted to visit. As it turned out, the locksmith had far more work than we had anticipated.

The house had a basement, a main floor, and a second floor. The basement contained a boiler-room, a laundry, and a utility-room. The main floor had a kitchen, a dining room, a living room, and a recreation room with all the appointments including bar and television. The top floor, we assumed, held the bedrooms. We assumed, because each of the three doors was adorned with a bright new powerful lock. The locksmith went to work with wax to make impressions for keys, while Willie and I did inspection downstairs. We found nothing of any vital interest except three loaded pistols artfully deployed; one in the china-cabinet in the living room, one in the whiskey compartment of the bar in the recreation room, and one in the refrigerator in the kitchen.

When the keys were ready for the bedrooms—we needed more keys.

Two rooms were the master bedroom, with separate outer doors but with an inner door, open, connecting the two rooms. The third room was furnished as a guest room.

The guest room had been transformed to an office, with a desk, a typewriter, correspondence (most of which had to do with negotiations for the purchase of a house in Surrey, England), ledgers with figures that had no meaning to us (except for the fact that the Jacksons—or Kisses—were keeping records), and a loaded gun in the upper right hand drawer of the desk. The door of the guest room and the doors of the master bedroom were equipped with inner steel slide-bolts four inches wide. Once bolted, the doors could not be opened from the outside. Each of the bedrooms had a television; the larger room had two closets; the smaller room one closet—we *assumed* they were closets because they too had doors that were locked with bright new locks, and again our locksmith went to work. When he opened those doors, he made keys for the front door and the rear door, and then he was finished, and the glazier was finished, and Adam Wembley took them, and himself, away, and then Willie and I were alone in the house on Marble Drive.

"Kiss?" I said to Willie.

Willie laughed out loud. "Some other time," he said.

"Stop with the jokes."

He was still laughing. "Man, you don't realize how funny that sounded."

"Looks like Kiss, doesn't it? All this obsession with locks?"

"Could also be a very careful Jackson, aided and abetted by a very careful and a very well trained Valerie."

Upstairs, the three closets of the two rooms of the bedroom revealed three massive steel safes, one in each closet. We did not touch them. The nighttable in each room contained two loaded revolvers, and one drawer of a chest of drawers was filled with boxes of cartridges.

"Christ," Willie said. "Like an arsenal. Three loaded guns downstairs—five of them up here. And enough ammunition for a small war."

In the guest room we looked over the ledgers more carefully. They were obviously in code but the figures were large figures, in the millions. Then we found a professional card, a Dr. Paul Scofield, with an address on West Wilshire near the ocean. Then we gave our attention to the correspondence. We learned that the Jacksons had purchased a house in Cobham, Surrey, but the actual details of the transaction were meager. We jotted down the name and address of the British broker, and then we closed up shop. We locked every door behind us including the front door by which we left.

At The Mansion a palpitating Marla cross-questioned us with all the fervor of an ambitious prosecuting attorney, and after we had been drained of all we had learned, Willie summed up masterfully:

"That type of house and the conservative manner in which they lived, they wouldn't be the target of professional burglars. Thus, basically, their precautions were against the possibility of the intrusion of an amateur, a tramp, or some delinquent juveniles, or some roving bungler; that sort of thing. Most unlikely, most improbable, but enough of a possibility, however remote, to be guarded against."

"And they sure guarded against it," Marla said.

"Since there was always some one at home during the day, nothing could happen then. In the event that somebody, somehow, would try to force his way in, there were enough loaded pistols around to discourage, promptly and effectively, any such attempt at forcible entry. At night, the bedrooms were locked and bolted from the inside. They could watch television, safe within an almost impregnable bastion."

"And those massive safes?" Marla said. "Would you call them a precaution against the intrusion of an amateur?"

"Fire," Willie said. "They were fire insurance. That was probably the real fear—fire. Fire can always happen, and what in hell can you do when millions of dollars are burning up? Those safes are the finest of their kind, no question about that, layer upon layer of steel and insulation—and that, without doubt, was their purpose."

"No more fear," I said. "That money's out of there now."

"What's our next move?" Marla said.

I made that move at once. I called in Betty Shulman and Harry Grant and told them they were going to England. I gave them the address of the British broker, and I told them I wanted to know everything about that house in Surrey. Then I showered and changed clothes and took one of the cars—we had eight on hire—and drove into Hollywood.

I have many friends among the movie colony, and I began an inquiry into Dr. Paul Scofield. I learned that he was a highly respected surgeon, that he had his own hospital on Wilshire, and that he was an intimate friend of Jerry Wolheim who was an intimate friend of mine. Jerry was a producer at MGM and I drove out to Culver City and talked with Jerry and briefed him on some of my problems. Jerry called Dr. Scofield, briefed *him* on some of my problems, recommended me in saintly terms, and arranged an appointment at Scofield's clinic for eight o'clock that evening, and at eight o'clock that evening a comely nurse brushed off other business and whisked me into his presence.

He was chubby, bespectacled, benign. He had wavy iron-grey hair and a wavy iron-grey Van Dyke. He smoked a curved pipe and he had a gracious, patient manner. After the amenities, I took up where Jerry had left off. I said, "Doctor, I'm not here for either of us to breach any ethics."

"Naturally," he said.

"Mr. Wolheim has told you the type of work I'm in."

"Yes," he said.

"Now my first question is whether or not you've had a patient named Richard Robinson Jackson. If so, then we can go on. If not, then I'm barking up the wrong tree."

He was seated behind a large desk, and I was seated opposite him. He smiled around his pipe, leaned forward, pulled a drawer of a card-index file on the desk, riffled through, stopped, leaned back in his chair.

"Yes," he said. "I've had a patient by that name."

"Do you remember him?"

"Distinctly."

"Good. Now, doctor, my world and your world are different and what I'm going to say may startle you." Jerry Wolheim had opened a wedge for me but I had to hack through. Surgeons can be stuffy and ethics can be stony. I had to blast, right off, with all my fire-power. I did it dramatic but I did it contained, with my voice pitched low and casual. "Richard Robinson Jackson," I said, "is a murderer."

That sat him up straight. "Beg pardon?" he said.

"A murderer. Not a crime-of-passion murderer, but a cold-blooded, criminal murderer. Not the murderer of a single individual, but a multiple murderer, and also a thief. In the planning and commission of a robbery involving millions of dollars, Richard Robinson Jackson murdered four men. I am one of the people who have been retained to accumulate evidence while he is under surveillance but before he is taken into custody."

He had small blue eyes but they grew large behind his spectacles.

"Just what do you want of me, Mr. Chambers?"

"Your impression of him, and what his business with you was. And I assure you, doctor, that I appreciate whatever confidence you repose in me and such confidence—"

"Yes, yes, of course. Jerry has spoken most highly of you." He laid the pipe on the desk and clasped his hands. "A murderer," he said softly. "Unbelievable."

"Why? Murderers are people. They don't have special stigmata."

"But he seemed to be such a pleasant man."

"Please go on, doctor. Your general impression."

"Quite a handsome man, tall—"

"We know all about his appearance, sir." I switched myself to plural, to the pompous, more impressive, semi-official, meaningless but pragmatic "we." "We are interested in your general impressions of the nature and character of the man," I said with all the grave pomposity I could muster. "We are fully acquainted with his appearance." And then a hunch hit, and I played it. In my business you never let a hunch go to waste. "Including," I added, "the mutilated first and second fingers of his right hand."

"Yes, yes." He was smoking the pipe again. "I'd say he was a pleasant man; he frequently smelled of drink but one cannot fault him for that—many people when visiting a doctor must fortify themselves, spur up lagging courage. He had a pleasant personality but not, especially, a stimulating one.

He did not speak much and when he did, well, I wouldn't say he was a . . . a cultured man."

My heart sank. Jonathan Kiss was Phi Beta Kappa, *summa cum laude,* a Master of Arts out of Harvard. Richard Robinson Jackson was a lush, a lout, a floater, a drifter. I pulled up a sigh and let it come out as, "What was his business with you, doctor?"

He laid away the pipe and bounced the balls of his fingers against the desktop. "Because of the circumstances which you have recited to me, and because of what Jerry has told me about you personally, I'm going to cooperate with you, Mr. Chambers. But please remember I will never testify to any of this in court, I have no right to; such material is privileged between patient and physician, and the law protects the patient . . ."

"Yes, of course, doctor, we appreciate that."

His fingers were manipulating the card-index again and his eyes flicked for data. "Mr. Jackson came here to my clinic on the nineteenth of June. He had suffered injury to his right hand. The first and second fingers had been severed to the second joint as a result of an accident with a power lawn-mower. An excellent tourniquet had been applied, and he had been driven here by his caretaker, a Mr. Casey. It was a clean severance without complications and the operative procedure was simple. He returned at intervals for dressings and he was discharged in six weeks. In one way though it was rather remarkable."

I had been dawdling at the back of my chair during the dull drone of medical history but now I pushed up front again. "Remarkable?"

"Perhaps remarkable is too strong a word."

"You said rather remarkable. Rather softens it."

He stood up. He was dismissing me. He had delivered his communication. He had had enough of me. So had I of him. But he had a hook in me.

"What was rather remarkable, doctor?"

So now the doctor became the professor, lecturing. They all do sooner or later. There is a subtle change in personality, preceded by a cough. He coughed. "Trauma," he said, "always causes a form of desensitization. Do you know what trauma is, young man?"

"Physical trauma," I said to teacher. "A violently produced wound."

"Very good. Capital. Excellent. Couldn't do better myself."

"Thank you."

"Trauma anesthetizes—nature's way of temporarily numbing the pain of a sudden wound. For instance, when you're severely punched. The first reaction at that point is numbness. The stronger the blow, the longer the period of numbness, you know?"

"I know."

Slowly and politely but firmly and inexorably he was shepherding me to the door. "The anesthetic reaction to trauma varies, of course, with each individual, but this was about the most extreme case of my career. Not only were the fingers anesthetized for quite a period of time, but the entire hand was numb." And at the door, I was stuck with his point of vantage. Heartily he said, "Well, goodbye, Mr. Chambers, I do hope I've been of some assistance."

I was being put out but I was not unwilling. He had offered all that ethics could permit him to offer. It might have been a big deal to him but to me it was nothing. So the guy—Kiss or Jackson—had got too frisky with one of our major cripplers, a power lawnmower, and he had sliced off a couple of fingers and the trauma had been real desensitizing. But the doctor had been courtly and courteous and in my racket we appreciate courtliness and courtesy, they are all too infrequent phenomena.

"Goodbye, doctor, and thank you," I said. "You've been very helpful."

Maybe he had been. If so, I didn't know it. Yet.

TWENTY-FIVE

THE REPORTS pattered in from Vegas and London, and they dovetailed neatly.

In Vegas the Jacksons were finally letting loose. Operating out of a top suite in a top hotel, they lounged, swam, dined, supped, shopped, clubbed, gambled and gamboled, indulging in a frolic of relaxation, and why not? A stupendous robbery had been successfully brought off and almost a year had passed and there was not the faintest tremor of repercussion. It was time to celebrate and they were now free to celebrate and they were going to celebrate, it appeared, for a month because they were booked at their hotel until the first of June.

From England we learned that, functioning discreetly through a staid firm of discreet London agents, they had purchased the house in Cobham, Surrey, for two hundred thousand American bucks which is a hell of a lot of British pounds.

The house had fourteen rooms, was completely furnished, had once belonged to an English duke, was set in the midst of thirty acres of rolling greens, had its own private cemetery, and the entire property was ringed within a twelve-foot-high spike-topped iron fence. The Jacksons were due at their home in England on June 15.

Willie and I had planned to make our first real overt move in Las Vegas but we were not in any hurry now because the Jackson's itinerary was clearly shaped for us: they would stay in Vegas until the first of June, they would return to the house on Marble Drive for a couple of weeks of mop-up, and on June 15 they would take up permanent residence at their estate in Surrey.

We did one more inspection of the house on Marble Drive, this time with Marla, but we found no more than we had found before except an old hypodermic in a bottom drawer of a dresser in one of the bedrooms.

"Don't tell me we can add dope to their list of iniquities," said Marla.

"Of course not," Willie said. "We've been watching them closely enough to know that nothing like that has been passed to them in all these months. This is probably a leftover from the prior occupants."

When we got back to The Mansion there was word from Vegas: Valerie was bedded down with a virus and Jackson was sporting around alone. At once Willie and I took off for Las Vegas leaving a protesting Marla to watch the store; and for two nights running, carefully but closely, we watched our man in action.

He wore excellent clothes and he carried himself beautifully. He spun around in a hired Caddy and he hit all the live spots. Despite the added weight he was a most attractive man and the ladies gave him as much attention as we did. Although I worked on Willie for an opinion as to whether he was Kiss or Jackson, Willie had no opinion; a year ago he had seen them separately and close up, but that had been a year ago. "If you weren't bugging me," Willie said, "it would be Jackson without question."

"But I am bugging you," I said. "For instance, the ladies flirt but the guy doesn't flirt in return. Jackson was a ladies' man, he'd figure to flirt. Not Kiss. Kiss was in love."

"But Jackson is married now and he's loaded down with loot. He may not want to risk any playing around. And this guy does drink like a fish. Remember that Jackson was a lush."

"But Kiss on a toot would be drinking too."

That left us nowhere, and the fact that the guy was gambling for high stakes in all the casinos left us in the same place, but on the third night steps were taken for more positive recognition. On the third night at two o'clock when he left a casino and started off in the Caddy a figure unwound in the rear and placed the muzzle of a gun at the nape of his neck. I was the figure and the gun was mine.

"Keep driving," I said. "Out toward the desert."

"What goes?" he said.

"Simple. A stickup. Keep driving."

"Okay," he said. "Just watch yourself with the goddam gun. I'm not going to fight you."

"Nice boy," I said disconsolately. I was not happy. The nice boy had a fine baritone but the slurred diction was far from Harvard. "Turn here," I said at the first break in the highway. "And drive slowly." Willie was in the car behind us, and I didn't want him losing us. It was a dark night and off the highway it was darker. "Put on your brights," I said. He did and we drove slowly until we hit another break, a dirt road to the right. "Turn right," I said. We drove along that bumpy road for about a mile and then I said, "Pull over to the shoulder and stop." He did that. "Now turn off your lights and get out."

He got out. I got out and faced him. It was dark and I was wearing my hat pulled low. Kiss or Jackson, he couldn't know me even if it weren't dark and I weren't wearing the hat down low: he had never seen me before.

"Keep your hands at your sides," I said, waving the gun.

Willie pulled up, put out his lights, got out, ranged up behind him, and leveled a judo-swipe at the back of his neck, not too hard. Hard, Willie could kill a man. Not too hard, our guy toppled like a chopped tree.

Willie brought out a flashlight and we went to work on

him. We pulled down his pants and pulled up his shirt and undershirt. The bastard had a lovely appendectomy scar. Willie grunted. I sighed. Willie went back to the car. I plucked some of the white hair from the guy's head and carefully placed them in an envelope. Willie came back with a couple of colorless plastic plates. Carefully, we took the prints of all his fingertips except the first two fingers of his right hand which had no fingertips. Willie took the plastic plates back to the car and waited there. I re-dressed the guy, took out his wallet, took out his money, and transferred that to my pocket. Then I replaced his wallet, sat him back in his car, joined Willie, and we started on the first leg of our journey back to The Mansion. We weren't worried about the guy worrying about us. He wouldn't make any complaint and he certainly wouldn't link us to any of his own activities. A stickup is a stickup, happens all the time. The guy would consider himself lucky that he had suffered no more than a pain in the neck. He could afford the loss of the money. His loss was exactly seven thousand three hundred and forty-two dollars, and his loss was Victor Mason's gain supplementing the expense account.

In the morning Adam Wembley went to work, and Willie and I went along with him. The white hairs in the envelope were brought to a research laboratory and we were told we would have a report in an hour. Then Adam took us to an expert who made photographs of the clear prints off the plastic plates, and then we went back to the laboratory and got the report. The white hairs were dyed. *They were dyed white.* Some were black, some were iron grey, but they had all been dyed white.

"Well?" I said to Willie in small triumph.

Dryly he said, "Don't look so pussycat. It could be Kiss who dyed his hair white to make him look like Jackson. But it could also be Jackson who dyed his hair white just like another might dye his hair blond or black or whatever. Certainly that white hair made him different, attractive."

"Maybe," I said, "but we've got his prints now. Kiss was bonded and Kiss was fingerprinted—"

"Now *that* would be decisive," said Willie.

"You bet," I said and they drove me to the airport and we pulled rank and paid out extra dough for a flight and the next afternoon at twelve-thirty I had lunch with Victor Mason and we lined up all the sights.

"Peter," Victor said, "I've a hunch it's coming to a head. You handle it any way you like but whenever you're ready, so am I. My decks are clear and I'm waiting for word from you. The minute you call me, I'll join you on the coast. But please remember, the last lap will be handled by us— you and me—alone."

"You bet," I said. "Who's the bonding company?"

"Client of yours. Wheeler Surety."

"Sloan Wheeler's outfit?"

"That's the outfit."

"Let me go to work, Vic."

"Go to work, pal. But please remember that I'm ready whenever you think it's time for the final move, and that's got to be before June 15, before they check out for England. Call me at any time, at any hour, day or night, whenever you think it's right."

"You bet," I said and left what was left of my lunch. "I'm on my way to Wheeler Surety and although Sloan is a client I think, while I'm en route, you'd better call so that I'll have carte blanche."

"You bet," he said and when I got to Fulton Street where were the offices of Wheeler Surety I got the royal treatment which meant that Vic had consummated the call.

"The Jonathan Kiss file," I said to Sloan Wheeler and produced the photograph of the fingerprints. "I need these prints matched up by one of your experts as a favor to Victor Mason."

"Of course, my lad," said Sloan Wheeler who knew on what side his bread was buttered and he pushed buttons and gave orders and hirelings panted as comparisons were made and then I died another little death as the expert said, "Sorry, but you have *not* brought us Jonathan Kiss' prints."

"Are you kidding?" I said.

The expert, a tiny man, grey and wizened, drew himself up to his full five feet. "My dear man, I've been at this work for more than thirty years, and I do not make mistakes. These are not Jonathan Kiss' fingerprints, and I am not kidding."

"Who handled this matter?"

Sloan worked the file, then smiled. "The best. Duffy Gaylord. And you know he's the best. You were one of his references."

Duffy was the best. I knew more about Duffy than his boss knew about Duffy. Duffy was Yale, typical Yale, more Yale than O'Hara could dream up Yale. Duffy was all soul and all integrity but Duffy had been irrevocably bounced out of his family because Duffy was a homosexual and Duffy was stubbornly homosexual and Duffy's family would not brook a stubborn homosexual, and so Duffy struggled out on his own. Duffy was no queen, no platinum-dyed freak, no screaming faggot. Duffy lived quietly with Reggie Blythe who was a chef at El Morocco. Duffy was young and beautiful and gay and charming, but circumspect and secretive and fearful of scandal. Duffy was the best, with soul and honor, and he bore his cross with quiet dignity. Duffy did not belong with a stuffy bonding company because Duffy had artistic talent but a buck is a buck and we must all eat, including Duffy.

"May I speak with him, please?" I said.

Sloan said, "He's no longer with us."

"Since when?"

Sloan worked the file again, then worked another file. "He left us four months after he had completed this Jonathan Kiss thing."   `

"Fired?"

"Oh no, he resigned."

"Took another job somewhere?"

"I have no idea."

"Well, thanks," I said and gathered up my photographs and went out into the spring sunshine and took a cab to Sheridan Square in Greenwich Village where Duffy lived with Reggie Blythe but neither of them lived there any more, and had not lived there for six years, and there was no forwarding address. I called El Morocco and learned that Blythe had quit six years ago.

That left me steaming up a cold trail and so I went to Forty-second Street and Lexington Avenue, to the office of Mike Rommel, a good private detective, and I gave him all the dope I had on Duffy and told him to find him.

"What do you want with him?" Mike said.

"Just want to know where to get in touch with him."

"That shouldn't be too tough."

I'm in the business and I knew what that meant. If the fee was good, the action would be fast. If the fee was bad, it would be routine skip-tracing in the normal order of business. I wrote a check to Mike for five hundred bucks and I said, "I expect to be in town for twenty-four hours. If you locate him within that time, let me know at my office or at my home. If it takes longer, this is where I'll be." I wrote out the address and the phone number of The Mansion.

Then I kissed Mike off and went to a west side station house and bailed out Detective-sergeant Leonard Wagner and took him to lunch, first lunch of the day for him, second for me. He was hungry and he was a big man and he ate like a horse and then he grinned and said, "To what do I owe the pleasure?"

I gave him the photograph of the fingerprints. "I want a favor," I said. "A full check on these prints."

"What else?"

"Nothing else."

"Look, Pete, I owe you a few favors, so I'll do this for you."

"I need fast action."

"I'll put it on the wires for you, urgent, but if you want a full check, it'll take some time."

"How much time?"

"I get through tonight at midnight."

"So?"

"By then I should have a report for you."

"Would you drop it off at my apartment?"

"Be happy to."

I paid the check and outside we shook hands.

"See you at midnight," he said.

"Thanks," I said, and he went off, and I took a cab to my office, and caught up on old mail, and then I went home and called Harkness and made a date for dinner with Carmen for eight o'clock, and then I took a nap, and at eight o'clock I picked her up and we went to Camilio's and she ate while I nibbled but I drank and she realized that I wasn't with it, that my mind was troubled, and after dinner she suggested that we go back to her place.

There we dimmed the lights and put on the television. She made drinks for us, and then went away to change. I took off my jacket, loosened my tie and opened my collar, and sat with my ankles crossed and watched the gunplay on the television, and then she came back in tight gold pants and a loose gold jacket, and I turned off the television, and I made a pass, and then another pass, and although she made with the elbows, she didn't fight me, and then we were necking, panting like two kids parked on the back seat of

Papa's car, and then I began to lose control, so I climbed out of it, because I was a swain.

We sat opposite one another, separate, heaving but talking, and I would have popped the question right then, right there, that night, but I was involved in a big one out on the West Coast, and one that could turn out to be dangerous, and you do not ask a gal to marry you when you might be dead before you're engaged. It would not be long now; I agreed with Victor Mason that it was coming to a head; if it turned out well and I got lucky there would be a big bonus in addition to my big fee, and so when I returned, if I returned, I would at least be in excellent financial shape to pop the question.

At eleven-thirty I put on my jacket and I pulled her to her feet and held her close and kissed her and felt her stomach squirming against mine and then still holding her, our bodies jumping, I said at her ear, "I'm out of my mind for you."

"Then why you go away?" she whispered.

"I've got to see a man about fingerprints."

That cut it. She broke away, laughing, the white teeth flashing, the smooth dark face darker, red-dark with heat, the huge black eyes moist and shining. "Ah, sad man, you are so funny man too. You will go back to the Hollywood?"

"Yes, I'm afraid so. But I expect to be back soon, quite soon, and then I'm not going away again, and I'm going to spend all my time with you."

"Oh? So?"

"And we're going to talk, honey. There's a hell of a lot of talking that I'm holding back."

"And when you return we will not hold back?"

"I'm hoping," I said.

And then she came to me, and kissed my forehead, and I cut out of there, and I walked in the spring night cooling out, and then I went home, and at ten minutes after midnight my bell rang and Lenny Wagner said, "I'm bone-tired, pal. I'm going home." He handed me a ten-by-twelve brown envelope. "Your report's in there. The subject was arrested once. Good night. Merry Christmas."

I had one drink first, a large shot, neat, before I sat down with the envelope. I opened it slowly and drew out the photo of the prints attached to which by clip was a short typewritten report. The subject had been arrested once, fifteen months ago. The subject had been booked for assault and battery. The case had appeared in Magistrate's Court but had been dismissed because the complainant had refused to press the charge. The subject's address had been 222 East Sixty-second Street. The subject's name was Richard Robinson Jackson.

That night I flew back to the West Coast.

TWENTY-SIX

I ARRIVED in a funk and I stayed in a funk as the days sped into weeks. If the guy had been Kiss we might have been able to deal with him: intelligence can serve two ways. But with Jackson there would be the usual hysteria, and that joint was an arsenal, and a shooting spree could leave all our parties dead, and like that how can you recover eight million dollars or any part of it? My hope was with Valerie: but would she be able to control the white-haired goofball? It was not good and it did not get any better. I had no word from Mike Rommel and when I called him on May 18, he said, "Duffy's not in New York, that I can guarantee."

"I don't want to know where he's not. I want to know where he is."

"I'm working another angle, and that may help."

"What angle?"

"Blythe."

"Blythe?"

"Blythe and Gaylord are like husband and wife. From Social Security and from a chef's helper at El Morocco we got a lead on Blythe. He's out in your neck of the woods, the West Coast. I'm pressing on that and I ought to turn up a break real soon.

I remained dour and dreary in my own private hole. Willie tried to cheer me but Willie wasn't built for it. Marla was, and Marla tried, but I remained cheerless.

On June first our pigeons came home to roost. Their roosting was resting, they had no real packing to do. They had clothes in their apartment in London and we learned that the closets in the house in Surrey were also stuffed with purchases. Afternoons, they took the sun on their patio, drinking to prevent dehydration; on occasion, they did gardening; on occasion, they drove out to the beach and swam in the sea. Evenings, now that they were free, they ate in the best restaurants; and nights, they enjoyed the talent in the best night clubs. And then on the morning of June 5, Mike Rommel called me.

"In the bag," he said.

"Where's the bag?" I said.

"Right there in your bailiwick."

"What bag?"

"They own a spot, a real big successful spot."

"Who owns?"

"Reggie Blythe and Duffy Gaylord. They're partners. Big shots now, very successful."

"What spot?"

"Tres Gay. It's a night spot on the Strip."

"You sure?"

"Sure I'm sure."

"Thanks, Mike."

"Don't mention it, Pappy."

Whatever it was, at least it was something. I put out a few preliminary calls and gathered in some information about the Tres Gay. Where most of the joints jumped with the jazz, the Tres Gay played it strictly romantic, and they stayed with it, and because they were different, they pulled in the customers. The food, I was told, was superb, but the music was square, but square becomes round, when the customers are hippies. Twelve fiddles wandered from table to table, and when the fiddles rested, four harps went to work, and when the harps rested, four zithers picked it up, and when the zithers were finished, the fiddles were back. String music, no drums, no percussions, no brass, no jazz: and because it was different, and because they stayed with it, and because they persisted, they had become established: the customers moved from the jazz to the strings, the hippies plunked down the stamp of approval, and the reputation was made—from there on it depends entirely upon the management. If management is serious, if it does not start cutting corners for quick profits, if it does not sell out for capital gains, then a spot becomes a joint, a joint becomes a place, and a place becomes a fixture, an institution—like Romanoff's, the Brown Derby, the Stork, the Stage, Voison, Colony, Twenty-One, Toots Shor's, Henri Soule's.

Tres Gay was a fixture.

"Marla," I said, "how would you like to go romantic to-night?"

"With whom?"

"With me."

"With you, anything; if it will rouse you out of your despondency."

"Anything?" queried Willie.

"Almost anything."

"I'm not asking for a flip of the lid, or id," I said. "I'm inviting you for an evening at the Tres Gay."

"A *caveat*, oh General," proclaimed Willie. "Fiddles affect Marla like raw meat affects a tiger."

"Tigress," corrected Marla.

"How does she do with zithers?"

"Slithers," said Willie.

"I'll risk it," I said.

"I'll go," said Marla, "provided we dress."

"We dress," I said.

"We go," she said.

We went.

We arrived, togged to the teeth, at nine-thirty. Marla wore a silver sheath that hugged her astonishing curves like horsehide hugs a baseball, and I was in there pitching in a white dinner jacket; nonetheless the man stopped us in the outer vestibule.

"Reservations?" he said.

"No," I said.

"Sorry, but we're full up. You may wait in the lounge if you wish."

"We wish."

The lounge was a large barroom with a soft decor of scarlet and black, crowded with well-dressed people. I said to our man, "I'd like to talk to Duffy, please."

"Yes sir," he said. "Would you like to order first?"

"First I'd like to talk to Duffy. Is he here?"

"He is always here, sir. He's the host in the restaurant proper. Who shall I say?"

"Peter Chambers."

"At once, sir."

He went away and I said to Marla, "That's the way a good joint should be run. No stall, nobody too big for the britches, no snobbery, and a courteous captain at the door."

Marla tugged at the little fur jacket she was wearing. "All dressed up and nowhere to spread out. I feel like a tablecloth without a table."

That caught me in the funnybone and I was roaring laughter when the gold-leather swinging doors at the far end of the lounge were pushed open by Duffy Gaylord and he pranced toward us in the tightest tuxedo ever devised by a Continental tailor but on Duffy it looked good. He saw us, waved, and hurried. He was very tall and very slim with bright blue eyes and bright blond wavy hair and he had developed a very stylish swish.

"Peter, dear Peter, sweetheart," he said and grabbed me and hugged me and kissed my cheekbone. "Oh, it's so damned darned marvelous to see you."

The leopard had changed his spots. The once shy Duffy was now the palpably gay Gaylord: he was a beautiful elf out of a special fairyland and he didn't give a hoot in Hades who knew it: he flaunted it, all the way from the highly-polished tinted fingernails to the enormous diamond cuff-links to the frilly-lace dress-shirt to the star sapphire on the index finger.

"And who is the lovely lady?" he asked.

"Marla Trent," I said. .

"My pleasure, Miss Trent. Please, won't you come in?"

"The man said there was no table," Marla said.

"There's always a table for Peter, dear Peter of my salad days. You two will join me at my very own table."

Marla looked at me queerly, and I shrugged helplessly, and we followed the lithe and dancing Duffy through the golden doors into the most beautiful room of any restaurant I had ever seen.

It was dusk, it was permanent dusk: twilight. The lighting was a cool cunning blend that made it appear as though the day had just ended, that the sun had just set. The high ceiling was a pale blue, with the twinkle here and there of a star. The walls were pink, festooned with fresh flowers, and the delicate odor of roses and gardens and meadows merged with the more aromatic odors of herbs and spices and food. It was a huge room, filled to capacity, but strangely quiet except for the music: it was soundproofed and all clatter was deadened. The tables were set far apart; there were tables and booths, all with sparkling white tablecloths and gleaming silverware, and each with a vase of flowers. Duffy led us to a semicircular booth on a dais in a corner.

"Order your drinks," he said, "and look over the menu, and it's all on the house. I must do a bit more hosting—I'm expecting some special people with special reservations—and then I'll join you and we'll have dinner together. Gee, I'm thrilled to see you, Peter." And then he bowed to Marla, and gracefully moved off, and then a waiter came with a bottle of champagne.

"Compliments of Mr. Gaylord," he said and popped the cork and poured and went away and we drank.

The zithers were doing a duet of the *Third Man Theme*. Marla removed her little fur and her white shoulders gleamed in the twilight. For the first time in weeks I felt relaxed.

"Just how well do you know the guy?" Marla said.

"He told you. We were friends in his salad days."

"Where?"

"Back in New York."

She tightened her brows. "*Good* friends?"

"Not *that* good, my love."

And we drank champagne, and then the zithers shifted to fiddles, and I began to peek down Marla's dress, and then Duffy came back, and he ordered for all of us, and we ate, and we talked.

"When you're gay," said Duffy, "you can't have a job. You have to be your own boss, then you're free."

"Weren't you free in New York?" Marla said.

"Hell, no. Ask Peter. In New York I was a mouse. I'll tell you something about New York, it stinks. It's got a reputation for being a metropolis, but it's a lousy little town, with a hell of a lot of people, but a lousy little closed-up provincial hypocritical town. Not like Paris, not like London, not like Rome—not even like here."

Marla had nerve. "You mean the gay world is not that wide open in New York?"

"That's a symptom, isn't it? Christ, out here half the town is gay, and nobody starts shaking bones about it."

"Duffy," I said, "you're sure a changed man."

"Why not, Pappy? I'm beholden to no one. I've got a quarter of a million bucks in the bank, I've got a restaurant for which we've been offered a half million dollars cold cash, I'm a character in the town, and I'm my own boss."

"How did it happen?"

"Reggie is the best chef in the world." To Marla he said, "Reggie is my partner. Reggie's back there in the kitchen, supervising, doing the work he loves."

"How did it happen?" I said.

"We always planned to open a restaurant. With Reggie in the rear and me out front, we couldn't miss. I have a talent for decorating, for hosting, for having a *feel* for people, and Reggie is a true *haut chef de cuisine*. How could we miss?"

"Seems you didn't."

"We serve the finest food that money can buy on the finest of china with the finest of flatware. We choose our captains and waiters with meticulous care. Reggie's always in the kitchen, working; and I'm always out front, working. Every year, July and August, we close and redecorate completely. Those two months we go to Europe, relax, vacation, and pick up new recipes with which to titillate the palates of our customers. The Tres Gay is now one of the top restaurants of the world, internationally known."

We had dessert, coffee, and brandy, and then I said, "Duffy, is there somewhere we can talk alone?"

The blue eyes blinked and a muscle twitched at the hinge of the smooth pink jaw. "Alone?" he said.

"It's important."

"To you? Or to me?" Success had given him authority.

"To both of us."

"And the lady?"

"The lady knows I want to talk to you alone."

"I know," said the lady.

The blue eyes stopped blinking and the jaw hardened. "Certainly," he said. He stood up and I stood up. "Please pardon us, Miss Trent," he said, and he led me to the rear and into a small elevator and we went up one flight and then he led me along a corridor to a large drawing room. "This is the office," he said. He brought out brandy and poured into oversized snifter-glasses. "The rest of this floor is, well, almost like a ballroom, where we have parties. Upstairs is our apartment. It's a three-story building. We own it." He sipped brandy and sank into an easy chair. "What is it, Peter?"

"It's Jonathan Kiss."

"Oh no." It was a groan. The groan delighted me.

I picked it up and stuck with it. I didn't know where I was sticking him but I poked, hoping. "Didn't you think that would come up, sooner or later, and bite?"

"No," he said. "At the beginning, perhaps. Now, no. What do you have to do with this, Peter?"

I laid it out like a mat, flat but bristly. "Kiss is suspected of a crime, a big crime. Any information you give me will be confidential, absolutely confidential. I'll use it as an axe to chop up Mr. Kiss, but that's as far as it'll go. But if it gets out of my hands, then you might have cops, and cops can bust this beautiful bubble of yours wide open." I was shooting buckshot hoping a pellet would hit where it hurt.

Plenty of pellets hit. The pink face took on a shade of chartreuse. He finished his brandy in a large gulp. He said, "Will you consider me a client?"

"What does that mean?"

"You're the expert and you're a friend. It's something I've wanted to talk about to an expert *and* a friend, some one whom I could trust. It's like when you've got a thing that you want to talk over with a lawyer, but a lawyer you can trust, who can take the burden off you. Dig, Pappy?"

"I dig, Duffy."

"May I be your client? I can afford to pay."

"You bought me my dinner. You're all paid up."

The pink was beginning to displace the chartreuse. He smiled and he got himself more brandy. He remembered that I was Peter Chambers and that I had backed him up when he was a frightened little fairy living on Sheridan Square with Reggie Blythe. "What do you want to know?" he said.

I kept it at the buckshot. "All about Kiss."

He sighed, sipped, smiled with more teeth. "I owe all to Jonathan Kiss."

"All what?"

"All of my present affluence."

"Don't tell me he fell in love with you."

It was a sucker remark but he was gentleman enough to let it go by. He studied the glinting amber of his glass and then he said, "Reggie and I had planned for something like this, but to make it we'd have to wait years and years. Reggie had ten thousand bucks by inheritance and he had saved an additional five thousand. I had a thousand bucks in the bank and a job with Wheeler Surety for a hundred and fifty clams a week. You can't open a restaurant on sixteen thousand bucks. You don't have a chance on sixteen thousand bucks. We were with it, we had studied it—others had tried and had flopped on a shoestring. A restaurant has to grow, be nurtured, mature. You have to have the mad money for the pull. The front money disappears fast, and if you don't have the mad money for the pull, you disappear with the front money. We weren't thinking on a big scale; we were thinking on a small scale; but you've got to have the mad money behind the front money to have a chance. We figured it real down close, but we wanted at least a year, on a small scale, to give us a chance to make it."

"And sixteen gees wasn't enough?"

"Not enough, as we learned by the experiences of others."

"How much would be enough?"

"Thirty thousand. Thirty thousand, operating on a small scale, and we'd have a chance. Sure we could make it big, we could make it quick—that possibility existed—but that possibility had ruined many others who jumped in, hoping for the quick success, and then flopping. We had studied the business, and we wouldn't take the risk, not with Reggie's life savings, and my thousand bucks. We would have to wait, living frugal, saving, until we had the mad money to back up the front money. It figured for years, before we weren't working stiffs, working for wages; before we'd have a chance to be bosses of our own, to live free, and to start up a restaurant with time for it to develop."

"And then Kiss came along."

"Came as a threat, but blossomed to bounty."

"Very poetic but you've lost me."

Duffy lit a long cigarette. "A big executive out of Harrison Safe and Lock was shifting to a new position as a big executive with Corn Exchange National. The latter job required bonding but the bonding was no big deal with this type of executive, simple routine, a quick check with the company for whom he was working, a couple of affidavits, his fingerprints, and that would lock up the file."

"And you were in charge?"

"Yes. He came in for a chat, and then I did my routine, and then I called him to come in, and he stalled for a few weeks, busy with business for Harrison Safe and Lock, and then one night the bell rang at Sheridan Square and it was the august Mr. Jonathan Kiss who had come a-calling."

"Unexpected?"

"But totally. I was alone, Reggie was working. He was suave, charming, lovely, and asked me out to dinner. Where do you think he took me?"

"I give up."

"El Morocco, where Reggie was working. One would think it was a coincidence, but it wasn't, it was psychology, only I didn't know it until we got there."

"And when you got there?"

"We ate in a nice little secluded spot, and then Kiss went into his spiel. He knew all about me, he knew all about the boy-bars I hung out at, he knew about Reggie, that we were living together, and that Reggie was working at El Morocco. He had done a check and he had me but good."

"I can imagine."

"No, you can't imagine because you're not queer. You can't imagine what it's like to live in constant fear—fear of exposure, fear of being fired out of a job, fear of ridicule, fear of not being able to earn a living. You must remember what a frightened little guy I was back there."

"Of course I remember."

"All I wanted was to be let alone. I wanted to live like a normal human being. I wanted to work at my job, and save my money while Reggie saved his money, so that sometime, somehow, we could break out on our own and be free."

"So what happened with Kiss?"

"First came the threat. Suavely, coolly—even kindly—he told me what he *could* do. He could get me fired out of my job. He could get Reggie fired out of his job. He could even get me arrested because he could swear that I had attempted to solicit him for immoral purposes. He was a big man, a big shot. I was a nothing. I would have to lose. I couldn't stand up against him. After he laid that out, pointedly and precisely; after he let me know what he *could* do; then he told me what he would do."

"What would he do?"

"He did it, right there. He told me that the new job with the bank would pay him twenty-five thousand dollars a year, and that it was worth a year's pay to him for me to cooperate. And he handed it over to me, in an envelope, right there, that night. Twenty-five thousand bucks, with instructions that within six months I quit Wheeler Surety."

"And you took his money?"

"You bet I did, Pappy. It was my opportunity to break out on my own, once and for all. It was my chance, finally, to establish myself. I could get out onto my own. Even if I'd have to do a term in jail afterward, it was worth it to me. And dealing with a big man like this Kiss, I doubted I'd get into any trouble, because he'd have to get into trouble first and he had demonstrated right then, hadn't he, that he was a pretty smart cookie."

"What did he want?"

"That his fingerprints didn't show up in the file at Wheeler Surety."

"But they are on file. I checked that bonding company myself."

Softly he said, "They're not his prints, Peter."

"Whose are they?"

"Mine," he said.

TWENTY-SEVEN

IT WAS three hours later in New York, but I called anyway. I roused Victor Mason from his dreams and gave him new dreams. I was convinced our guy was Kiss. If he had finagled one set of fingerprints, he had finagled the other. I now knew how he had done the one, I did not know how he had done the other, but I was convinced our guy was Kiss. I compressed my facts over the phone but I delivered them all. He told me to hang on while he used another phone. When he returned he informed me that he would be at The Mansion tomorrow morning at eleven o'clock California time. Then he gave me instructions. I was to pay off the staff and disperse them. All of the cars except one were to be returned to the rental company. Marla and Willie were to go back to New York. All of this was to be accomplished tonight and early tomorrow morning. I was to be alone when he arrived at eleven o'clock.

He was the boss and he was paying. He had a right to give instructions and it was his due that they be strictly complied with. When he arrived at eleven o'clock—ten minutes after eleven—I was alone.

It was a hot, steamy, sunny day. He was pale, grim, perspiring. I took him directly to the Observation Room and let him have a peek at the telescope. Our people were pottering about the garden, exercising. Kiss was barefoot, in bathing trunks. Valerie was in sandals, shorts, and bandana.

"Soon they'll go in for lunch," I said. "Then they'll come out clean and showered and changed and rest on the patio whilst lapping up sunshine and whiskey."

"He sure doesn't look like Kiss," Mason said.

"He's maybe forty-fifty pounds heavier. He's saffron-dark from a year of sun. He's crew-cut with white hair. Sure he doesn't look like Kiss."

Mason went away from the telescope.

"How about a drink?" he said.

I brought whiskey and ice and glasses and soda and water for both of us. He took off his jacket and tie and opened his collar. He did not take off the shoulder-holster he was wearing. I gave it no notice. His shirt was wet, pasted by sweat to his body. He dropped ice into a glass, added Scotch and soda, drank it all thirstily, made a new highball, and sat down with it. His black hair was tousled, glinting with perspiration. His wide mouth seemed wider, set at the corners, grim. The planes of his face sagged; he looked tired, depressed, drooping; he had lost weight. But the large grey eyes were clear and alert and intense, strangely intense.

I made a highball, licked at it, left it, lit a cigarette. "Vic," I said, "I don't know what you have in mind, but a normal operation will produce the results for us."

"Like how?" he said without enthusiasm.

"Our killer's Kiss, no question."

"So?"

"We move in with cops and take him. With what we've got, interrogation, even by the rankest amateur, will break him down in an hour. Then we're home free."

"You're trying to talk me out of what I've got in mind, aren't you?"

I stayed stupid. "I've no idea as to your intentions."

"But your intentions are cops."

"We've got him. It can't miss."

"Except that the whole deal blasts wide open, and you know damned well that's just what we don't want. If he's arrested, there'll be a trial. At a trial, naturally, he'll defend. He can't win, but *we* lose. The whole bit becomes public scandal. Christ, are you trying to con me? If we would have wanted cops, we wouldn't have retained you. We would have had the United States government working for us. A bank job is Federal. We'd have had the F.B.I. We wouldn't have needed Peter Chambers and Marla Trent and William Boyd Winkle. Good as they are, I think even they would admit they're not quite as good as the F.B.I."

I tried again. I limped along another tack. "We can treat with him. He'll deal, once he knows all we've got on him. We'll give him a piece off the top as ransom, but you'll get back most of the loot, and that's what you've been after, isn't it?"

"He's too smart, and too dangerous."

"What does that mean, Vic?"

"He'll understand, once it's private—without cops, without law—he'll understand just why it's private. That piece off the top will be far greater than what's left at bottom."

"You're a business man, Victor. When you're in a bind, you settle." Now I let it out a notch further. "You don't want to settle with him, do you?"

"Would you, if you were in my position?"

"I'm not in your position."

He drew on the ball again, set it down, stood up, and walked. "The guy killed four people. He killed three bank guards, and this bartender, this Ritchie. I don't know Ritchie —didn't know Ritchie—and one of the bank guards was a new man. But the other two, I knew them, even knew their families, the wives and kids. Omit that. Skip that. That goes to the emotions. Even if I didn't know any one of them, this guy, this Kiss, murdered four people, four human beings. Do I deal with him? Do I give him the bulk amount of perhaps eight million dollars, as a prize for murder?"

"And would *his* murder square it?"

His voice was thick. "Then you do know what I have in mind?"

"I'm not going to be a party to it, pal."

It was out now, ugly, open as a wound.

Victor Mason sat down again and drank his whiskey. Murder makes a taint, even at preliminary, at premeditation, even with justification. There were lines on his face, sagging, and the skin beneath his eyes was haggard. "What difference who is the executioner?" he said. "He's a murderer. If we deliver him, the State will kill him."

"But he'll have the right to present his defense."

"Defense? *Defense? What* defense? Christ, Peter, don't *you* go Pollyanna on me. You're an experienced, worldly, bitter, sophisticated man. And you're a highly intelligent man, and above the nonsense that children have dinned into them in high school. The man is a murderer and a murderer knows he risks death as a penalty. You've killed people in your lifetime."

"Yes, but in a sense, unavoidably. I've never tried to play God."

"God?"

"Judge, jury, and executioner—all in one—that in a piece is as of God."

"So now you're trying to go religious on me."

"I'm trying anything—everything—to talk you out of it."

"Nothing will help you."

"I'm trying to help *you*."

He fought me. "Thank you. I don't want your help."

I fought back at him. "And if and when he's dead, how does that fit with the business end?"

"I'll deal with her. They're lovers, in love, thank God, in a joint operation, with joint accounts and joint ownership. In joint ownership, when one is dead, the survivor owns wholly."

"And what will you have to offer her?"

"Her life," he said.

TWENTY-EIGHT

AT TWELVE-THIRTY they were out on the patio having fun in the sun with frosted drinks. They were a handsome couple, clean-bodied, smooth-tan, and dressed in white. He had changed to white tennis shorts. She had changed to white sandals, white snug shorts, and a white bandana.

I put away the binoculars.

This was it. Point of climax.

"I'm going in," I said.

"I'm going with you," Victor Mason said.

"I'm going in alone."

He put on his jacket. "I'm not paying you to be a hero."

"I'm going in alone," I said.

"Now, why?"

"Maybe I can separate them, divide them, put a wedge in."

He was silent for a moment. Then he said softly, "Yes, that would help—for my purpose."

"I'm not trying to help your purpose." I started for the door.

"I'll drive you," he said.

"Good enough. But you stay in the car."

"Right outside the door."

"Good enough."

Downstairs he said, "Aren't you forgetting something?"

"Like what?"

"A gun."

"I'm not forgetting anything."

"But you told me yourself that house is an arsenal."

"So what? I'm on a peaceful mission."

"You can get killed on a peaceful mission."

"You can get killed faster if you carry a gun."

"I'm carrying a gun."

"You're not on a peaceful mission."

We drove without talking. He was tense at the wheel, his hands gripping tightly, his face creased in thought. I preferred not to know what he was thinking.

He stopped in front of the house and I got out.

"Good luck," he said.

I didn't answer. I walked. My thighs were stiff, my back was rigid, there was an ache in the muscles of my calves. The patio was in the rear. There was a flagstone path at the side of the house that led to the rear. I walked, mostly on the balls of my feet, keeping off my heels. It was a short distance but it was a hell of a long walk. Finally, I turned the corner of the house.

She saw me first. She dropped her glass.

"What the hell!" he said. Then he looked toward where she was looking. At me. "Yes?" he said. "What do *you* want?" He said it gruffly but not belligerently. He was fluffing off a Fuller Brush salesman.

"Hi," I said quite cheerfully. "How are you, Mrs. Kiss?"

He was spread out on a chaise lounge. She was seated on a metal chair. His head swiveled to her. "You know him?" he said.

"He's . . . he's Peter Chambers."

"Peter—who?"

"The man . . . the man who helped me when my husband . . ."

He smiled. He did it well. "Oh. Yes. Peter Chambers." The guy was good. I had to tip the hat I wasn't wearing to him.

"I was in the neighborhood," I said. "Figured I'd drop by."

She stood up. Her figure was as beautiful as ever. But not her eyes. Fear made her eyes ugly. "In the neighborhood? But how could you know . . .?"

"My name is Jackson," he said.

"Yes." She gulped, stood very straight. "You startled me so, Mr. Chambers, for a moment I lost my manners." She smiled. It was ghastly. "I . . . I've re-married. This is my new husband. Mr. Richard Robinson Jackson. Ritchie—Peter Chambers."

"Hi," he said.

"Glad to know you, Mr. Kiss."

"And I'm glad to . . ." Then it got to him. He came up out on the chaise lounge. He was a big guy. The smooth suntanned chest was wide and strong, and heaving. "Not Kiss," he said. "Jackson. Re-married, the lady said. The first husband was Kiss. I'm Jackson."

I showed off a little. "The first husband was Davenport."

"Yeah." There was no tinge of Harvard in the diction. The guy was very good. "First Davenport, then Kiss, then me. How long have you been in the neighborhood, Mr. Chambers?"

"Long," I said.

"Would you like to come into the house, Mr. Chambers?"

Come into my parlor, said the spider to the fly.

I was playing for keeps, and I had to go all the way. I was playing for a bonus of approximately eighty thousand dollars and I was playing to prevent a good friend, Victor Mason, from becoming a murderer. I was playing risky poker but I had the case-ace in the hole. My ace was Kiss himself: Kiss was highly intelligent. I have a great respect for intelligence, tremendous respect. Had Kiss been a dummy, I wouldn't have been there imitating a hero. I was risking my life on Kiss's intelligence.

"I'd love to come into your house, Mr. Kiss."

"Jackson."

"I keep calling you Kiss, don't I?"

"Seems you do."

"I'll keep on calling you Kiss, if you don't mind."

"I mind."

"We'll discuss it in your parlor," said the fly to the spider. "This way, Mr. Chambers."

It was cooler in the house, but hot. I sat down on a hard chair and spread my knees.

"Valerie," he said, "get something cold for Mr. Chambers to drink."

"Of course," she said.

"Oh, no glasses there," he said. "I'll get a glass here."

"Yes," she said.

She went toward the kitchen, to the refrigerator. He went to the china-cabinet. She would come back with an ice-cold gun. He would come back with a luke-warm gun. I would sit and show no surprise and if I played my poker properly I would win that pot and if I won that pot, I would win them all.

She came back with an ice-cold gun.

He came back with a luke-warm gun.

Both guns were pointed at me.

"There's another one," I said, "in the bar in the recreation room. Then there's one in the right hand upper drawer of the desk in the guest room, and two in each nighttable in the bedrooms, and there are boxes of cartridges in a chest of drawers in one of the bedrooms."

He grew pale beneath his tan and there is no color more sickly.

Thickly he said, "What do you want?"

"Whatever I want, Mr. Kiss, I want *you* to take notice that, despite my knowledge of all the loaded guns in this fortress, I came here in good will as can be evidenced by the fact that *I* have no gun."

"Touch him," he said. She started toward me. He stopped her. "Don't go near him with the pistol," he said. She placed her pistol on a table, came to me, gave me a fast but gentle frisk, then backed away and retrieved her firearm.

"He's telling the truth," she said.

"I have other truths to tell," I said.

"What do you want?" he said in a voice muted by bewilderment but with, at last, a faint touch of Harvard coming through. "Why are you here?"

"I'm here to give you dignity."

"You're here to—*what* the hell?"

"I've lived with you for a year, Mr. Kiss. I know you almost as well as I know myself. You're a brilliant man who performed a remarkable crime. It has backfired and you're washed up. I'm here to give you dignity. You're entitled."

He moved back until his legs touched a chair. He sank

into it but the gun remained pointed at me. "What do you want?" he said.

I drew in a long breath. The next line of this dialogue was all-important. It had to go all the way through, into his psyche, into his soul, and it had to take root.

"I want you to kill yourself, Mr. Kiss."

Her breath sucked up a gasp. His broke out in a form of laughter.

"First I'll kill you," he said.

"Why?" I said. "Because I want to give you dignity? Because I want to spare you ineffable disgrace, prolonged agony? Because I've fought with cops to permit me to come in here alone to talk with you? You're an intelligent man. I'm doing for you what I would have wanted you to do for me, had I been in your spot. Why should you want to kill me?"

"Cops?" he said.

"They're all around here, waiting. Right outside your door, right in front, sits Mr. Victor Mason. I pleaded with them to let me come in here first. I gave them all sorts of reasons —that I wanted to prevent a pitched battle, gunfire—but there was only one reason. I want to give you dignity. You're entitled."

"Go look," he said to her.

She went to the window, slanted the venetian blind, peered.

"Victor Mason," she said. "In a car. Alone."

"And all around the place," I said, "hidden, deployed, armed, are cops, dying to come in here the moment I give the signal; or, without signal, if I stay in here too long."

"My God," he uttered and he was finished.

I dressed it up. "They know all about it, Mr. Kiss. The murder of Jackson, the phony suicide, the switch in identity. They know you locked your apartment with an extra key, slipped out of the building during the excitement, got yourself a crew cut, went to Jackson's apartment, dyed your hair white, cleaned up there, packed up and moved out, even disconnecting the telephone—as Jackson."

"How?" he muttered. "How?"

"They've spent a year on it, all the way from the apartment on Thirty-third Street off Park Avenue, to the three safes here in this house, to the banks in Beverly Hills, Vegas, Paris, Rome, Zurich, all over the world. They even know about your house in Surrey."

"How, how?" he kept mumbling but the gun he held was still pointed at me. And the gun she held was still pointed at me.

"You've been tailed for a year, by top experts. You've had a year's attention from craftsmen, the best in the profession. That holdup in Vegas, for instance, wasn't a holdup. A swatch of hair was yanked from your head and laboratory analysis disclosed the hair was dyed. We didn't find the dye here in the house, it's probably in one of the safes. And that night of the holdup, your fingerprints were taken."

"Fingerprints," he said.

"Even that gorgeous set-up you prepared so long in advance is demolished. They've got Duffy Gaylord, and Duffy squawked his brains out."

It never fails. When you're going good, bonuses happen. When you're going bad, nothing will happen. I was going good. Bonuses broke out like a rash. "You clipped off the first two fingers of your right hand in a supposed accident. It was no accident. You used a hypo with novocaine to anesthetize the hand, and they know why."

She talked. "Why?" she said.

"So that he could have a different handwriting, is why." And to him I said, "They even know why you had Marla Trent Enterprises do the tape-recording in addition to the photos—the tape-recording that never showed up. You studied that tape, you lived with it. You're a guy with acting talent. You learned from that tape. You learned to talk like Richard Robinson Jackson." I stood up. This was the last pot in our game of poker. The face-cards were overpowerimg. He couldn't possibly know where I was bluffing. "Do you still want to kill me, Mr. Kiss? Because I came in here, at the risk of my life but depending upon your intelligence, to give you your dignity? Do you want to kill me, Mr. Kiss?"

"No," he said.

"Thank you," I said.

"I thank you," he said and put the gun to his head and splattered his brains across the room.

She screamed and threw away the weapon and came at me with the weapon she was more accustomed to using. Her bare arms encircled my neck, her breasts rubbing against my chest. Her tongue lapped across my mouth, licked at my ear. "Help me," she whispered. "Please, please. You. Only you. You'll never be sorry."

I was starved for a woman and she was all woman. I stiffened but I backed off, disentangled from her.

"You'll help me?" she said. "You will?"

"Yes."

"You'll never regret it."

"I've got to get you out of here."

"Whatever you say."

"Go upstairs. Pack everything into a bag."

"My clothes?"

"No! Stuff that can be incriminating, that can hook you to the Kiss operation. The guns, the cartridges, the ledgers, the correspondence, all that stuff. Do you understand?"

"Yes."

"His suicide will have to be reported. There'll be local cops. Clean out everything. Into the bag. Now go. Move."

I watched as she went up the stairs. I watched the long smooth tanned legs and the undulating buttocks, tight-white in the shorts. I watched until she disappeared and then I sighed and looked at Kiss. He was heaped across the chair, leaking blood, the gun still in his hand. I stooped and picked up the gun she had thrown away, skirted around Kiss, and went to the recreation room. There I took the pistol out of the whiskey compartment of the bar and, carrying two guns like a fast-draw sheriff squeezing out a career on the television tube, I went upstairs to the bedroom.

A leather valise was open on the floor and she was busy filling it. I tossed in the two guns as my donation and sat down in an armchair and waited. Finally she said, "Done."

"Everything?"

"All in there."

"Close it up." She closed the bag. "Get dressed."

She had no shame. She had nothing to be ashamed of. She undid the bandana and let it drop. She unzipped the shorts and stepped out of them. She kicked out of the sandals and lifted her arms high and stretched, standing on tiptoe. The demure little lady had not taken her sun in the nude. The breasts were white. From the navel down to the tops of her thighs she was white. All the rest of her was gold-tan. Suddenly she came at me, wrested me to my feet, slid her arms under mine, and scraped her fingernails into my shoulders. "Now, now, please," she whispered, "now, take me, have me, please, now, now."

"You're crazy."

"Crazy excited. Crazy to make love. Now. Now, now."

"Kiss is dead downstairs."

"But we're alive. You've never had what you're going to get now."

"Yes I have, baby. Remember me?"

"You had a sample of nothing. Take me now. You'll never be satisfied with anyone else."

"No good. Mason is outside. He can bust in at any minute."

As suddenly as she had come, she pulled away. "Your loss," she said. "You talked yourself out of it."

"Get dressed.'"

She dressed as though I weren't there. She hooked on a small bra. She wore no panties. She slipped on a garter belt and then, sitting on the edge of the bed, she smoothed on sheer nylons. Then she slid her feet into high-heeled pumps, stood up, got a dress, drew it over her, buckled on a belt, and she was finished—almost. She combed her hair, applied perfume, touched on make-up, took up a little clutch-pocketbook, said, "Whenever you're ready."

I took the suitcase and we went downstairs. At the door she slid her arm through mine. We looked like a honeymoon couple ready to check into a hotel.

"I'm depending on you," she said.

"Depend."

"You promised. You're going to help me."

"I said it, didn't I?"

"How?" I was about to open the door but she restrained me. "What are you going to do for me?"

I used Victor Mason's line.

"I'm going to give you your life," I said.

TWENTY-NINE

THE DEATH of Richard Robinson Jackson was indentured upon the records without complication as a suicide. Inquest produced the testimony of Mr. Victor Mason of New York, Mr. Peter Chambers of New York, and Mrs. Valerie Jackson, formerly of New York. It was adduced that Mr. Mason, visiting with Mr. Chambers, had accompanied Mr. Chambers when they had called upon the Jacksons at noon. The Jacksons had then been invited to Mr. Chambers' rented house for lunch. Mr. Jackson had declined but Mrs. Jackson, an old friend of both Mason and Chambers, had accepted. When they had returned to the premises at two o'clock, they had discovered the body of Jackson and had immediately called the police. Jackson had been in a depressed state for months, suffering stomach pains, nausea and vomiting. He had been morbidly convinced that he had cancer but he had steadfastly refused to see a doctor. He had a fear of doctors. The last time he had visited a doctor, last June, it had been a surgeon, Dr. Paul Scofield, but that had been as a consequence of an accident which had resulted in the partial amputation of the first two fingers of his right hand.

Thus the public records had Jonathan Kiss a suicide in New York and Richard Robinson Jackson a suicide in California and the public records of both states were wrong. Jackson had been murdered in New York and Kiss had killed himself in California; the locale of each demise had been switched but they were now nonetheless both dead while Valerie Dayton Davenport Kiss Jackson was very much alive but, as Victor Mason carefully explained to her, on sufferance.

"An accomplice to murder is just as guilty as the actual murderer," Mason told her.

"I had nothing to do with the murder of those bank guards," she said. "I wasn't an accomplice. I didn't know he had any intention to kill them."

"You knew damned well he planned the robbery?"

"Yes."

"Well, how did you think he was going to manage that? Just stroll in and take the money?"

She made no answer.

"And you delivered Jackson to him, didn't you?"

Again no answer.

"You knew he was going to dump him, you knew he was going to kill him. Honey, in a court of law, you're dead. You can squirm around here with me, trying to think up technicalities, but the most callow of district attorneys couldn't miss out on a conviction. At worst, you'd get the electric chair. At best—with your shape, your legs, your eyes, your winsomeness, and the most expensive of lawyers—you'd get twenty years to life. Do you want that?"

"No."

"You know what I want?"

"Yes."

"You'll cooperate?"

"I have no alternative."

"Okay, let's go over those ledgers again. Carefully."

The ledgers proclaimed Mason a pessimist. He had estimated that the claimants reporting their losses had padded them up for a fat million. They had padded them up for a comparatively skinny $300,000.

"Pessimist," I said.

"Please," he said happily. "Call me a one-third pessimist."

The actual heist had amounted to $8,300,000. The ledgers disclosed that over the year the Kisses had expended approximately $300,000 and that included the purchase of the house in England. That left a cool—frigid—$8,000,000 exclusive of what could be obtained on a re-sale of the house. The money had been fairly evenly distributed amongst all the banks except for the bank nearest the house in England. There, in Surrey, in large bills, reposed one million dollars.

Mason questioned her closely and her answers incriminated her further. There had been love between her and Jonathan Kiss but there had been more: there had been a mutual lust for great wealth. Within the first year when they had gone together—even before they had been married—Kiss had discovered this in her and she had discovered it in him and they had admired it, one in the other, and then slowly, as his confidence in her had ripened, he had hypothetically expounded his plan, and she had become avidly interested, and after they were married she had become an active confederate.

"It was your job to produce the fall guy," Mason said and he sounded as though he were fighting an emetic.

"And all-important that job was," she said, proud, strangely, even now. "He had to be right, just right. Same color eyes, some grey in the hair, similar skin tone, same general build, same general appearance. And the body had to be hairless and with a scar from an appendectomy."

"That must have taken a hell of a lot of doing," I said.

"It did."

"And a hell of a lot of sleeping around—to check up on the intimate details."

Her smile was lewd. "I couldn't complain about that chore, could I? Whoever it was, he had to be handsome if he looked like Jonathan. And in a sense it was a challenge, getting the man to bed."

"Not much of a challenge with you as bait," I said.

"Wasn't your husband jealous?" Mason said.

She flared. "Why? Why should he be? Jealousy is a form of insecurity. Jonathan was secure, totally secure. He knew I loved him and that any other man was manure as compared to him."

"But did you enjoy?" I said.

"Sure I enjoyed."

"And Jonathan knew you enjoyed?"

"I didn't lie to Jonathan, ever. Sure he knew."

"And it didn't bother him?"

"Of course not. Why should it bother him that in the course of business I was having fun. He knew that I loved him and couldn't ever possibly love any other man. He was a man, Mr. Chambers, a *man*. A man, 'a true man, with full confidence in himself, doesn't worry about the competition, doesn't worry about—"

"It must have taken a long time," Mason said.

"What?" she said.

"The search. The search for the sucker."

"Two years. And we devoted ourselves to it, believe me. We had to look, of course, in special places, sort of downstream. Lower depths sort of thing, you know? And then, even when I tested a man, he would then have to be one without real connections, without ties, one whom I'd be able to manage. There were times when it got close, and then the guy would turn out to have a wife, or a sweetheart, or was engaged, or something."

"And then there was Ritchie," I said.

"There was Ritchie," she said.

And Mason had had it. He drew her back to the ledgers and to a discussion of pecuniary matters but there was one last matter still bugging me and I opened it up again.

"Do you know about the fingerprints?" I said.

"What fingerprints?" she said.

"Jonathan's fingerprints turned up in New York as the prints of Richard Robinson Jackson."

She was proud again. "He thought of everything, didn't he?"

"He sure did," I said and went along with her by not pressing the fact that whatever he had thought of was now part of the debris of debacle.

"He was a brilliant man and you can't deny that."

I stayed along. "I wouldn't attempt to deny that."

"Baffled? Baffled, Mr. Chambers?"

"Completely."

"If ever there was any question as to his identity, his own fingerprints could have proved that he was who he said he was—Richard Robinson Jackson. And yet, actually, it was simple. As Jonathan once said, 'Whatever is complex has a base of simplicity. It is only the end result that appears complex.' "

"And how did Jonathan achieve this end result?"

"Through the operation of his principle of simplicity."

"Christ, *how*?"

"On a Friday night I had Ritchie passed out cold in the apartment. But out—cold! Finished! Then Jonathan came up and changed all his credentials for Ritchie's. Then we went out to the street, started a brawl of our own, and he beat me, really hit hard, until I was bleeding and screaming and the cops came and he was still fighting and they subdued him and arrested him, on my complaint, and booked and printed him for assault and battery—as Richard Robinson Jackson. And then in the morning, in Weekend Court before the Magistrate, I suffered a change of heart and refused to press the charge and the Magistrate dismissed him and we went back to the apartment and changed up the credentials, but the prints remained on file as those of Richard Robinson Jackson."

We flew her back to New York and we stayed with her and then for our trip Mason arranged for the use of his own plane, a large one, with an alleged crew of six. Of the crew one was the pilot, one the co-pilot, one the navigator, one the radio man, and two—huge silent men—were supposed to be engineers but in my estimation they were bodyguards for just in case. None of them knew what we were flying for. All they knew was that they were flying us.

The itinerary was simple but as backbreaking as a misfit chiropractor. We went to a bank, we picked up cash in two strong satchels, we flew back to New York with it, and then we went out to the next bank. Mason was not taking any chances; there was no layover; the money was returned in the straight line that is the shortest distance between two points: from the bank where it lay to the bank in New York; and thence out to the next bank.

First we attended to the United States banks, and then the foreign banks: we saved the last for Surrey where the house was. When it was necessary to stay over for a night, I would check into a hotel with Valerie as Mr. and Mrs. Peter Chambers and Mason would take a nearby room, but he would stay with us, and one of us—Mason or I—remained awake while she slept. Mason and I each carried a gun (and I imagined the two "engineers" did likewise). On the plane we gave her full freedom: she chatted and flirted with the crew all six of whom were young, strong, and good-looking.

And so seven million dollars were transferred back to the Corn Exchange National, and even the crew and the "engineers," who invariably stayed with the plane, grew thinner and tenser under Mason's unswerving drive, but he flourished, growing rosier and ruddier and more expansive and more talkative. And then at last, on a hot rainy June 29 in England, we were on the last leg of our odyssey.

The plane and the crew stayed at the London airport. Mason and Valerie and I, wringing wet through contact and osmosis with incessant rainfall, traveled by cab to Surrey. There in the bowels of the vaults of an old bank we packed one million dollars in big bills into our satchels and then the cab delivered us to the house in Surrey where Mason said, "Do you have whiskey here?"

"I have everything here," Valerie said.

We wetted our insides to reduce the effect of the wet on our outsides. In a huge cavernous drawing room Valerie sat behind a wide carved desk and Mason sat near her and I sat on a cushiony divan and lapped at whiskey while Mason wrote out the prescription for the end of the sickness.

"Peter will take the bags back to the plane and go on to New York," he said, "while I stay here with you."

"You'll stay with me?" she said almost coyly.

"You've been a good girl," he said, "and we're almost finished and we know that, forever, we can depend upon your discretion."

"You really trust me, don't you?" she said.

"Not in the least."

"But you just said—"

"That we can depend upon your discretion, because that discretion involves *you*. One peep, and you open up the hornet's nest. There is no statute of limitations for murder—that hangs over you for the rest of your life. So if you talk, if you even squeak, you're shoveling the dirt for your own grave. I believe by now you understand that."

"You've made it damned clear, Mr. Mason, and you've repeated it until I'm sick of hearing it."

"Better sick than dead."

"Why are you going to stay here with me?"

"Only in my capacity of collector, my dear. This house was bought with the bank's money. You'll sell it—while I'm with you—and turn over the proceeds to me. Then we'll be all finished and quit."

"And high time."

"Haven't you enjoyed my company?"

"It's disgusted me."

"And vice versa, my dear."

"Now, now, kiddies," I said over my Scotch. "Let's not get into a battle at this stage of the game."

"How's the game going to end for me?" she said.

"I'm going to be kind," Mason said.

"Yeah, you, kind," she said. "You're not a man, you're a machine. A cash register."

"The cash register has ticked off your life to you. It will add to that. Upon the completion of our business here, I will give you five thousand dollars—because I'm a man and not a machine. I can't just leave you here with nothing. My advice would be for you to stay here, in England, and start fresh. The deed to this house is on file?"

"Yes."

"You have copies of the papers?"

"Of course."

"Where?"

"Right here in the desk."

"I'll take them."

She opened a drawer of the desk but she did not come up with copies of papers. She came up with a gun, a huge black-muzzled .45.

"If you move you're very dead," she said.

We did not move. Even a wild shot from a .45 can make a very large hole.

"Oh, I've been waiting for this minute," she said, "planning for it, praying for it."

"Honey," I said as casually as I could manage, "you're out of your ever-lovin' mind. Don't you have troubles enough? Must you creep in again, before you've even crept out."

"I'll do the creeping, creep." She stood up and came out

from behind the desk and leaned on it. "And I'll do all the directing here. First, stand up. Both of you. And, careful."

We stood up. Both of us. Careful.

"Now drop your guns to the floor. And remember, if you start any fireworks, I'll finish the fireworks."

Mason glanced toward me. I nodded. She was talking. Amateurs always talk. If we kept her talking, we had a chance. We dropped our guns to the floor.

"Now kick them toward me."

We did just that. If she stooped for them, I hoped that Mason would know enough to jump her. I was too far away.

She did not stoop.

I kept her talking.

"Honey," I said. "What sense?"

"I'm going to kill you both," she said.

"Repeat. What sense? The crew knows we're here. You'll be out of the frying pan and into a real fire."

"The crew doesn't know what it's all about. I've talked with them. I've a hunch nobody knows what it's all about—no cops ever showed up. I've a hunch that the bank wouldn't—couldn't—publicly admit that its vaults were looted of more than eight million dollars."

She was bright, but she was talking.

I was delighted to note that Mason, shuffling, moved a step forward.

"So?" I said.

"So after I kill you, I'll go to the airport and tell the crew that you sent me to tell them to go home. I'll tell them that we're to take up our journey without them, that you two have already left. They think that the three of us are joined together in some sort of mission. I'll tell them that we expect to be gone for several months. Oh, they'll believe me. They don't know that I've been a prisoner and I'm certain they don't know a thing about this house."

She was so damned right—all around the mulberry bush. But Mason took another step toward her and I kept her talking.

"Somebody'll find us and then they'll find you. Cripes, by now I'd imagine you'd have learned you can't run from murder. Kiss was brilliant and even he couldn't make it."

"I'll make it."

"How'll you dispose of us?"

Mason had moved up another notch.

"I'll bury you, that's how. There's a cemetery right here on the estate."

"Then what'll you do? Just live here as the mistress of the estate?"

"I'm not that stupid."

"Nobody ever said you were stupid, baby."

"Don't baby me."

"Nobody ever said you were stupid."

"Yugoslavia," she said.

"You go—*what?*" I said.

"Yugoslavia. It's a country."

"Oh."

"My mother's living there, and she's well connected. Jonathan had instructed me that if it went bad, if I had to run, I was to run there. Well, that's where I'm going to run, but instead of running broke, I'll run with a million bucks, and once there—pouf! I'll disappear. It's an iron-curtain country—"

"Semi-iron, you know, like tin or something, but . . . " and then Mason jumped!

Who can define bravery? If I'd have been in his position, I'd have jumped her too, and I make no pretense to bravery. When you jump at a .45 you can get killed by one bullet. On the other hand, if you stand still that bullet can find you more easily, and even the amateurs cease talking once the sadistic thrill of prolonging the torture has run out.

Mason jumped and caught her and they bounced to the floor in a swirl, legs flying. The man was strong but the woman was desperate and they fought for the gun, panting, rasping, twisting, flailing, and then the shot sounded and Mason stood up and I bent to her and she had a hole like a tunnel beneath her left breast but she was still holding the gun.

I stood up. "Finished," I said. "End of chapter."

He had recovered his breath. He did not look at her. "There goes the house," he said. He shrugged. "Well, we tried. Okay, let's clean up here."

We collected our pistols and we cleaned up, thoroughly and accurately, with emphasis on fingerprints and then we got out of there. We walked for a long time with a million bucks in the dark rain, and then we took a cab. Once he said, "The Lord works his miracles in strange ways," and he said nothing more, and I said nothing, and then we were at the airport and we went into a cafe for coffee.

"Please remember we were never at that house," he said.

"Of course not."

"We did our business in Surrey and came back to the plane."

"Yes."

"And you'll so inform Trent and Winkle too."

"Yes."

"No sense our getting involved in this."

"No sense whatever."

"It'll be a long time before she's found alone in that house."

"And when they find her?"

"They'll find a suicide, what else? They started that cycle and completed it, didn't they, Mr. and Mrs. Kiss?" He drank coffee, set down the cup. "As a matter of fact, that's precisely what it was. We gave her every chance but she fought away from freedom. The death-wish is inscrutable and certain forms of suicide are impelled by the unconscious. She pulled a gun on two armed men. Did she think she'd get away with it?"

"Maybe she did."

"But damn, she knew what she was risking. It was a million bucks or it was death. She didn't get the million bucks. She got what she deserved and she got it, as it turned out, by her own hand." He pushed his cup away. "I'm not a hypocrite and I won't pretend a sympathy I don't feel. She was spawn of the devil and she's in hell where she belongs." He touched my arm. His hand was heavy. "Time to go home," he said.

THIRTY

WE TOUCHED down at Idlewild at ten minutes after ten of the morning of June 30, already blazing hot. At eleven o'clock Victor Mason added a million dollars to the special account at Corn Exchange National. At twelve o'clock in the offices of International Guarantee at the Empire State Building, Victor Mason wrote two checks, each in the sum of $80,000, one to me and one to Marla Trent Enterprises. I took his money, shook his hand, beat a path to my bank, and deposited my loot. Then I rode a cab home and called Marla Trent at Marla Trent Enterprises.

"Come and get it," I said.

"Get what?"

"Like eighty thousand bananas. Our business is done."

"Or begun," she said.

"Pardon?"

"Where are you?"

"My apartment."

"I'll be there at eight o'clock."

"Eight o'clock?"

"Hell, lover, I've got to prepare. We're going to celebrate. Hang on to everything."

"Bye."

Suddenly reaction hit like a house caving in. Suddenly a year's work was terminated and I was exhausted. Suddenly I just sat by the telephone, as though waiting for a call, and just sat there.

Then I stood up, peeled off my clothes, tottered to the bed, and dropped into it. I turned with a groan like an arthritic old man, set the alarm for six, closed my eyes and was sleeping. In a minute the alarm rang and it was six o'clock, but I was refreshed.

It was hot. I had not even opened the windows.

I did not open the windows. I pushed the buttons of the air-conditioners and then went off to shave and shower.

When I came out, it was still hot. I pushed more buttons on the air-conditioners and they started to wheeze like over-fed matrons after a polka. Being a detective I quickly deduced that they were out of order; hell, I hadn't used them since last summer. I called the repair service but got answering service which informed me that repair service knocked off at six o'clock but please leave your name and address and you will get your repair tomorrow. I left my name and address, and opened the windows. In hot weather in New York open windows are an anachronism, and I enjoyed the change. I got an unaccustomed whiff of fresh air. It was hot, but a little scented breeze wafted over from the park.

I called the Harkness for Carmen but Carmen was gone.

I called the Waldorf for Carmen but Carmen was not at home.

I called the Stage Delicatessen for food and had a meal sent over. I ate and then I prettied up for Marla and at eight o'clock my bell rang and I had Marla in a lovely blue dress with white buttons down the front.

"Hail," she said. "How are you?"

"Hale," I said. "And you?"

"Slightly stoned."

"Black Russians?"

"Many."

"How are your inhibitions?"

"I have none. But first, my check."

I gave her the check. She put it into her little white bag and laid that away and turned and smiled at me. I smiled back with pleasure and she was a pleasure to smile at: tall and extravagantly curved, simple in the blue dress without stockings and with high-heeled white pumps, complex in the unfathomable expression about the gleaming blue eyes.

"Do you have champagne?" she said.

I pointed. "Everything. In the bar."

"I'll make Black Russians."

"Help yourself."

She started across the room, toward me. "They're potent."

"So am I."

"Are you?" She took my face in her hands and puckered my lips and sucked them into hers in a kiss that had all my good resolutions wavering. Then she let go and said in a small voice, "Damned hot in here, or is it us?"

"Us, and hot in here."

"What about the air-conditioning?"

"It's on the fritz."

"Are the windows open behind those venetian blinds, just so we don't suffocate?"

"Open."

"Hot," she said and unbuttoned the white buttons and removed the dress and stood there proudly, almost defiantly, glowingly naked except for tiny fishnet red briefs and a tiny fishnet bulging red bra. Marla Trent in a scarlet fishnet Bikini would have caused a panic on the French Riviera, in my apartment good resolutions came tumbling down. I wasn't married yet, I had not even asked; hell, I had a right to be unfaithful, once, just once, Carmen or no Carmen. I started my move but she stopped me.

"Go take a bath," she said.

That certainly stopped me. "Bathe? I——"

"Symbolic," she said. "Like washing off all that's gone before."

"Yeah. I dig. Women."

"And I'll change the sheets and the pillow cases."

"Symbolic," I said.

"And then I'll prepare the Black Russians."

I shrugged and toddled off for my symbolic ablutions and

when I came back properly dressed in a towel the Black Russians were ready but she was not. I drank one Black Russian, I drank another, and I was beginning to feel them and getting anxious to feel the new sheets, but the tease was on. "I'm going to take a bath too," she said. "Symbolic."

"So go," I said.

"Sweetie," she said, "you're no child, you're a sophisticated man. Relax. We're going to have a long life together—I hope." She was seated in a deep armchair, her legs crossed, her knees high, a Black Russian in a long-stemmed glass in her hand. "Tell me about your trip with Mason."

I told her about our trip.

"And you and that Valerie checked into the hotels as husband and wife?"

"Mason was always with us."

"Yeah," she said. "And at the end, she was let loose scot free."

"It was part of the deal."

"And did she smooth that deal with a little sex?"

I was beginning to steam. "No."

"Not even a teensy-weensy little bit?"

"Nothing." The Black Russians were beginning to work.

"And you didn't want any part of that?"

"Part of what?"

"Part of that bitch?"

"No."

"Weren't even curious, were you?"

"There was nothing to be curious about."

"Why not?"

"That curiosity had been satisfied long before." It was out. Blame it on the Black Russians. Blame it on the tease. Blame it on pique. Blame it on nosiness that was none of her business. Blame it on the manner of her cross-questioning. Suddenly I didn't care.

She stood up and sat her Black Russian on the bar. "You lied to me, you bastard, didn't you? You're a cheap little man after all, aren't you? You told me you'd never been with that bitch. You did, didn't you?"

"Knock off." I'd had it. I rose up in my full dignity, or as dignified as you can rise up attired in a towel. "Having fun?"

"No."

"The cross-examination finished, counselor?"

"All finished."

"So forgive, forget, skip the whole bit, and let us start afresh like the two pristine dolls we both are. You go take your bath symbolic while I set up the new Black Russians."

"Like hell I will, like hell you will." She stepped into her shoes, wriggled into her dress, buttoned all the buttons. "Remember what I once said to you, doll?"

"You've said many things, doll."

"Men will never understand women." She took up her little white bag. "Thanks for the check, and thanks for nothing." She came to me and kissed my forehead. "It's been most instructive." Then she left like a lady without slamming the door.

I sat down in my towel.

In a few minutes, naturally, I was glad I had remained faithful to my Carmen. In a few minutes, naturally, I came around to thinking that I *had* remained faithful to Carmen, in spirit as well as in flesh. In a few minutes, naturally, I believed that *I* had maneuvered the conversation to the point of Marla's departure. By then it was time for more Black Russians and it was also time to stop wearing a towel. I put on shorts and slacks and socks and loafers but remained bare on top because it was warm. Then I went to the bar and closed my eyes trying to remember the recipe and then it came to me. Champagne, vodka, and creme de cocoa, but I did not know in what proportions, so I dreamed up my own proportions, two-thirds champagne, one-third vodka, one-sixth creme de cocoa, and to that I added a splash of bitters just for the hell of it. I shook up my proportions with ice to a foaming fizz, poured, tasted, and it was delicious. I had a large shakerful and I was about to settle down to getting lively drunk when the bell rang and instantly that posed a problem.

How could I square up my conscience if Marla had had a change of heart? I had worked myself up to being a hero with me, but now, already, I was palpitating with the recollection of the white body in the red Bikini. What man is a hero against a beautiful body in a red Bikini and how long can his heroism remain rigid against the pressure of other rigidity? I decided to play it cool but if it got hot I would let the chippies fall where they may. I put on a righteous smirk and opened the door but my righteousness slipped because my guest was not Marla Trent.

My guest was Carmen Valesquez.

It was my night for champagne because cradled in her arms

like a baby was a magnum of the bubbly.

"Hail," I said staying with the script.

"Ah, I am so delighted you are home. I have brought for you a gift."

She handed me the bottle and I closed the door behind her. She was wearing a short black silk cape. She took it off and she was wearing a tight black silk dress cleaved down the middle like the hoof of Satan. She lifted her hands to fix her hair and the mountains pressed against the valley. She was the only woman I had ever known with mountains that made Marla's mountains look like hills. This was my night for peculiar travail and I was fighting a losing battle against my libido. I unbuttoned my eyes from the glitter of the sheath and deposited the magnum on the bar. "Thank you for buying me a present," I said.

"Oh no, I did not buy it. It was given to me."

"By whom?"

She came near me. She smelled sweetly of wine. All in character this night. She was stoned as a statue.

"It was a party. For me."

"Who gave it?"

"At the hospital. For farewell."

"Farewell for what?"

"It is over. I am leaving. The year is finished. Tomorrow I go home to Colombia."

"I'll be going with you."

"Dear sad man, always so funny. You love me, do you not?"

"I think by now you know that."

"I know it." Her hand, hot, touched my arm, cool.

I suddenly realized I was naked from the waist up.

"Hold everything," I said. "I'll get a shirt."

"No, no," she said. Lightly, she kissed my chest. "You have a smooth lovely body," she said.

Boy, the approach persisted in being cockeyed this night.

"How about you?" I said.

"Smooth, lovely."

I looked at her eyes. She was loaded.

"You never showed me," I said.

"I will show you," she said and at once she pulled the zipper of the dress.

In pattern? Crazy night?

The dress came off and there she was in black pumps and

white briefs and nothing else. The brown body gleamed as though oiled. She came to me quickly and put her arms around me and drew my face down to hers and kissed me. "It is for us, tonight," she whispered. "Our night, tonight, for us, together. I have so longed for this night."

"There'll be many nights."

"This night. Tonight." She released me, flashed the bright white-toothed smile. "Why you not open the bottle?"

"No need. I have drinks prepared."

"Prepared?"

"I must have divined you were coming. It's a champagne drink, a mixed drink with a champagne base. Powerful."

"So? It is called what?"

"Black Russian."

"Oh, not. I will not have it. Communist drink. Not. So sorry."

Love and politics mix like oil and water. I got off that bit with alacrity. "No, no, no, no," I said. "That's just a name, the American name for it, a good old American name for a good old American drink." I poured from the shaker into a glass and brought it to her. "Taste."

She tasted. "Delicious." She drank it all.

I took the glass, poured again, brought it to her again, and this time she sipped, and I ran my hand down along her spine. She quivered, then she said in her husky voice, "You will go to take a bath."

I jumped. Fairly leaped. "Bath? I've taken a bath. I've showered and I've bathed and—"

"No, please," she said softly, "it is for . . . how to say . . . to wash away all before . . . to have, so to say, a new beginning."

"Yes," I said mournfully. "Symbolic."

"Ah, you are so wonderful, so sweet, understanding."

I had had a recent training in this understanding. "Thank you," I murmured, and then as though struck by a sudden bolt bluely descended I said, "The sheets and pillow cases are fresh, but maybe . . ."

"Ah, you are so dear, so fine. Yes, dear love, I will change them. You go."

I went. I bathed. I did the whole bit. I had never been this scrubbed in my life. Then I got out of the tub, cleaned it, and drew a new bath for her. I learn quickly. Well, fairly quickly.

When I came out dressed fresh in a new towel, only one low light was burning, and I stumbled through dimness to the bar, while she stumbled naked to the bathroom for her symbolic bath. There was very little left in the shaker and I drank that directly from the shaker and then I went to bed, my heart thumping like a virgin's, and then she came to me, kissed me and held me and I said, "I love you."

"I know. I believe. Love me, my love."

"I want to marry you."

"Yes," she said. "Love me. Tonight, this night, we will love all night, all night."

"I want to marry you."

"Yes. Love me. I have saved this night for us."

"I want to marry you," I said holding her off stiff-arm and she finally heard me.

"Marry?" she said. "It cannot."

"It cannot what why?"

"Marry, it cannot."

"Why not? What's wrong? I love you. I thought—"

"I am married."

"You are—what?"

"Married, I am."

I sat up. I crossed my knees, Indian fashion. I rocked like a Yogi saying his prayers. I said, "The guy that came up periodically from South America?"

"Yes. But please. It is not of matter now. Now it is for us, this night. Once, us, together, I have tried not for a year, I cannot help, I am human, it has never been with another before. I wish you, I want you, one night, this night, all night, for us. Tomorrow go home."

"Tonight you go home."

"What? What is?"

"It is—nothing."

Sadly, I climbed out of bed. Wearily, I dragged on clothing. Lugubriously, I ruminated. Marla Trent had said that men will never understand women. Marla had expressed a basic principle to which I had to agree. But Marla had never expressed the necessary corollary, the converse: nor will women ever understand men. The proof was being voiced from my bed. Women seem to believe that all sensitivity is reserved for them. No matter how they cloak it, no matter even their assumed unconcern, no matter all delicate and lilting phrases, women always believe they hold the ace: they depend with fanatic certainty upon the brute male animal instinct. Carmen Valesquez had saved one night, one last glorious night, for us. Unilaterally, she had saved up for one great big beautiful bursting night of love. She lay naked and ready and seething and irresistible and I was refusing. What manner of man was I?

"What it, Peter? What is wrong? What is the matter?"

"Get dressed," I said.

"But why? What is?"

Who needs it with lectures, and who am I to lecture? I couldn't possibly marshal the words. We are all inadequate with words when we have the great need for words and so my words were: "Look, once upon a time, like a year ago, I asked you to take your dress off, remember?"

"Yes, but now—"

"Now I'm telling you to put it on. Please get dressed."

Silently, sullenly, uncomprehendingly, she did as she was bade, and then I locked up the barn and I took her home and I kissed her off and that was ended.

My watch said eleven o'clock.

Without a Marla and without a Carmen and swacked on Black Russians and soured on all women, I was alone with my grief and I pondered where to go to grieve most pleasantly. The psyche is entitled to fitting grace. Lorenzo's was certainly the place to complete the cipher of the lamentable cycle, and so, after one huge accelerating sigh, I zeroed in, cipher psyche cycling, upon Lorenzo's where the jazz was jumping, the smoke was heavy, and the customers were thick. Lorenzo led me to a narrow booth and squeezed me in and said, "Your wish, Mr. Chambers?"

"Champagne."

"Ah, we are celebrating?"

"Celebrating. Champagne. The best in the house."

"At once," he said and he went away and the waiter came with the bucket of ice and the bottle of juice and he exploded the cork and I drank from a wide-mouthed glass and I stared at nothing and I tapped my toes to the music and then Lorenzo returned and he bent to my ear and he said, "Company? Would you like company?"

Champagne shot from my mouth in a fine spray and then I said, "Brother, my brother, this is where I came in."

"Not quite," he said, "because this time it is the lady who is asking."

"Asking?"

"To join you."

"What lady?"

"That lady."

He gestured discreetly toward a large circular booth not ten feet away. At one side of the circle sat the producer Leland Logan and his wife and at the other side sat the director Otto Kydudreck and his wife and between them, alone, sat Anna Esther Wing.

She waved a small wave.

I waved, large, like a brakeman flagging down a train.

It got through to Lorenzo.

"You wish," he declared.

"I wish," I verified.

"It will happen," he said and he went to the circular booth and assisted as she squirmed out. She was wearing a shimmering silver Chinese-type gown that covered her body, uncoveringly, all the way up to the neck. It was slit up the sides and the bare flash of the flesh of the slender tapered legs was more exciting than all of the brazen deep-down decolletage of all of the overdressed underdressed lady-customers in the joint. Lorenzo seated her opposite me and he went away and immediately my knees clasped hers under the table.

"Hi," I said.

"So good to see you," she said in her soft breathless voice.

"Me too," I said.

"When you came in, so unexpectedly, I virtually trembled."

"I'm trembling now, baby."

"I'm not joking."

"Nor am I."

"I've thought a great deal about you."

"Me too." That was ambiguous so it wasn't a lie.

And then she said with emotion. "I do want to express my profound admiration for you?"

"Profound admiration? Me?"

The blue eyes burned seriously. The delicate breathless voice was down to a whisper. "I offered myself. Do you remember?"

"I hope the offer still holds."

She ducked that. "You refused because you were being faithful to a girl. I think that's beautiful, wonderful. Perhaps I'm cynical but I don't believe there are too many men around like that. It's one of the reasons I've never been able to get you out of my mind."

"No more girl."

"You're free?"

"No more girl," I said and my hands clasped hers over the table. "I've been reading about you. All sorts of things have been happening, haven't they?"

"Thrilling things."

"We've a lot to talk about, you and I."

"I'd love to. But not here. This is no place to talk."

"Can you leave?"

"Of course I can leave."

"I have a place to talk."

"Wherever you say."

"The air-conditioning is broken down."

"I'll go wherever you say."

"One condition."

"What condition?"

"That I don't have to take a bath like symbolic."

"Pardon?"

"Sounds like Chinese, doesn't it?"

"I don't understand Chinese."

"Twice tonight I've taken baths symbolic."

"I still don't understand."

"Still Chinese."

"Please. Let's go talk English."

"Yes, ma'am," I said.

We went home and talked English.

But we took baths. I insisted.

I even changed the sheets. And the pillow cases.

I wasn't kidding, I wasn't being spiteful, I wasn't being cute, I meant it. The apartment was hot, and that was my excuse, but that's what it was, an excuse. I was infected. I wanted to talk English washed clean of the past, completely.

Symbolism is insidious.

It's our newest disease.

If you recognize it, run.

It's contagious as hell.

www.ingramcontent.com/pod-product-compliance
Lightning Source LLC
Chambersburg PA
CBHW070023260626

47159CB00005B/1937